THE TEASE

LAUREN BLAKELY

COPYRIGHT

ABOUT THE TEASE

I swear I'm a good girl.

I didn't go to the exclusive, after-hours masquerade to kiss my dad's best friend. I didn't even know who the masked man was when he touched me like I was his every fantasy.

But when I learn exactly how off-limits my new lover is, I do my best to avoid him the next time. Except, he has his sinful sights set on me, even when he discovers who I am. *Just one time*, he whispers. *Then we'll pretend this never happened.*

Seems the enigmatic, gorgeous single dad I've known by day is a very dirty man after dark.

But one night turns into a stolen weekend, giving me a taste of so much more. When it ends, we vow to stay apart.

We could never work.

He's focused on raising his young son, and I can't let my already damaged family break more. But the caring, possessive man keeps coming back to me, and these secret nights tangled up together are turning into tender moments that make my heart thunder.

And soon, this tease of a forbidden romance is making me want so much more than I can ever have...

DID YOU KNOW?

To be the first to find out when all of my upcoming books go live click here!

PRO TIP: Add lauren@laurenblakely.com to your contacts before signing up to make sure the emails go to your inbox!

Did you know this book is also available in audio and paperback on all major retailers? Go to my website for links!

For content warnings for this title, go to my site.

THE TEASE

A VIRGIN SOCIETY STANDALONE

By Lauren Blakely

1

HUSH HUSH

Jules

My friend Scarlett is begging me to fill in for her tomorrow night, but really, she doesn't have to ask twice. The second she called and asked, *"Can you play piano at The Scene?"* I was all in.

"Yes," I say as calmly as I can while I hustle past the turnstiles on Fourteenth Street.

"Thanks. I forgot all about my shift at the bar," Scarlett says, then hesitates. "And can you still play Gershwin? They're big on 'Rhapsody in Blue.'"

"My fingers remember all the jazz standards from my childhood," I tell her as I rush down the crowded steps to the platform, dodging harried New Yorkers racing up. Showtime's at eight for a critics' screening for a new TV series I worked on. I can't be late, but I don't want to press pause on this call and take a chance Scarlett might ask someone else to sub.

I soothe her worries even as I enter the belly of the subway beast. "I can play a ton of masquerade songs."

As an incoming train on the other platform rattles in, she's unexpectedly silent before she says, "Oh. I didn't think I said it was a masquerade?"

Shoot. Did I just give myself away? But I've kept my own secrets for years. I've *had* to keep them. "With a name like *The Scene*, I took a guess," I say confidently.

Another pause, then she speaks. "Well, good one, babe. Anyway, the parties are kind of hush-hush with the whole masquerade thing, and they're also kind of risqué. So I wanted to make sure you're definitely free tomorrow night and...well, that you're comfortable with it."

Oh, sweetheart. You have no idea. "I'm great with masquerades," I answer in the same tone I'd say *I'm great with people* at a job interview.

"Oh good. I thought you might be, since we've been clubbing," she says with a naughty little lilt in her tone. "And every time I see you, you always look like someone different."

Well, that's kind of the point.

I check for my train, peering down the tunnel but not getting too close to the tracks. The phone connection will sputter out any second, and I don't need to tell her the extent of my wardrobe and wigs to prove I'm the woman for the gig. She already knows my credentials. Knows, too, I helped pay for my own college by teaching piano. Still, I want this gig badly so I need to assuage all of her concerns. "The only thing on my schedule tomorrow night was putting on a sea-clay eye mask and listening to a playlist. So, I'm totally free to help out. I've got you," I tell her, selling myself subtly.

I'm not about to disclose the real reason I am bursting inside and already counting down the hours.

"Thank god. I can't believe I spaced. We're already short-staffed here, so my boss was going to kill me. But let me know if I can help with anything," she says, then hesitates. "Except, Jules..."

"Yes?" I ask tightly, hoping she's not backing out of her offer now.

"It's important you don't use your name. The members like the privacy and figure if they don't know yours, you don't need to know theirs."

"I'm a vault," I say, and nothing in my life is more true than that.

"And the dress code is *costume light* for the musician, so it's up to you if you want to wear one. But the mask is a strict requirement. Not the sea-clay variety though."

"I'll make sure I wash it off before I go," I deadpan.

She laughs, then adds, "I know some websites with overnight delivery for masquerade masks." Scarlett is in full-on helpful mode now. "And I can recommend some cheap costume shops too."

My friend doesn't have to recommend a thing. I'm a junior TV producer by day...whoever I want to be by night.

"I know where a few are too," I add as the rattle of the downtown train grows louder.

"You're a goddess," Scarlett says with obvious relief, then adds that she'll text me more details, like the theme and the secret password.

Bring that password to Mama.

As I hop onto the train, I mentally flick through my closet then rein in the grin of all grins when the magic words land on my phone.

The rest of the night, I fight like hell to focus on the screening—and not on *The Scene.*

After the longest and the shortest workday—I was nonstop from eight to six coordinating the upcoming location shoot for a hot new show the production company I work for developed—I stare at the Albrecht Mansion on the other side of this elegant Upper East Side block, freaking out that I'll be exposed.

I'm supposed to be the confident one in my friend group. The bold one. That's what they call me, though if they knew my sister I'm sure they'd call me shy. But now my mind whirs too fast for me to be bold.

Camden's by my side. She walked here with me, and while she's not attending, I can't just head into a naughty masquerade without a good pep talk from my bestie. "What if they figure out I'm not just a piano player?" I ask in a whisper.

"Who's *they*?"

I gesture subtly to the mansion. "You know. The... organizers. The people in charge," I say quietly.

She arches a brow. "Fear of authority much?"

Just a little. "Well, you've met my dad." He might have changed careers now, but once a cop, always a cop.

"First, you're legit allowed to be here. Second, no one knows you've been *dying* for an invite for months," she says as she tosses me a knowing smile.

She's right on all counts. I'm seriously glad she walked over here with me. My overactive mind starts to settle. "You're right. And I can't believe I finally got one," I say as I gaze up at the mansion, which is stunning, in a Vanderbilt kind of way. Ivy crawls up the burnished red bricks. A soft summer breeze rustles the trees hugging the staircase that leads to imposing double doors, the dark polished wood gleaming in the twilight. The doors are staffed by two big, burly men in black suits, muscles bulging. No one is getting past them without an invitation.

"I can't believe I've walked by this mansion a million times," I say as I soak in the secret society feel of this entire summer night. "And I had no idea what went on here just off Park Avenue."

"That's New York for you. City of Secrets." Camden likes Manhattan's mysteries too.

"It sure is," I say to the one person who knows most of mine.

Camden was with me at Revel House in SoHo, a converted church turned into a nightclub, the night we danced till dawn and heard whispers about The Scene. Words like *sophisticated* and *costume* and *never use your name* intrigued me to no end.

Since then, I've searched for details, chased down clues, eager for an invite. Rumor has it these after-dark fêtes aren't just masquerades. They're elegant opportunities for people with the same desires to meet.

Everyone who walks past these doors wants the same things.

And tonight, *everyone* includes the piano player.

I draw a deep breath, clutching my shiny gold mask more tightly. It's the price of admission, and I'm willing to pay.

I spin to face Camden. "How do I look?" I ask, flashing a *check my teeth* smile.

"Disgustingly perfect," she says, faux annoyed. "No lipstick on your pearly whites."

"That's the worst," I deadpan, but inside I'm grateful that I look good on the outside.

"I still can't believe you just happened to have this sexy number in your closet," she says, her bright eyes traveling in obvious approval from the gold sandals to the white dress visible through the gap in my cape, to the matching glittery headband. The only thing that doesn't match is my silver anklet. It's not part of the ensemble, and no one will see it under my dress, but it's with me. *Always.*

I strike a playful pose, getting into the spirit at last. "A girl should be prepared for a costume party. I can't just count on finding the perfect things at retail the night before." It takes hunting to find my recycled pretties, but I do.

"Next time you find something that screams 'hot rocker chick' for karaoke night, get it for me."

"Done," I say. I love finding clothes for my friends, and gifting them.

"Anyway, stop stalling. I need to get to work, and you need to go in there. And seriously, thank god Scarlett thought of you and not, like, the grandpa at Bloomingdale's who plays old songs for shoppers." Then she gasps. "Ooh, what if he's in there tonight? In a mask? And he tries to seduce you?"

I roll my eyes. "Enough of you."

"Exactly. *Go*, you goddess."

That's the idea. My goddess costume seems perfect for the party's theme—*old-fashioned, but with a twist.*

The old-fashioned comes from the character I'm playing from mythology—a Greek goddess. As for the twist? Well, that's just a play on hair. My chestnut hair is hidden under this golden blonde wig, with long, luxurious locks, softly curled, one side twisted in a gold clip.

I'll blend in best like this, fully in costume. I don't want to draw attention to myself tonight at the party. I want to do my job, entertaining the crowd, while taking mental notes of my fantasies as they unfold before my eyes.

The voyeur amongst them.

But I have to be cautious. I can't mingle. I'm not really a guest, after all. I'm staff, and there's a difference. I'd do well to remember it.

If I pull this off, though, maybe then I'll get an invitation for real.

With that in mind, and my itty-bitty purse in hand, I head up the steps and undo the button on my light summer cape—I didn't want to telegraph to all of Park Avenue that I was headed to *The Scene*—then toss it over my arm. In one smooth move, I slide on the gold mask.

As I cinch it into place, my gaze lands on a man turning onto the block. He's hard to look away from, since he's wearing the hell out of a three-piece suit and a phantom mask.

Oh, yes.

Modern suit for the twist. Dark, broody character from literature for the old-fashioned.

A thrill rushes through me. Does he like the same things I *think* I like?

My pulse skitters with hope, but I won't find out tonight. I'm here to observe how the beautiful, rich, and naughty like to play. I'm not rich, but I'd like to feel beautiful and naughty.

I quickly switch my phone to Do Not Disturb—I don't want anyone interrupting me while I play—then climb the final stairs to the mansion.

"Hello," I say to the bodyguard twins, as calm as can be.

One of them stares at me with hard, unflinching eyes. "Name?"

Scarlett's warning flashes through my mind. But it's easy, so very easy to leave behind Jules Marley, buttoned-up, twin-set and glasses-wearing good girl by day.

"Aphrodite," I say.

The man checks his iPad, then nods. First test passed, and I feel more victorious than I should. With a blank face that hides my giddiness, I give him the secret password. "I read a good book last night."

Well, I did.

He opens the door. "Enjoy."

Oh, I plan to.

2

SEX NOSTALGIA

Finn

This is my first evening out in months.

Between late nights with my laptop, closing deals, and reading past bedtime with my seven-year-old—I'm a sucker for the *just one more page* plea—I can't remember the last time I went out.

Alone.

When the invitation from the club landed in my email asking if I was interested in reactivating my membership—the one that'd been dead for years—I clicked yes impulsively.

One quick Google search later and I'd ordered the mask and had it delivered to my brownstone in an hour.

God bless New York and instant access to everything.

A masquerade at The Scene sounds like a perfect

escape tonight, since my kid's with his grandparents this weekend. *"Bye, Dad,"* he called to me so easily as his grandparents drove away.

Dad. I'm still getting used to that word, but it feels so damn right.

And so does *this*—catching a glimpse of a gorgeous masked goddess heading into the Albrecht Mansion. She looks utterly at home in that costume. Like she *is* a goddess.

From the other end of the block, I stare shamelessly at the beauty, something I can do freely now that I'm divorced.

Look.

Something I can enjoy again too. The shape of a woman, perhaps soon the feel of a woman.

But she's gone in seconds, scurrying through the open door to the same destination I'm headed.

Perfect.

I'll see her inside soon enough. As I near the mansion, my phone trills. I go on alert, grabbing it from my pocket in case it's Zach or his grandparents, needing something, anything. But it's not them. They've got their shit together.

It's my lawyer. I'd much rather be off the clock on a Friday evening, but I don't have that luxury—not when my brother and I are trying to close the biggest deal of our careers, and I'm the lead on it.

"Hey there," I say as I answer.

"Hit a snag in the paperwork," my attorney begins, wasting no time.

Fucking love him for skipping niceties. "What's the story?" I ask as I turn the other way.

After taking off the mask, I spend the next thirty minutes pacing around the block, sorting out details that I thought we'd put to bed. "I'll send you the new contract late tonight," he finishes.

"But I won't look at it till tomorrow," I say.

He laughs. "Sounds like someone has a good night planned."

A man can hope.

I say goodbye and end the phone call, then do my best to shove that business deal out of my mind for a couple hours.

Tonight is for escape at last.

With a goodnight text to my kid and a thanks to his grandparents, I silence the phone. I return to the mansion and give the password to security. Once upon a time in my twenties, I used to wonder what the security guys thought about parties that cater to certain tastes.

But then, life happened, and I stopped caring so much about what other people think. Besides, everyone has a secret. Some just wear theirs.

Like it's yesterday, or really a decade ago, I head up the grand stairs, past the twinkling lights curled around the banister. The soft lilt of Cole Porter pulls me closer to the grand ballroom, but so does an overwhelming sense of nostalgia. Is it weird to feel nostalgia for a— well, let's call it what it is—a kink matchmaking extravaganza?

But sex nostalgia is a thing, evidently, and I'm

feeling it big time. When I turn into the ballroom and drink in the sight—revelers in top hats and tails, gowns and ruffles, satin and black silk, with masks everywhere —the nostalgia disappears entirely.

I'm not longing for the past anymore. The past *is* the present once again, and it's a feast for the senses from the clink of glasses to the chimes of laughter, to the floral perfumes mingling with the buttery aromas of whiskey and the sweet pear scents of champagne.

I inhale it all.

As the mellow notes of "Night and Day" fill the room, a tuxedoed man wearing a simple black mask walks my way, giving an inviting nod as he nears me. "Good evening," he says in a familiar baritone. "Welcome to The Scene."

Then he walks right past me.

Damn, this mask I've got on is good.

I clear my throat. "What does it take to get a fucking cocktail around here?"

He immediately spins on his heels and shoots me an apologetic smile. "I'll send a server to you right away, sir."

I rein in a grin, working the asshole act hard. "How about you take my drink order right now?"

Service is important to my buddy Tevin. But so are manners. I haven't quite crossed the line yet, but I'm toeing it.

"Of course. What would you like?" he asks.

"Pabst. Served upside down. In a keg. It was the spring of—"

He groans in laughter. "You asshole." My college

friend claps my back affectionately. All is forgiven. "It's been..." Tevin's gaze drifts down to my left hand. *Naked.*

"Yeah, it's been a while," I say with some resignation, some relief, then waggle my bare fingers.

He lifts a brow in question. "Are congratulations in order?"

If he'd asked me a year ago when my wife called it quits, I'd have said no fucking way.

But now that the ink is newly dry on the divorce papers, all I can say is a big, truthful "yes."

Maybe a hell yes. I'm finally crawling out of the black hole of my marriage.

"Then congratulations, man. Especially since you're back here. So I'd say the drinks are on me tonight," he says, even though this isn't a cash bar. We've all paid handsomely for the beverages. "Macallan?"

"You know it," I say, and Tevin heads off to the bar. He runs these parties with his wife, Kiara, who's surely here somewhere, likely in a costume that makes her easy enough to recognize too.

As I wait for him to return, I hang back at the edge of the ballroom, checking out the crowd. I'm feeling at home a little more, thanks to the vibe. That's the point. A familiar atmosphere but a chance to meet new people with the same tastes I have.

Like my goddess. There's something about her...

With a laser focus, I survey the party for the beauty, enjoying that no one recognizes me. Anonymity is a wonderful thing, a lovely escape from the weight of the day and the heaviness of the past. It's a cloak, too, to search for her.

She's not mingling though. She's not at the bar either.

The music shifts to "Rhapsody in Blue," and I turn toward the grand piano set in the corner of the room, the romantic tune calling out to me.

Yes.

That's her—behind the keys.

And just look at her. I stare unabashedly at her masked face—those lips, those fucking lush lips— for another few seconds till Tevin returns, hands me a tumbler, then says, "To your return to the land of the living. You were a phantom for some time, man."

Can't argue with him there. I lift the glass. "I'll drink to that."

* * *

An hour or two later, I've refreshed my drink, chatted with old friends, exchanged pleasantries with new ones, and tried valiantly, but failed miserably, to not stare at the woman at the piano.

She bites the corner of her cherry-red lips as she plays, moving her body sensually with the music. Her hair, too, is driving me wild, all curls and waves twisted up on one side. She'd better have a break really fucking soon.

I take a final swallow of my Macallan when she looks up again from the ivories. Her masked gaze meets mine from across the softly lit room. Electric candle-light plays with shadows, but even in the half-light, our eyes lock. There's a catch in the music, a faint pause, then her lips press together.

Like she's swallowing a sigh.

Or maybe the pause in the tune was intentional, because when she ends the number, she segues into the familiar opening notes of "Music of the Night."

I'm not the only phantom here. But hell if I'm going to let any other man take his chance. Screw waiting for her to take a break.

Waiting is for other men.

A server sails by, and I set my empty glass on the tray, then weave through the crowd, past taffeta and finery, past promises of late-night trysts, past men kissing women, and women kissing women, and dark deeds negotiated in darker corners.

"May I join you?" I ask when I reach the other side of the piano.

She glances around, scanning for someone. Tevin? Kiara? Or just permission to...interact? That I can give her, since I know my friends won't be bothered by the musician talking to a guest. "They won't mind."

She swallows, then asks skeptically, "Are you sure?"

"I promise."

She's quiet for a beat, clearly thinking while she keeps playing. She's artful with the tune, extending the opening notes, letting them repeat like a soundtrack to her thoughts, perhaps. "And why should I believe you?"

To her, I'm just a stranger in a mask. "Because I don't want you to get in trouble." I keep my answer simple, suspecting that's what she needs.

"Why's that?" It's another challenge, but her tone's softer. Maybe she's letting down her guard.

I'm not about to admit that the way she wears that costume, like it's who she is deep inside, caught my eye from down the block. Then, when I arrived in the ball-room, her music caught my ear. She's a woman in tune with her senses. That's what I've missed. That's what I crave desperately.

She deserves a direct answer though, and, perhaps, proof that I'm worthy of her. "Ever since I saw you walk past those doors, I haven't been able to get you out of my head."

"Oh," she says softly, then dips her face. "You saw me walk in?"

"Couldn't look away," I say, and her lips curve up. My god, I want to wipe the red lipstick off her mouth right now. "Still can't."

Life is short. Time is precious. I'm not here to fuck around.

She raises her face, meets my eyes, and plays on. "I saw you too."

I smile at the acknowledgement of our instant attraction. "Good. Then, I ask again—may I join you?"

With a flirty smile, she plays past the opening notes at last. That's a hell of an RSVP, and I take it, moving around the piano to the bench. I drink in the sight of her, from her creamy skin to the graceful column of her throat, to the mouth that I'm obsessed with already.

And her magnificent tits.

She ought to be worshipped in bed, and then, ideally, teased all night long.

But most of all, her dark eyes intrigue me. They sparkle with hidden wishes I want to grant.

She scoots over a few inches, and I slide right next to her on the bench. There's a sliver of space between us, and she tips her gaze to the keys. "I've never played this as a duet," she says softly. There's a double meaning to her words. I'd like to find out what's underneath them.

And frankly, under that gorgeous fucking dress.

"First time for everything...but," I say, then dip my face closer to hers, "I have a confession. I can't play a single song."

"You tease."

"You teased me with this song," I counter.

"Did I?" she asks faux innocently.

"You absolutely fucking did," I say, admiring her nimble fingers as they fly.

"Or maybe I just like *Phantom of the Opera*."

"If I'm doing this right, you sure do."

"I guess we'll have to find out if you are."

She's making me work for it, and oh hell, will I ever. "I'm up for the challenge."

I don't know her at all. But I know this key detail— she likes to play, and I don't just mean the piano. There's a cat-and-mouse energy to her. A sense of gamesmanship was evident when she began playing "Music of the Night," almost like she was summoning me from across the room.

Plus, I know from years ago that piano players here aren't required to go full costume. But she did. And this choice of hers to dress like a goddess is so deliberate. So sexy. She might be playing the piano, but I suspect she wants to play other roles too. "I bet you were an excellent piano student once upon a time," I begin.

There's a subtle hitch in her breath. "I was."

"I'm sure you listened and played perfectly during the whole lesson," I say, emphasis on *lesson*.

She nods eagerly. "I was very good."

"Did you have a good teacher?" I ask, feeling her out.

As her fingers fly, she turns her face slightly to me, her lips parted with...excitement. "He wasn't...strict enough."

Yes. Fucking yes.

As the song nears its end, my expression goes stoic. Intense, as I slide into the role she wants. "Show me 'Für Elise,'" I demand. "I told you to work on it last week."

"I'll play it for you. The way you like," she says, like a good student, and I stifle a groan from her responsiveness.

She slides right into the Beethoven. With her chin tipped up, her face mostly hidden, but her gaze locked on me, she asks, "Am I doing it right?"

I burn inside. Talk about a double meaning. But I stay in character. "No."

"What am I doing wrong?"

I lower my voice, move closer to her ear. "You need to play it perfectly...even with distraction," I tell her.

"Distract me," she whispers.

Gladly.

I slide a hand across the small of her back over the silk of her gown.

As her fingers caress the keys, mine roam up her body, traveling across the fabric of her dress. I've missed this. This kind of touch. This kind of moment.

I reach her neck, tracing a line up her soft flesh all while she plays, and revelers drink champagne, and partygoers dance, and others eat, and some kiss in corners.

And here, behind the shield of the piano, I *crave.* The feel of her, the taste of her, the scent of her. Like a lush garden, the kind you'd want to fuck in.

But when she speaks again, her voice is a little confessional, and not at all in character. "I don't want to ruin my chances here."

Maybe this is her dream job. I don't want to ruin that for her either. I drop the demanding tone. "Do you want me to stop?"

"No. I want you to keep going," she says, being vulnerable now. "That's the problem."

Then I'd better find a solution, and sometimes the first idea is the best one. "When's your break?"

"In ten minutes."

My mind cycles through options then quickly lands on one. "Meet me on the rooftop patio. I'll clear it. Take the stairs behind the library."

She shakes her head instantly, then asks, "How about the library instead?"

There's worry in her voice. But I don't dwell on it. "The library is perfect. I'll make sure no one's there."

"Will you grab my hand and pull me into a dark corner?"

I'm crackling with desire as I growl out a *yes*. I leave, heading to the library in seconds.

3

A LESSON

Jules

I didn't come here tonight for *this*. But, really, I suppose I did come here precisely for an encounter.

Ten minutes later, as the music flips to a recorded playlist, I slip away from the piano, weaving through the boisterous crowds of randy souls, heading down the hall, scanning for...security? I don't even know what I'm checking for. Who I'm trying to avoid.

But mostly I don't want Scarlett to get in trouble for my desires, ones I've kept hidden since college a few years ago. Ones I don't think I'll be hiding much longer. I shouldn't act on them. But that *shouldn't* isn't strong enough to stop me.

Servers scurry by carrying trays, but no one gives me a second glance as I head down the hall. I guess the costume does the trick. Perhaps I'm just Aphrodite gliding toward the library, thankful, oh so thankful, that I'm not heading to the rooftop.

I check the time on my silenced phone in my clutch purse. With my heart beating in my throat, I glance around and behind. *Coast is clear.* With one final check, then just one more, I reach for the knob of the door, open it, and step into the alcove of a dimly lit room that smells of old books and faraway tales.

Before I can turn into the space, a hand tugs mine.

The man can follow directions. My pulse spikes with excitement.

I spin around, my skin tingling as he locks the door, then pulls me away from it, playing the part as I asked. When we reach a corner, he turns to face me, his back to the books.

It's sensory overload with him, and I want to savor every detail so I can enjoy this moment, but I want to remember them too so I can write them down later, starting with his scent. It's smoky and floral but also dangerous. His cologne is like orchids and leather set on fire.

It reminds me of something, but I'm not sure what.

More than half his face is covered, so I can't tell much more about him when I'm looking at him straight on than what I caught from his profile while on the piano bench. Except what I suspected. He's not a boy. Silver flecks color his stubble, and some crinkles line the corners of his green eyes, hungry behind the mask. For a flicker of a second, his jawline feels familiar. Like a memory of a memory but there's no time to place him. Besides, I don't want to be in *my* head. I want to play a part.

When he threads his fingers through mine, I can feel the heat of his desire. "Is this the lesson you've been wanting from me?"

I think I'm going to melt. We only have a few minutes. But we'll have to make the best of it. "Yes. Before anyone comes home," I say, dropping my clutch to the wood floor.

His eyes gleam. "You've been driving me crazy for months," he says, building onto our role-play.

"It's only because you're so stern with me."

His hands reach for my face. He's careful with my mask but nothing else. His fingers grip my chin possessively. "Do you know how hard it is to teach you? To watch you play? To look at your hands when all I want is to put mine all over you?"

I gasp. I want to linger in these roles, but the clock is ticking. "No. How hard is it?"

He tugs my face closer to his, inches away. "Impossible. And I could be in trouble if anyone hears us."

"Then I better be quiet," I tease. *Make me be quiet.*

"Really fucking quiet," he commands, then drops his lips to my neck, moaning like he's been dying to kiss me there all night. His murmurs and groans make me wet as he travels up my throat. Then, he kisses me. A fierce, hard kiss like he's claiming me. I shiver from head to toe as his mouth covers mine, as his hand holds my face, as his arm ropes around my waist.

My mystery man takes my kisses like they're thirsty gulps of water in the desert and he's parched for me.

His thumb strokes my jawline, then travels to my mouth. He breaks the kiss only to press his thumb between my lips.

I shiver. Then suck.

If I thought his groan was feral before, it had nothing on this new sound. Raw, animalistic. A message that he wants me to suck his cock so badly. He's easy to read. Easier to please as I wrap my lips tighter, draw him deeper, show him what I'd like to do to him.

"Yes, fucking yes. This mouth has made me crazy all night. From the start of our lesson."

I lift my chin, then with equal parts thrill and nerve, I ask for what I want. "You should make me be quiet now."

His smile is filthy, his intent filthier as he covers my mouth with his and tugs the silk of my dress higher and higher, till his hand travels under it, then up my thigh.

A pulse beats between my legs, an ache for him. One he eases when his fingers tease at the waistband of my lace panties. He slides his palm down over the fabric, finding the damp panel.

Make that...*soaked*.

He moans into my mouth, then wrenches away from me. His voice is deep and raspy with desire as he asks, "Did you wear this lace to torture me?"

"I did. Did it work?"

He grabs my hand, slams it against the outline of his hard-on. Thick, eager. My mouth waters for him. "Yeah, it worked," he says, then he covers my mouth with his palm.

I shudder.

Taking my hand off his dick, he moves us around, pushing me roughly against the shelf. The spines of old books dig into my back as his fingers glide through my slick flesh while his other hand keeps me quiet. Like that, with my sounds captured, he fucks me with his fingers. Thrusting, playing, then sliding his thumb along my pulsing clit.

"You're so wet for me. Such a naughty girl," he says as he strokes faster.

I grip his hips to hold on, wordless at his sexy reprimands.

"You need to stop tempting me so much during our lessons," he continues.

I tremble, my pussy aching.

"Or I'm going to have to make you come again and again and again till you beg me to stop."

Orgasm torture. Sign me up. My mind goes hazy. My knees wobble. His deft fingers fly. Crowding me, he presses his strong frame to my side, rubbing against my hip.

This man. He's dry fucking my hip while fucking me with his fingers. "That's what you do to me," he rasps in my ear as he strokes maddeningly torturous circles on my clit.

I can't speak and I love it. I love the game. Love the play. Love the pretend as his mouth travels down my neck. I ride his hand, seeking my pleasure. "Kiss me while you come," he urges.

I nod fiercely, then rock into his hand as he drops his other palm then slants his mouth to mine, swallowing my cries of pleasure. I shake and shudder, coming hard on this stranger's hand as we pretend.

I gasp in his arms as he eases out then brings his fingers to his lips, sucking off my taste one finger at a sensual time.

I'm turned on again from the sight of him tasting me. I'm aroused, too, by one dangerous possibility. I grab his wrist, check the time on his watch. "Four minutes," I say, biting my lip.

"What do you want to do, my naughty girl?"

I drop to my knees.

4

VERY UNGENTLEMANLY

Finn

I don't want to think. I want to fuck her lush lips.

But I can't let her kneel on the hard wood floor like that, ruining her costume, hurting her knees. The couch across the room, with the small rug in front of it, is just too far away.

Instead, I whisk off my jacket. "Use this," I tell her, bending to arrange it on the floor right in front of her.

"Such a gentleman," she says as she adjusts herself on the material.

"Sometimes, but not always," I say.

She lifts her chin brazenly. "Show me the ungentlemanly side."

A fire ignites in me, blazing nearly out of control as I unzip, take out my cock, and rub the head against her lips. "You're dying for my cock, aren't you?"

"I thought about your dick while you taught me

'Für Elise,'" she says, then licks the tip like I'm a decadent piece of candy.

A hot burst of pleasure shoots down my spine. And if she wants ungentlemanly, she'll get ungentlemanly. "Open wide. Need to fuck that pretty mouth."

This masked beauty devours my dick with no hesitation, no toying around, just a purposeful awareness of a ticking clock.

She sucks the head, flicking her tongue then drawing me deep. Intense, powerful sucks. Then seductive, teasing licks, all while I indulge in the top-down view of those fantastic tits. "Yes, take it. All the way," I urge.

She curls her hands around my hips, tugging me closer. Then, I'm holding her masked face in both hands, fucking her mouth, and giving her a warning. "Coming," I mutter, ready to pull out if she wants that.

But her fingers tighten on my hips and she holds me in place, my pleasure in her hands and mouth, my release in her throat.

I squeeze my eyes shut, the world spiraling away as ecstasy throttles me in its wicked grip.

My legs shake. My hands rope through her hair.

I pant hard for several buzzy seconds, then open my eyes as she's adjusting her hair and her gold mask. I must have knocked it off when I grabbed her face. But she's got it back on now, covering her up, and I offer her a hand. She rises, then licks her lips, and smooths the material of her dress as it falls back down around to her ankles. I catch a glimpse of a silver anklet.

It's almost familiar, like I've seen something like it somewhere.

Then, the fabric hides it and she comes in for a quick kiss, that heady scent of her perfume infiltrating my senses once again, and it's chased by the smell of lilacs. Flowers and sex, and she's scrambling my head again. "Bye."

Wait. She's leaving? Holy shit. Her break is already up. There's so much I need to say to her.

In seconds, she's racing to the door.

My mind's a fog of lust, but I manage to call out a question. "What's your perfume?"

It feels important. I don't even know why, but it does.

"Summer Day," she says, then slips out the door and snicks it shut behind her.

I don't leave right away. I just stand here against the shelves, heart thumping, pulse racing.

Mind...floating.

That was completely unexpected, and the hottest night I've had in ages. I stare at the books across the room, the only witnesses to our stolen moment. They wink back at me. Cheeky fucking stories.

Yeah, I know, books. It's been a while.

I run a hand across my scruff, trying to reactivate my brain. Figure out what's next.

Need to get her name. Her number. Another night. One time with her is not enough. I want to undress her, spread her out on my bed, and devour her sweetness all night long.

When I look down to the floor, her gold clutch purse flickers on the wood next to my jacket.

My naughty Cinderella.

With the treasure in hand, I zip my pants, grab my jacket and head down the hall to the bathroom to straighten up. When I've pulled myself together, I return to the ballroom and the sound of "Que Sera, Sera."

Whatever will be, will be.

Nope. Not leaving another encounter with her to fate. She's the first woman I've kissed since my divorce. The first woman who's ignited my senses in some time. I weave through the crowd, heading straight to the piano, but Tevin stops me with a firm hand on my arm.

Shit. Did he see us? Not that we did anything wrong, but as someone hired by the club, she was worried. I don't want my piano player to get in trouble, especially since I promised her she wouldn't.

"Are you having a good night?" Tevin asks.

"The best," I say, without cracking a smile that'd give too much away.

"Will we see you again?"

"When's the next one?"

He tells me, and I make a split-second decision. "Yeah. I'll be there," I say.

I take risks for a living. I run a venture fund with my brother, and my entire career has been built on the foundation of gambling big in business. No reason to play it safe in my personal life now that I finally, maybe, have one again.

He peels away, and I resume my path to the piano,

setting her clutch on top of the baby grand. "You left your glass slipper," I say as I drink in the sight of her one more time.

To anyone else, she wouldn't look well fucked. But the absence of her lipstick thrills me. The few hairs out of place excite me.

She tries to hide a smile. "You found it," she says, then darts her gaze around the room like she's checking for prying eyes.

I don't want to ruin a thing for her, and really, there's no need to bother with names or numbers right now. I'll get them next time. Because I fully intend for there to be another night like this. I bend closer, then whisper in her ear, "I want you to come again. *On me.* I want to do very ungentlemanly things to you. The next party is in two weeks. I'll be here, waiting in the library for you to take your break."

She looks my way, her eyes unreadable, her lips tight. She says nothing as she maybe weighs the request.

Fine, so this is another challenge. I'm up for it. "The theme is Speakeasy. I'll wear navy suspenders. I bet you have a flapper dress that'll drive me wild."

Her breath catches. That hitch sounds like a yes.

"Wear it," I tell her. Her subtle gasp says she likes orders. "Without anything under your skirt." Her eyes widen, and I savor the look as I pause, then add, "And I'll take care of you completely."

Her answer comes in a shudder and then a question. "Will you finish what you started tonight?"

It's a wonder I don't haul her back into the library right now. "You have my filthy word."

* * *

"Let me get this straight. You built a tree house? An entire tree house in one weekend?" I arch a playfully skeptical brow my son's way as we walk through Gramercy Park on Sunday afternoon.

"No. We did it all in *one day*. And it has the best stuff in it. It has a game room, and a lookout tower, and a lab," Zach says.

And, evidently, ample space for one seven-year-old's very active imagination. I wonder how big this tree house actually is. I'm guessing it's only one regular-size tree house room, but it becomes whatever he wants it to be. I wonder, too, how important building a tree house is to him. I'm still learning all these details. I *relish* learning them.

"And what did you do in it?"

"Well, first we did some experiments in the lab. We made a volcano and watched it explode," he says, and that sounds fun. Way more fun than the Saturday I spent reviewing the terms of the upcoming acquisition.

Though maybe not more fun than my Friday night. But I am *not* going to think of my goddess while I'm with my kid. Zach spent the weekend with his maternal grandparents just outside the city. Normally, or what passes for normal after less than a year spent together, he spends time with them in Scarsdale a few nights a week. But he starts science camp tomorrow in the city, so he'll be with me for the next seven days. Since it's five in the evening, I suppose I should have settled him into our home —*our,* that's another strange thought, but a good strange thought—but when Zach begged me to take him swimming at Uncle Nick's, it didn't take much arm twisting to get me to say yes.

Sometimes I'm a pushover. I hope that's not bad.

When my brother's Art Deco building comes into view, Zach's little feet rev up and he darts ahead of me, but I grab his hand before he takes off running down the block, powered by copious seven-year-old energy.

"Stay with me, dude," I say.

"Okay, Dad," he says, but it's not a grumble–it's an acceptance. Just like he's accepted me easily as his father. Well, not when I first met him eight months ago. But soon after that, we got into a groove, and he started calling me Dad instead of Mr. Adams. Thank fuck. Only my grumpy dad is Mr. Adams. "Anyway, did you know Grandpa has a whole tool shed, with hammers and everything? He's super handy."

Well, considering I barely know the grandparents who'd been raising him for the last two years, I had no idea. "That's cool."

But does that mean I need a tool shed? I have a tool-box. Isn't that enough? I can fix things. As if my fire-fighter dad would have let me leave his house without knowing how to hang a bookcase, spackle a hole, or repair a leaky faucet. "You know, your dad is pretty handy as well," I say.

And competitive too.

Zach shoots me a quizzical look. "Can you build a tree house?"

It's a simple question, not a challenge, but I know tonight, I'll be googling how to build a tree house in a tiny yard in the West Village. "I can," I say. "But I can also make the best forts ever."

His green eyes pop wide open. My eyes. The kid has *my* eyes. The first time I met him it was eerie to see the similarity. Now, it's just...cool.

"Can we make one tonight?" he asks as we reach Nick's building.

"Sure," I say. I'm still bad at saying no.

We head inside and he picks up the pace. I shake my head. "Inside feet," I say. At least I draw the line there.

Zach nods like a good little soldier and resists running across the marble floor. When we reach the elevator, his eyes light up with glee. "Can I press the button?"

Things I don't understand about kids—the need to be the one to press the elevator buttons. "Were you helpful with your grandmother this weekend?"

"I set the table for dinner," he says earnestly.

That's good. "And were you polite with your grandfather?"

"I thanked him for the tree house," he says.

Stroking my chin like I'm weighing his good deeds, I finally say, "You can press it then."

"Sweet!" He stabs the penthouse button, and a minute later, we're off and he's rushing down the hall to my brother's home. I should tell him to stop, but fuck it.

I ran like a demon as a kid too. I don't mind seeing his rocket-fueled feet.

He raps on the door three times, but Nick answers on the second one, holding a couple of pool noodles in each hand. "Look what I got," he says, looking far too pleased.

Dammit. I wish I'd thought of noodles, but Nick's been at this parenting thing a lot longer than I have.

"Noodles!" Zach shouts, a battle cry for fun. He asks if he can go change, and Nick points to the guest bathroom. Zach scurries off, and I shut the penthouse door behind us.

"Noodles are the way to a kid's heart, I guess." I make a mental note.

"Well, pools are too. Hell, your pool in Miami is still the way to my thirty-nine-year-old heart," he says.

I do like that infinity pool in my second home. Could even see playing a *pool guy* scene there with my naughty piano player, pretending she owns the place, and I found her sunbathing with her top off, and she begged me to service her...

But I shake off those thoughts.

There's a time and place for those, and it is not when I'm about to pull on swim trunks.

Since there's no downtime with a busy seven-year-old, the three of us head to the indoor pool a few minutes later. Nick's building has one and the price tag reflects it.

Works for me.

Zach jumps in first, all limbs and elbows as he splashes. I'm right behind him, making a bigger splash.

Things I've learned in the last few months of trial-by-fire parenting—you can't walk into a pool with a kid. You must make an epic entrance.

He surfaces, laughing at the big waves, then turns to my brother on the ledge. "Do a cannonball, Uncle Nick!"

Like anyone needs to ask my brother twice. He heads to the deep end and complies, making a tsunami across the chlorinated water. Zach paddles to the edge, grabs his goggles, and yanks in one noodle.

"Takes after me," Nick says, and he sounds as proud as I am, even though he's got a kid of his own. But Nick was a swimmer in high school and college, and like me, he's enjoying finding the similarities between us and this new addition to the Adams family. "It's still wild to see you with a kid."

"Yeah, it is to me too," I say, with fondness for this new life, but some sadness, too, over how it happened.

Last summer, my wife of six years left me. We'd spent years in therapy, so the demise of our marriage was a surprise to no one, including me. The big surprise in life came a few months later.

I was running on the High Line with my buddy Tate when my phone rang with a Westchester County number. I answered it in case it was one of our portfolio clients for the venture firm, but the voice on the line was a stranger.

"This is Candace Irving. Any chance you were in Rome in September eight years ago?"

Startled, I stopped running. The surreal question belonged in the opening scene of a page-turning thriller. The kind where someone's identity is stolen, his life hacked, his world upended.

I sat on a bench, my heart racing faster. Tate joined me while this woman I didn't know shared more details, beginning with the fact that she was Nina Irving's mother.

The hair on the back of my neck stood on end. I hadn't known her last name. Nina was simply the captivating free spirit of a woman I met one night in Rome way back when. I was thirty-two, traveling for business. I met her in a piazza, and we spent one glorious night together. I knew very little about her except that she was an American working in Europe as a wedding and boudoir photographer, but she'd impulsively taken the weekend off to go to Rome with friends. By the end of the evening, she'd been in my hotel room.

In the morning, she was gone, catching her flight to Amsterdam where she had work for the week.

One hot night. Only first names. Nothing more.

Except, it wasn't just that.

As I learned from Candace, Nina wound up pregnant. She tried to find me, but not very hard, they said. With only a first name, she had no success, though she knew I worked in venture capital and lived in New York. But the free spirit in her believed everything was meant to be, that she was destined to be a single mother. Her parents believed otherwise, and when Nina died of a brain aneurysm when Zach was five, they became his guardians and took on the mission of tracking me down, eventually finding a news article online about a deal my company had inked in Rome right around the time when I'd have met Nina.

"We want him to know his father," Candace said simply.

The skeptical part of me figured they wanted his father's money too. That since they knew who I was, they'd want a payoff.

But they never asked. They wanted Zach to know his father and to be raised by him in tandem with them. One paternity test later, and I was sharing custody with the retired bankers in Connecticut.

Life is weird. I'm forty and a new dad to a seven-year-old. This is everything I'd wanted during my marriage—and it came *after*.

Zach tosses me a noodle and issues an order. "Chase me on my seahorse. Both of you," he says.

Well, then.

Nick and I comply, motoring after him until Nick's fiancée strides into the pool area. Nick pops off and swims to the edge of the pool. He parks his elbows on it, a stupidly swoony look on his face—which is how he looks *every time* he sees Layla. "You off to the store?" he asks her.

"I have a quick sesh," she says, then gives him a playful pout. She runs several makeup shops and does in-store makeup tutorials. "Then, it's poker night."

"Be sure to win big, sweetheart. Come home with the whole pot," he says to her.

"I'll take my girls for everything."

Nick wags a finger. "And don't let Jules beat you this time."

She heaves a sigh. "Hey! It's not my fault. She has the best poker face in the group."

"No, you do, beautiful. You do."

With his pep talk done, she stands and waves to me. "Have fun swimming," she calls out.

"Good luck with the card sharking," I say. "And taking your friends' money."

"I'll do my best," she says, then leaves. When I spin around, Nick's back on a noodle, paddling toward Zach.

Ah, hell.

I can't resist.

I catch up to him quickly, then mouth to Zach, *watch this.*

I drop my hand on Nick's head and dunk my little brother—younger by a year. Zach cracks up, and the sound is wholly gratifying.

When Nick resurfaces, he narrows his eyes. "You'll pay for that."

"Still worth it." I horse around with my kid and my brother, focusing on family and not on after-dark fêtes that take my mind off all the things I haven't had these last few years.

All the things I've missed.

When we return to his penthouse an hour later, my clothes are missing.

Fucking little brothers.

Well, this swimsuit is dry enough. I call a Lyft and head home with Zach, wearing only my swim trunks.

Zach laughs the whole way.

5

ALMOST PERFECT

Jules

Things my dad taught me—be direct when you want something.

Things my mom taught me—lubricate a request with a gift.

I go with Mom's guidance when it comes to asking Scarlett if I can fill in for her in another two weeks.

After I finish my Krav Maga class on Sunday afternoon, I pop into a candle shop in my Chelsea neighborhood to snag a gift, then I head home to take a quick shower. Under the stream, I rehearse what to say when I stop by Scarlett's bar in a bit. I hate walking into situations unprepared.

What if I'm tempted to shout *I sucked a guy's cock in the library the other night and I want to do it again?* What if I go on and blurt out every single personal detail about my encounter in front of all her customers? What if I reveal all my dirty dreams to...ugh...everyone?

My pulse skitters wildly as the awful images whirl. Suddenly, I'm picturing saying all those things. It feels so likely, as if I absolutely will do this, until I take a breath.

In for four—then out for a long count of eight. And again, as the hot water runs over me and I face the intrusive thoughts straight on. Labeling them for what they are. I can handle them. As the water patters against the tiles, I do my homework from my therapist.

These thoughts are not up to me.

They will just float through my mind and go away. I won't act on them. I accept them instead of fighting them.

A few minutes of talk-back and I feel mostly better. I get out of the shower and dry off, then put on lotion, taking my time as I get more distance from the thoughts.

I'm calmer when I head to my favorite place—my closet.

I'll be meeting my friends later tonight, so I pick something fun to wear, opting for a pair of black denim shorts I snagged from my favorite vintage shop, along with a lavender crop top. Since the weather's not too hot yet, I grab a blazer that was once owned by some lady boss.

In the mirror, I strike a pose, assessing. If my sister were here, I'd ask her opinion.

I listen for Willa's voice, but it's grown faint through the years.

Just tug the blazer toward your shoulder. Don't be afraid to show a little skin.

She was the *real* bold one. That was the problem. I'm the planner.

That was the problem too.

I'm almost ready to leave, but I need one more thing. I grab my anklet from the drawer of my jewelry box and fasten it on. It's thin, with little silver stars dangling from it. Willa gave it to me for my eighteenth birthday seven years ago. When we learned all their possible meanings, we became obsessed with ankle bracelets, gifting them to each other constantly, trading them back and forth, then pretending they meant different things. Ridiculous things, all of them ultimately boiling down to anthem—*fuck the patriarchy*.

I flip the bird on her behalf, then grab my beige journal from my nightstand. A reminder of *why* I'm making this request of Scarlett will do me good.

Why I'm going to such lengths for another time with that man.

Opening the journal, I take out the card I keep in there, setting it down on the bed, before I flip through the pages. I re-read the details I logged in the journal about Friday night.

Leather, orchids, fire. A teacher, a phantom, an ungentleman. A tailored jacket for your knees. A request to come again. Then, with the pen from the loop holder, I add a few more words, written as fragments, like a haiku out of order, so no one can decipher it. *Make me be quiet. Sometimes, but not other times. Flapper dress and...nothing.*

The memories make me shiver.

"Done," I say, then pick up the card and tuck it safely back inside and lock up the journal. I grab the gift for Scarlett, dropping something I snagged for Camden into a bag too. On the way out of my pint-size apartment, I stop and sniff the gardenias I picked up at the farmers' market. They're fragrant, peachy. Flowers have always made me happy, so they're my little luxury.

They also settle me before I head into unusual situations, so I take one more hit, then I walk the few blocks to Better Days, powered by determination.

After pushing open the door, I march to the counter where my friend is uncapping two Modelos and sliding them to a pair of women, both wearing ripped jeans. When they go to a table, Scarlett turns to me, her bright blue eyes sparkling.

"Hey, babe," Scarlett says, stretching out her inked arms for a hug that doesn't quite happen across the counter. "You're my heroine!"

I lean in to receive the almost embrace. "That's me. How was your shift?"

"Crazy," she says with an eye roll. "But it's all good. Everyone got their booze so the world kept turning."

"What more can you ask for?"

"A better boss," she mutters under her breath, then sweeps her gaze from side to side and launches into a litany of how strict her boss is about the schedule, and how now he wants her to work every Friday.

"That sucks," I say, sympathetically.

"You're lucky you like your job."

"Definitely," I say.

After a pause, she asks quietly, "So, how was it?"

"It was fantastic," I say in my job interview voice, and I don't at all say what I feared I would. I rarely do. That doesn't stop the thoughts from coming though. But I understand them now. I've learned how to handle them so they don't have as much power over me as they once did. I know, too, that I'm in control of my words and my deeds.

I dip into my canvas bag, grab the lavender candle and set it on the bar. "Just a little thanks."

"You didn't have to do that," she says, but her upbeat tone tells me she likes the gift. It's her signature scent, and I picked it especially for her.

"It was fun." I draw a quiet, fueling breath. Here goes nothing...and everything. "And hey, I heard there's another one in two weeks." I keep it breezy, easy, and in a lower volume I add, "Any chance I can fill in? Especially with the way things are around here." I gesture subtly to the crowded bar.

Her head tilts. "Really? But why?"

I shrug like it's no big deal, when it's *all the deal*. "It's a Speakeasy theme. And you know me. I just really like looking at the costumes," I say with a smile.

I'm not lying. I *love* dressing up.

Scarlett seems to consider it for a second. "Sure. I heard from the couple who runs it that you were really good on the piano."

I was really good on my knees too.

"Thanks, babe," I say, then leave, a smile blooming bright and wide once I'm out on the streets of Manhattan.

Too bad, Dad. Looks like Mom was right.

* * *

Another thing my dad says is there are no good reasons to be late, only excuses. So I'm early for poker night as I exit the subway twenty minutes after leaving Better Days then walk a block over to a sleek stretch of Madison Avenue lined with pricy boutiques and chichi cafés.

I spot Camden walking toward me. Like me, she's carrying a canvas bag. She's in charge of snacks tonight. I'm responsible for liquor, and my tote holds a boxed sauvignon because boxed wine is more fun. Also, wine openers suck.

I cross the street and stop to give her a hug. When I let go, I reach into my bag for *another* bag—a purple one—then hand it to her.

She arches a brow in question but takes the bag with avid eyes. "What's this?"

"Only the very thing you asked for," I say with a grin.

Opening the purple sack, she gasps. "You didn't."

I shrug, pleased. "I did."

She paws at the paint-it-on vegan leather pants, the faded black tee with the cut-up neckline, and the studded wristband—the rocker chick outfit she wanted for karaoke. "Seriously. You didn't have to do that," she says.

"I know. But it was so very you." I don't make a ton of money, but I like to spend my extra on my friends, and, well, on my OCD therapist, Shira.

"Then I will wear the fuck out of this," Camden declares with a smoky purr, then squeezes my shoulder. "Now, gimme all the details," she says as we continue to our mutual destination.

"I told you everything yesterday," I remind her. We turn onto Harlow's picturesque block, walking under a canopy of honey locust trees. "Or was it so good you want a repeat?"

I know I do.

She rolls her eyes. "Hello. *Your request.*"

"Oh, right," I say, embarrassed. Maybe I'm a little overeager to repeat the juicy details of the hottest sexual encounter of my life. Not that there are many contenders, but still. "Scarlett said yes. I can fill in for her again in two weeks. Well, twelve days, but who's counting?"

Camden's eyes flash victory signs. "And now, *Masquerade All The Way: The Sequel* is officially green-lit," she says, clearly amused as we pass a brick brownstone that looks like it belongs on the set of a rom-com flick. "It's longer, dirtier, and full throttle."

"You should write movie trailers."

"And *you* should play chess with those moves you pulled off to make part two happen. I swear, you're always thinking."

More like overthinking. "Except chess is boring."

"But your sex life isn't," she says.

"Potential sex life," I correct.

She grabs my elbow, stopping me on the pristine sidewalk—pristine by New York standards—before we reach Harlow's building. "Is he...*the one*?"

Camden knows me better than anyone—she doesn't mean *the one* in a love-story type of way. Still, the idea of *the one* is difficult for me to embrace. If there's one person for you, then there's one person who can hurt you the most. One person you can lose.

But *the one* for a first time in the bedroom? "Hell yes," I say, feeling so damn certain.

Her eyes light up. "Are you going to tell him it'll be your first time riding a D?"

Even though I'm twenty-five, I'm not precious about my virginity. I wanted to sleep with my college boyfriend, Brandon. Planned to, in fact. But he played the cruelest mind games in a sick ruse to get me into bed on his timetable, not mine. I didn't let him win, but his twisted tricks shut me down. For a few years after college, I was wholly uninterested in having sex or participating in the games people play to get it.

But I did *think* about sex. Sometimes too much. To the point where I'd be in a work meeting, and out of nowhere, I'd imagine having sex with the people my boss and I were talking to. My thoughts were out of control and distressing because I didn't want to be thinking about those people in a sexual way and I didn't understand why I was. It was like an uncomfortable dream you fight to wake up from.

I tried counting to make them stop. I tried repeating innocuous words to distract my brain from them. I tried ignoring them harder.

Finally, I confessed them to Google. And the answer was one of those *lightbulb-on* moments.

You have OCD and it's manifesting as intrusive thoughts.

I finally went to therapy, and it's been for the best. Shira's helped me with much better strategies and techniques, than my counting compulsion. She's also helped me to see that my other fears—like balconies, rooftops, and subway platforms—come from the same place.

I used to think I was a freak for having these awful thoughts touch down in my brain. I used to think I was a freak, too, for craving a little domination in bed, a little playacting.

Shira's helped me see that there's nothing wrong with the desire to pretend I'm someone else during sex.

And that my intrusive sex thoughts aren't the same as my true desires.

I've separated them now. I can tell the difference between uncomfortable thoughts and exciting fantasies.

And I've finally found a man whose fantasies seem to match mine.

But if I'm going to see my phantom again, I suppose it's best to start with a base level of honesty—something Brandon never gave me.

Resolute, I nod to Camden, answering her question. "Yes, I'll tell him, but not in a big-deal type of way."

"A take-me-or-leave-me way," she says, understanding completely. Before I can reply, the click of shoes grows louder behind us, and a familiar voice calls out, "You better have good snacks."

I turn around. Layla walks toward us wearing a short-sleeve pin-up blouse that tells me she had a makeup event this afternoon.

"As if I'd bring anything less than the best," Camden says as the keeper of the snacks.

I've known Layla for a couple of years and Camden for my whole life. I adore them both, but there are different levels of access.

So when Layla reaches us and asks brightly, "How was your weekend?" Camden takes the question, telling a story about a song request she got last night at the lounge where she's bartending and moonlighting as a torch singer. She chats more about it while we head inside Harlow's building. On the way up to her place, I try to decide how much I'll say when the poker questions inevitably turn to everyone's weekend.

Including mine.

Really though, how much *is* there to share anyway? I don't even know that man's name. But I want to.

"Oh my god, fuck you," Layla says, slumping deeper onto Harlow's orange couch as she points at me. "I can never beat you."

Harlow nods sympathetically. "No one can, sweetie."

"But you should keep trying," I deadpan as I scoop up the chips from the table, thanks to a fantastic bluff on a pair of twos. Layla folded with a pair of kings. Bummer for her.

She shoots lasers at me with her bright blue eyes. "I've been trying for months. Since we started playing. And I swear I thought you had a full house or something. I was telling Nick and Finn just hours ago that you have the best poker face."

Camden's brow knits as she dips a hand into the bag of chocolate-covered orange slices. "Who's Finn?"

"Nick's brother. He was over at our place today. Well, they were swimming with Finn's kid."

The talk turns to the weekend again, coming back around to me with Harlow asking, "What did you do this weekend, J?"

Even though it was inevitable that the chitchat would return here, I'm *never* sure what to say when conversations get too personal with anyone other than my bestie. It's so much easier to talk about other people than to talk about myself. I'd rather listen.

"Oh, you know," I begin, trying to keep it light, but I feel like a little sneak, which I hate. It reminds me of terrible days long ago and of things said and unsaid that still pierce my heart.

"No, I don't know," Layla teases as she reaches for her glass of wine and takes a drink. "Did you make or break dreams all weekend, Jules?"

"Bridger says you're his secret weapon," Harlow adds affectionately.

I do love the secondhand praise from my boss,

Harlow's fiancé. Part of my job at Opening Number, the production company I work for, is to read scripts for Bridger and provide coverage on whether we should pass or not on those shows.

"Definitely, I broke some hearts," I say, taking the easier answer, then I tuck a strand of my hair behind my ear, feeling fidgety.

I wish it weren't so hard to tell them about the party—to tell them how I felt and what I want and then ask what they think. To analyze it together, turn it inside out, and then somehow feel better for having shared the experience with all my good friends.

But a nagging voice asks...*what if?*

That's the problem. Telling someone one thing opens the door to them learning more things—things they could use against you.

Like plenty of people have done. Like, say, Brandon. And, hey, how about my parents too? Yeah, that was real fun.

"Lots of scripts," I add. "Then, I did some planning for the final episodes of *Happy Enough*."

"Spill," Layla demands.

With a smile, I shake my head. "Can't give up trade secrets," I say. That's one of our most popular shows, based on books by the romance author Laura Paigeley, and it's heading toward the end of its successful second season.

"Fine, fine. So, basically a typical weekend for you," Harlow says, bumping her shoulder against mine. It's a move she does with Layla. A friendly move.

I miss big friend group moments fiercely, so the

move inadvertently does the trick, opening me up more. "And I filled in for a friend of mine who plays piano."

Whew. That wasn't too hard to say.

"Oh cool. Where did you play?" Harlow asks.

"It was kind of like a private party," I say.

In tandem, Layla and Harlow both sit up straight, instantly attentive. "What kind of private party and how do I get an invite?" Layla asks.

"Well, I can't really say," I answer as memories rush through my mind, heating my body all over again. My cheeks warm.

"Oh!" Layla's lips part in a gasp.

"What?" I ask, a little alarmed.

"You're blushing," she whispers.

So much for my poker face.

"What *did* you do at the party?" Harlow asks, her tone dripping with curiosity too.

"Or should I say...*who*?" Layla adds.

I don't have to share all the details. But this conversational pawn? I can move it a square, and dammit, I *want* to move it a square. "There was this guy. He was... interesting," I say.

They are literally on the edge of their seats, and it feels good to have an audience for a story again. It's been a long time.

"How so?" Layla asks.

I smile, a little demurely. "He was...bold. Direct. The kind of man who knows what he wants. Know the type?"

Layla fans herself. "Um, yeah."

"Right. You're living with the type," I add as Camden grabs the deck of cards. It's her turn to deal. "And let's just say...we slipped away during a break, and we had a very good time."

There. That wasn't so bad. *Very* ought to cover a lot of what happened in the library.

"And?" Harlow asks, staring pointedly with those big green eyes that would con a bone away from a dog.

"I'm supposed to see him again. So we'll see how it goes."

Camden shuffles more loudly this time, perhaps knowing I've reached my limit. It's not the first time she's saved me. "C'mon," she says. "We have a card shark to take down, girls."

They try, but I still win the game.

I've got my poker face back on. It's safer that way with almost everyone.

One more day.

The next week, as I walk to my dad's office on a Thursday evening, I remind myself I only have to make it through one more day till *The Scene*. Somehow I've managed to survive nearly two weeks of production coordination for *Happy Enough*. But I've also been working extra hours, reading the scripts Bridger gave me for our new dramedy, *The Rendezvous,* which is shooting now and slated to air on an upstart streaming service. That project came directly to him since he's become known as a producer with a great sense for international shows. One of his first hits took place in Paris, and I wish I were working on this one too. The writing is sharp, and the inclusive cast of characters intrigues me—Black, white, queer, straight, and all shapes and sizes.

Bridger says there aren't any open producer positions for me, but that hasn't deterred me from staying up late and offering him tips for the upcoming location shoot in Paris, like where the heroine's flat should be, and info on securing it for the time we need it.

I've spent later nights prepping for *The Scene.* I have my outfit picked out and my mask chosen. My tunes practiced, thanks to the keyboard at my apartment. Scarlett put me in touch directly with the organizers, who sent me the details, including arrival time and password. I had no chill when I saw their name pop up in my email. I squealed.

All I have to do is make it through dinner tonight with my dad and his wife, then a day of work tomorrow, then it'll finally be time for my take-my-V-card-please date.

Will my date be gangster or Gatsby in his navy suspenders? That tease of a man only told me *one* piece of his costume. I picture him in a vintage suit, shedding his jacket, his suspenders, then asking me to ride his cock.

Yes, sir.

But best to bleach those images away for the next few hours as I enter my father's office building. He's a former cop who went to law school several years ago and is now a corporate attorney.

On the way up in the elevator, I mentally review the evening ahead with my dad. What I want to talk about over dinner. The things in my life I'll share with him.

Hmm. That'd be work, work, and more work. So much better than talking about the day we all went to grief counseling after Willa's death.

I shudder, then slam the door on those terrible memories.

When I reach his floor, I smile at the firm's receptionist. "Hi, Anita." She knows me since I see him for dinner regularly.

"Hello, Jules. Tate's just finishing up with a friend, but he said you can go in anytime."

"Sweet," I say, then I run a hand down my twin-set sweater. It's short-sleeved and mint green with an embroidered cherry on the front. Very mod and vintage —perfect for the TV biz with its artsy vibe. I paired it with a black pencil skirt, and I have my glasses on. I like to wear them at work and save my contacts for going out and for friends.

I head down the hall to my dad's office, but when I near it, something stops me.

A voice.

And it's not my dad's.

A dart of worry pricks my chest as I listen to the next thing the man with my father says. "Saturday morning? I don't think so, Tate," he says in a deep, raspy tone that makes me shiver.

Which concerns me.

Because...I should not be shivering at my dad's office.

Maybe I'm hearing things. Maybe this is a new symptom of my OCD. I walk cartoon-character slow, keyed in on the voice.

"Oh, c'mon. You're going to slack off?" my father goads, but he's clearly baiting the guy in a buddy sort of way.

"Yeah, I'm a slacker," the man says dryly, and my shoulders tighten with worry.

"Better not be. We have that bet with the other triathlon team."

"Well, I'd hate to lose," he says.

"Perfect. Then I'll see you this Saturday at the crack of dawn so we can kill it," my father says in a lighter tone than he ever takes with me. I tiptoe closer now, a few feet from the open door. They can't see me, and none of the paralegals or lawyers are walking down the hall. The office is half-empty at this time of the evening.

"Appreciate the hard sell, but not this Saturday," his friend says, drawing a line in the sand.

My heart climbs up my throat uncomfortably. *No, please, no.* Just let them sound similar.

"I guess someone has a *fun* Friday night planned," my dad says, a little too dude-bro for my tastes. I picture my dad lifting his eyebrows, asking what's on tap for tomorrow night. Gross.

"We'll see," the man hedges, but I can hear the smile in his voice.

In it is the echo of other words. Words like...*Open wide. Need to fuck that pretty mouth.*

And...*I want you to come again. On me.*

I want to scream. This can't be happening. My father's running partner—the guy he does triathlons with—*can't* be my phantom, my Gatsby, my Friday night secret date.

I draw a deep but quiet breath, then take one more step.

"You better show up Sunday morning, then," my dad says.

"You do know when we win that bet, it'll be because of me," the man counters.

That voice.

"Fucking show-off," my dad says with a friendly scoff.

"It's not showing off if it's true," the man says.

I wish my OCD brain was playing the meanest trick on me with some new and awful intrusive thought. But I know it's not. Still, I need to be sure if it's really him. If I just peer carefully into the doorway, I can see most of Dad's desk, but he won't be able to see me.

Praying I'm mistaken, I peer carefully into the office. My father sits at his desk, cracking a rare smile as he chats with the man across from him.

In slow-mo, like I'm watching through horror-movie fingers, I turn.

I. Die.

I roll my lips together, sealing up all my screams. That jawline covered in scruff. That hair, thick and brown, with a few silver streaks. Those broad shoulders.

I'd know that half profile anywhere.

Even though I only saw him in the dark, that's the man I kissed at the masquerade. The man who made me come hard by the books.

The man whose cock I sucked good and thorough... is my father's best friend.

Finn Adams.

I swivel around, race-walk down the hall, then duck into the ladies' room.

I guess I'll risk being late this time.

6

BACKING OUT

Jules

My father finishes a bite of his salmon, washes it down with water, then asks, continuing our dinner conversation, "And what did Renata say about your track record with Opening Number?"

Is your best friend still married??? Because I'm sick to my stomach right now. Like, I want to die.

I'm twenty-five, so it's not like I hang out a lot with my father and his buddy. They only became friends a few years ago. It's not like Finn came over to barbecues when I was a teenager, or, worse, to piano recitals when I was in braces.

I shudder at those thoughts but strive to keep my poker face as I answer his question about the executive I've been working with at Webflix, the streaming service that carries *Happy Enough.* "Well, I didn't exactly say *here's my track record.* Instead, I did what she asked me to. I ran the budget for the show they're going to carry."

My even tone doesn't give away the relentless loop playing in my head. *My father's best friend wants to fuck me and I'm pretty sure he's married.*

I can barely take another bite of this mushroom risotto. From across the table, my father's wife watches me as I push food aimlessly on my plate. She's poised like a cat, staring at my dish.

But before the only-eats-salads health nut can jump in, my dad continues down work-talk road. "You should find ways to let her know, Julia," he says. He's the only person who calls me by my given name. I've been Jules forever. "We made sure you landed a job at one of the top production companies in the world for a reason—so you could have the job you've always wanted."

We?

He's trying to take credit for my job with Bridger? Fine, he introduced me to Bridger when I graduated, and Bridger hired me as an intern. But I had to prove myself. I had to work my way up, and over the last three years, I've done that on my own terms.

But I don't point that out. I don't plan to tell him, either, that I've been dying to work on *The Rendezvous.* He'd probably call Bridger and diplomatically suggest he move me onto that show, saying Streamer would be lucky to have me working on its flagship production.

No thanks.

Besides, I have a bigger mission at this meal—

moving the conversational chess piece to the guy who's no longer a phantom. I already googled Finn while I was in the ladies' room at my dad's office. He's not on social, so I didn't find anything that would tell me his current relationship status. No photos of him recently, but plenty over the last few years at charity events with his wife, Marilyn.

Who I met a year ago.

Dad had texted me at the last minute to join him at a nearby restaurant with some of his friends. When I arrived, Finn rose, shook my hand, and said, "Good to see you again, Jules. This is my wife, Marilyn."

My chest caves just thinking of those words. He didn't have a ring on at The Scene, because of course he didn't have a ring on at a kink masquerade.

I even contemplated texting Layla to ask if Finn's married, once I'd put two and two together and realized my Finn is Nick's brother. She's mentioned Finn in passing a few times, including at poker, but of course I hadn't known he was the *same* Finn. Or my phantom. But even now that I know, there's no reason why I'd ask her. If he is married, I don't want to let the cat out of the bag that he cheats. And I definitely don't want my friends to think I'd hook up with a married man because I wouldn't knowingly do that ever. I don't want to do that unknowingly either.

"I'll find a way to let Renata know," I tell my father, though I won't, but I add, "Anything else you think I should do?"

Dad motors on about work ethics, reminding me once again that I shouldn't ever be late to work, like I was late for meeting him earlier, and then it hits me. *Earlier* he and Finn were talking about training. All I have to do is ask my dad about running.

When there's a pause in the conversation, Liz sets down her fork next to her plate of lettuce, then asks, "And how is your risotto?"

That's not what the carb hater really means. "It's great," I say quickly, then look at my dad. "Hey, how's your triathlon training going? You're still running every weekend in the park?"

It's a bit obvious but maybe not too obvious.

"Great. We have another race coming up in a month," he says.

"Who's we?" I ask, acting confused. "Oh, that guy you train with? What's his name?"

He huffs, clearly frustrated with me for forgetting. "Finn Adams. You've met him a few times, Julia."

Score one for me. I led the witness, and the witness is an attorney. "Right. I think...with his wife?" I ask, scrunching my brow.

Liz shakes her head, cutting in with, "They're not married anymore."

Thank god. I breathe freely for the first time since I heard that sexy, raspy voice an hour ago.

"Oh, that's..." But I don't add *too bad* because who really knows? And if I say *that's good,* I might be at the risk of smiling so hard my cheeks crack.

"Yeah, it's for the best," my dad says, then zooms right back to the subject of work, peering closely at my sweater. "Are you wearing those sweaters to work?"

"I look professional, Dad," I say defensively as I fiddle with the pearl buttons.

He eyes the embroidery on the front of the sweater. "A cherry?"

I tug it closed. "I work with creatives."

"Just make sure you don't wear sweatpants to work like all the other young people do," he says.

Seriously? "I don't wear sweatpants to work," I say, and he launches into a riff about how people dress today.

Why is a daring, edgy man like Finn friends with my hard-ass dad? My dad's not fun. He doesn't scream *good-time buddy*. But then, he seemed different in his office when I overheard him talking to Finn. He was relaxed, sarcastic. They needled each other in the way good friends do.

Oh shit.

Does my dad go to those parties too? Are my father and Liz kinky? What if Finn and my father are kink friends? I think I'll just die right now, because that thought is more terrifying than my father himself, who's scary on the best of days. A stern, no-nonsense man who has been strict with me ever since he married Liz, who's strict with herself.

Which means...Finn can't ever know who I am. He'd never mess around with Tate Marley's daughter. No one wants to piss off a friend, let alone a friend who's a former man in blue.

I have less than twenty-four hours to figure out what to do about The Scene.

"Her outfit is nice, Tate," Liz cuts in, coming to my defense, which rarely happens.

"Thanks, Liz," I say, appreciative and a little surprised.

"It's perfectly professional," she adds, then goes on as an HR executive about office dress codes these days, which is kind of boring, so I return to the drumbeat in my brain.

Of all the men in New York City, why did my father's best friend have to be the one who lit me on fire? Why did he have to be the one I'm dying to see tomorrow? Why, fucking, why?

I push my risotto around some more, then Liz pauses and shifts gears. "Jules, you're not eating much?" She's trying, but she can't hide the hope in her voice.

She's tiny and toned and exercises a ton. She never eats dessert, never stays up late, never misses a Pilates class.

I'm curvy with big tits. And yeah, I work out, too, and have the toned arms to prove it. But salad won't make my boobs or ass smaller.

"I'm not on a diet, Liz. I'm not very hungry," I say.

Finding out the guy you want is your father's best friend? That will kill anyone's appetite.

* * *

The second I'm on the subway heading to Chelsea, I tap out a text to Scarlett.

Jules: I am so sorry but something came up and I can't fill in tomorrow night after all.

I stare at the draft, my thumb hovering. I feel terrible letting her down, but I can't go anymore. This way, Finn will never know I was the piano player. I'll just be the naughty girl who disappeared into a summer night with a perfume that drove him so wild he asked for its name. He'll never know he kissed his best friend's daughter. It's nicer that way. If he learns who I am, he might be twisted with guilt about it. Guilt sucks. I can't let him feel that way. Nor do I want to irrevocably alter his relationship with my dad. But as I re-read the message, another type of guilt pricks at me.

I want to be a woman of my word. I don't want to leave Scarlett hanging, especially when I'd asked to fill in. So I hit erase and try again.

> Jules: Something came up for work. Is there any chance you can still do tomorrow night?

> > Scarlett: What??? Babe, I'm out of town with my sister. She stole me away for a girls' weekend.

My chest hollows out, emptying to nothing. Then, it fills up again, topped off with jealousy.

> Jules: Don't think twice, then. I'll make it work.

I drop my head in my hand as the subway rumbles to Chelsea, dreading tomorrow night.

7

SOMETIMES AN ANKLET IS JUST AN ANKLET

Finn

Something has been nagging at me since yesterday, but I can't think what it is. As Zach rushes out the door of my—*our*—West Village brownstone, tearing off to meet his grandmother waiting on the sidewalk, I cycle through possibilities. Did I pack everything he needs for the weekend? Definitely. I even signed him up for another camp next week. Got the confirmation earlier today when we were at the park.

But I don't think *this thing's* about Zach. It's more like a sense of déjà vu that's been dogging me since I visited my buddy's office twenty-four hours ago. More specifically, since I glimpsed a woman ducking into the ladies' room as I left. No clue why that would stick with me. I barely saw her, but something about her felt familiar.

Best to let it go, especially since Zach's flying down the steps.

"Slow down, buddy," I call out. Too late. He's already jumping off the last step like he has wings.

When Zach hugs Candace like he missed her the most, my heart squeezes painfully. Maybe that's what I'm missing—*years*. He's known her his whole life. She must be more like a parent to him than I am.

She hugs him back fiercely, like a mom would do, which is the role she's effectively played since Nina died.

But as much as she loves him—to the moon and back—we never fought over custody. From the start, she told me she wanted to share custody with me if I wanted it.

If.

I wanted it all, but I took half. That felt fair.

Her husband Michael still motors around the house and the yard, but he has a heart condition, so she worries that Zach's days with him are numbered.

Well, they're both in their late seventies, and Zach is seven, so she's not wrong to be planning ahead.

I walk down the steps as the sun dips toward the horizon. The clock is ticking. I'm not antsy for them to go, but...I am really fucking antsy to see my goddess again.

Once Candace is free from Zach's octopus hug, she ruffles his dark hair. Did Nina do that? Probably. Does Zach remember his mother's touch?

No.

His words, not mine. When I showed him the picture of his mom boosting him up on a jungle gym at the park—a shot Candace gave me for Christmas—

Zach took a quick glance at the shot and said, "I bet we had fun that day."

Zach *bet*. But he didn't *know*.

I filed that under things that make me sad, especially since I actually like my parents. I see them often.

"You ready, cutie-pie?" Candace asks Zach.

"I bought a new rocket kit for Grandpa and me. I sent it to your house. Did you get it, Grams?"

Shaking her head in amusement, she looks my way. "He's ordering his own rocket kits?"

That's not normal? "Yeah. Well, the Internet's pretty easy to use," I say a little defensively.

"This world. I swear," she says, then turns to Zach. "Yes, I thought your dad sent it."

"Well, he knew I got it. I bought it on his phone the other night."

Zach hurries to the hatchback, but before he yanks on the handle, he zooms over to me for one more hug. I give it to him happily. "I'll come get you Sunday night," I say, rubbing a hand on his back.

He'll be mine again for another full week in the city, and next weekend too. We've had a blast these past five days, and my tiny yard is proof, still covered with the lava from the volcanos that we erupted. Mount Loa has nothing on this father-son duo. But I also took him to the movies and then spent the early evening hunting down superhero costumes.

I've been busy, and that's what I've wanted for years.

I head up the steps and inside, where I shower then get dressed. Once I'm ready, I walk through the kitchen, my gaze straying to the window that overlooks the tiniest of backyards.

The littlest tree house in the city looks awesome there. Maybe I'm not so wet behind the ears with this parenting thing after all.

I take off, leaving this part of my life behind for now. For the rest of tonight...I'll be someone else.

The man I wasn't able to be for most of my marriage.

* * *

Sometimes, your mind plays tricks on you. You remember a restaurant as being incredible the first time you eat there. Then you return, and the same dish just isn't as good. As I head into the Albrecht Mansion that evening, dressed in slacks, a button-down, and navy suspenders as promised—a little Gatsby-esque, complete with a black Art Deco mask—I temper my expectations.

Life has taught me to expect little, even when I want much.

A few years of marriage spent trying to please someone unpleasable will do that to a guy. Make you stop...hoping. Marilyn was a miser, doling out tiny portions of love and sex and happiness to a starving man.

When I want to feel voraciously.

My jaw ticks at the invasion of annoying thoughts

about my ex. I don't want to spend an ounce of energy tonight on what went wrong in my romantic life. The answer? Nearly everything.

Just for one night, I'd like to experience the rush of connection. The thrill of returned intimacy. The heat of hot, hungry sex.

But only after she's begged for it.

That's what I want most. To drive that woman so wild she's crying and begging for me to send her over the edge.

And just like that, I've figured out what's been dogging me. The huge mistake I made two weeks ago. When I left the party that night and arranged to meet her again, I screwed up big time. I thought meeting her in the library during her break would be enough.

Her break won't be long enough for the things I want to do to her.

My goddess might think I like role-play, and, sure, I do. But role-play is simply the start of what I crave.

It only scratches the surface of why I go to The Scene.

With the same desire that drives me to work countless hours when I'm *this close* to acquiring a new app, a new content play, a new online site, I stride up the steps, propelled by renewed purpose.

I'm determined to get my woman. I want an entire night with her, and when I get her alone during her break, I plan to propose just that—to take her home.

I turn the corner, heading down the hall, the piano music catching my ear. I tilt my head, a little surprised. I'd have expected something jazzy again, from the roaring twenties era to suit the theme. But instead, the song is "Crazy in Love."

The modern tune draws me down the hall and into the glittery room, transformed into a speakeasy. Already, the room is crowded, the corners occupied with women in flapper dresses kissing men in fashionable tweeds. In the far corner, a woman in wide trousers and a silky blouse is being kissed by two men. Wait. Now three.

The Scene isn't a sex club per se. There aren't rooms you can reserve with thrones or St. Andrew's crosses. The Scene is more of an anteroom. When you step into the private parties, you know everyone you meet will be into something...unconventional.

Almost everyone's into role-play, but The Scene serves other kinks too. The events aren't always masquerades but often simple cocktail parties catering to those into voyeurism or BDSM. I prefer the masquerades, since I've found role-play is the appetizer to what I like most in bed.

And what I like most requires time. Lots of time.

Hence my rookie mistake the other week. But I'll correct it soon enough because there she is at the baby grand in a darkened corner. My pulse surges the second I set eyes on her.

Someone understood the assignment. Her hair is short tonight. She wears a jet-black wig, cut straight at the jawline, and a shimmery black mask, covered in silver stars.

Wait.

Stars.

That sense of déjà vu taps on my shoulder. Was my déjà vu that I've been thinking of her?

Well, no shit.

I thought of her nonstop since I left the Albrecht Mansion two weeks ago. I can't get her out of my mind. Every night, she goes to bed with me. Every night, I take my cock in my hand and imagine the things I want to do to her body. The attention I want to lavish on her.

I roam my hungry eyes over her behind the piano. Her black dress is sleeveless, 1920s style, exposing the pale skin of her strong arms. I can't see the length of her outfit from here, or her legs. But I let myself picture black strappy heels. Something incomparably sexy that I'd tell her to leave on as I spread her out on the bed so I could feast on her for a good long time.

My skin heats at the sight of her. And I just...*need*. I need to touch her, taste her, satisfy two endless weeks of lust and longing.

Two weeks that felt like forever.

I watch her from across the room for a few minutes, willing her to look my way. She has to look up, right? But even when she shifts from one song to the next, she keeps her head down, focused on the job.

I swing over to the bar to get a drink. A pretty woman in an emerald fringe dress and a feathery black mask sidles up against me. "How's it going, handsome?"

She says it in that speakeasy side-of-the-mouth way. Don't want to be rude, but I don't want to lead her on either. "It's going great," I say, then nod goodbye and return to the ballroom with my whiskey.

Normally, I'd circulate, but I've already found the woman I want, so I'm content to watch. She's heads-down through a few more songs. Tevin swings by, and we chat as I drink, but I steal glances at the musician all the while.

She never lifts her gaze. Never searches the room— it's like she's trying to hide in plain sight.

My gut swirls. When Tevin leaves to chat with others, I've got a sinking feeling. She doesn't want to see me. What I don't know is why.

I'm not going to cause a scene at The Scene, but I need to know if I'm wrong.

If I'm reading something into nothing.

I check the clock. If her break is the same time as two weeks ago, it's coming up soon. When the clock strikes nine-fifty-five, I make my way to the library, but I don't go inside.

I lean against the doorframe, gaze from behind my mask down the hallway. I'm casual on the outside, coiled tight on the inside. When the music stops at ten, my pulse quickens. A minute later, the tap of feminine shoes sounds on the marble floor.

She's heading down the hall at a rapid pace, her gaze locked on the door at the end.

The restroom.

I feel like a stalker.

Hell, I am a stalker.

Especially since she turns her masked face to the left, avoiding the library side completely. She doesn't want to see me, and that pisses me off. Just say it to my face.

I had enough games in my marriage. I won't play them anymore.

I study her like I can find the answer *on her*. My gaze travels up and down her curves, from the mask covering her eyes to the fringe on her dress swishing against her knees to the stars dangling from her silver anklet.

Wait.

Déjà vu slams me harshly into yesterday evening at Tate's office, but the details aren't clear. I scrub a hand across my jaw, trying to activate the memory fully.

But now that she's seconds away, I'm torn. Figure out what's been nagging at me or find out why my mystery woman is ditching me.

I'm tempted to grab her hand, toss her over my shoulder, carry her into the library, and ask w*hat the fuck?* But I'm not going to push a woman around.

I step out of the doorway. "You're avoiding me," I say, using words, only words.

But she flinches, then stumbles. I dart out a hand, catching her wrist before she falls.

Her breath catches. "Oh." It comes out shuddery.

"Aren't you?" I ask.

Her gaze drifts down to my hand on hers, but she doesn't try to shake it off. "I don't know what you mean," she says, her voice not quite her own. It's as if she's trying to hide it, pitching it down.

But fuck games. "You haven't looked my way the whole night," I say.

"I've been working." Her tone is neutral, but a little

shaky under the surface like she's fighting to stay that unaffected.

I'm scaring her. She got cold feet, and I'm fucking scaring her.

The dating world is shitty enough for women. I don't need to be a demanding, aggressive prick. Resigned to being stood up, I let go of her and raise my hands in surrender. "I'm sorry. Forgive me. Have a good night," I say, then I step around her, but my eyes land again on her anklet.

That's...

The woman racing into the bathroom yesterday at Tate's office.

"Your ankle bracelet," I say heavily, dread swirling in my gut.

Her eyes widen behind her mask. She gulps. Oh hell.

Yesterday, Tate said he had to meet his daughter for dinner. I swear I saw her rushing down the hall, catching only a fading glimpse of her legs.

That woman was wearing *this* anklet.

I grab her hand again, and this time I do jerk her into the library, shutting the door and locking it behind us. I rip off my mask. "Are you...?"

With a pained expression, she slowly removes hers —revealing my best friend's beautiful daughter.

She's even more stunning with her mask off.

8

LIKE A GOOD GIRL

Finn

I slam my fist against the wall. "Fuck," I grunt, then shake out my hand. My knuckles burn. I can't believe my bad luck. "I've done nothing but think about you for the last two weeks," I grit out.

"Join the club," she says dryly, handling this much better than I am.

But it's not funny to me. I stare harshly at the beauty in front of me. "Do you have any idea how much you've been on my mind?" I ask, but I'm not angry at her. I'm pissed at fate.

"No. How much?" It's a challenge and a genuine question.

I stare at the most gorgeous woman I've ever seen. I've met Jules a couple of times. I didn't give her a second thought because I was married then. But yes, in an intellectual way, I registered that she's pretty, that she's witty, and that her glittering brown eyes held a hint of...*something* in them.

Something I couldn't name then, but I can now. *Curiosity.*

"Nonstop. You've been in my head for two weeks. Fifteen minutes in the library, and now you're lodged here," I bite out, tapping my temple.

Her lips twitch in a hint of a grin. "Well, you spent two songs with me on the piano too. Don't forget that."

I groan, annoyed and turned on all at once.

This is what I'm talking about. She's a delicious flirt as well as the most responsive woman I've touched. It's impossible not to want her. "That's the problem. I want more," I say, but inside, I'm torn apart by loyalty and lust. They're both terribly powerful.

She lifts her chin. Strong. Defiant. "I wanted that too," she says, fearless but seeming resigned to our new reality.

Still, her boldness is kerosene to my desire. I should not be so close to her. I should not stand this near to her.

I spin around and pace across the ornate carpet in the library, dragging my hands through my hair like I can rewind this awful twist of fate. "You're the first woman I've touched since my divorce. And you're—" I stop, choking on the words.

When I turn back, Jules is looking down at the floor like she's done something wrong. That won't do. I stalk back over to her, aching to hold her, fighting to resist her. "It's not you. I just can't believe this," I say softly, metering my frustration. I can't let her think she's the reason I'm mad.

She raises her face again. Her eyes are tinged with regret and disappointment. Everything I couldn't see earlier when she played, I see plainly now.

She was never avoiding me.

Carefully, I ask, "Tonight. When you wouldn't look at me...were you protecting me?"

A sad nod. "I didn't want you to know. I thought it would be safer if you never knew who I was."

"Safer for *me*?"

"Yes. I didn't want you to carry that with you."

"Carry what?"

"Guilt. I didn't want to ruin your friendship with my..."

Yeah, I can't say *your father* either. I should. But with her this close, with her so alluring, I can't let myself think of my best friend.

The man who raised her.

"You hardly know me and you wanted to protect me. And him," I say, kind of amazed.

"I know what it's like to lose a friendship," she says, her voice strong but forged from pain—that's clear.

This woman. What she must have been through. I met Tate after he endured the hell of his youngest daughter's death, something this resilient woman faced too—she lost a sister.

And here she is, trying to save me from hurt, from guilt, from loss.

I should walk away. I should take the gift she's giving me.

Really, I should.

But I don't. I close the distance, drawn to her.

She's next to the ladder against the shelves, that shiny dress showing off her bare calves and her lovely throat and teasing me with the skin I want to kiss.

I should not want my best friend's twenty-five-year-old daughter. "I should go," I mutter, without making a move to do so.

"You should," she says, not pushing me to go either.

I inhale her. That flowery perfume is driving me wild. It makes it hard for me to think straight. "It's so goddamn frustrating that I've been thinking nonstop about having you, and now I can't," I say.

"I wanted it to be you," she says, seeming equally annoyed, equally pissed at fate.

But then I replay what she just said. *I wanted it to be you.*

And I have to know. "You wanted *what* to be me, Jules?"

Her eyes blaze with truth and desire. "I wanted you to be my first."

I close my eyes for a heady, hazy second. Holy. Shit.

That's what I'd thought. I just needed to be sure.

"Are you okay?" she asks.

I open my eyes. I'm not at all *okay*. I'm wound tight, strung like a high-wire electrical line as I weigh the terrible and beautiful choices.

On the one hand is loyalty.

On the other hand is...*her.*

What if she picks someone else for her first time

and he treats her poorly? What if he doesn't worship her body? What if he doesn't take care of her?

Worst of all—what if he isn't...me?

I growl from deep inside my soul. Something primal rips through me, declaring she's mine. I huff out a harsh breath and hold her face tight in my hands. "I can't stand the thought of another man being your first," I say.

"You're possessive," she says, then nibbles on the corner of her lips. "Mr. Adams."

Ohhh yes.

She's playing again. Saying it like I'm her boss, perhaps.

I swallow roughly. "I am, Miss Marley. I want what I want."

"And you want...your secretary." It's not a question. It's a glove thrown down.

"It's so wrong, but I do. I really fucking do." I have never been more turned on in my life. My lips crash down on hers and yes, fucking yes.

I can taste my goddess again.

She tastes like midnight and gardens. Like flowers and heat. Like a woman who needs *this* man.

There is no one, not a man on earth, who can give her a first time like I can.

I kiss her hard, thoroughly, deeply.

Most of all, I kiss her with an absolute devotion to her pleasure.

When I let go, her lips are beautifully bruised and I've made my choice.

I adjust the strands of her jet-black wig. "Spend the

night with me. No one will know. Just you and me. Come to my place. I'm in the West Village. I'll make you come over and over. With my tongue, my fingers, my cock. I'll make you breakfast in the morning. Then, we'll pretend it never happened. What do you say, Jules?"

She trembles, which looks like a yes. Except, her brow knits, which tells me a no is coming. "I need to know something first," she says, clearing her throat.

"Okay," I say tentatively. I don't want to promise anything till I know what she's asking.

With a wince like it hurts, she asks, "Does my father go to these parties with you?"

I laugh once, relieved. Of all the things she'd ask, I wasn't expecting *that*. "No. Never," I reassure her. "He doesn't know I go either. Our friendship isn't about...*this*." I wish I didn't have to acknowledge his existence at all right now, but I get her concern.

"Okay," she says evenly, but she doesn't sound enthused.

"Are you sure?" I ask, stepping back, giving her space.

She blinks like she's fighting off something. Winces again. Finally, she exhales audibly, seeming resolved in whatever she's decided. "Yes," she says, then closes the distance between us and grabs my suspenders. "I'm sure you're a very bad idea, Finn Adams. But I want you anyway. I've been wanting you since the other night. For the last two weeks, I've been planning on you fucking me."

That is music to my ears.

"I'll send a car for you later. Once you're done." I nod to the door. "Give me your number, then get back out there and finish playing." I lean in, brush her hair over her ear, and whisper a seductive command, "Like a good girl."

But she makes no move to go. Instead, she smiles like she has a secret. "I don't always follow orders like a good girl though."

I tilt my head, intrigued, especially since I *think* I know where she's going. "Tell me what you did."

"I'd rather show you," she says, then takes my hand, slides it up under her dress, pressing my palm against the damp panel of her panties.

My bones vibrate with lust. All that sweetness will be mine soon enough.

"You disobeyed me," I say as I trace one finger along the lacy fabric.

She shudders. "I did."

I stop at her clit, drawing a circle over it with my thumb, making her gasp. "Then I'll need to take these home with me."

Her eyes widen with a wicked kind of excitement. I peel off her panties, stuff them in my pocket, then send her back out to play.

9

WHAT DID YOU DO TODAY

Jules

The Lyft can't get me home fast enough. I have so much to do before the car Finn's sending for me arrives.

As the driver swings through the city, I tap my toe against the floor of the Nissan. Traffic is light at this hour, but not light enough for me. I want to fly home.

Nibbling on the corner of my lip, I review everything I need to do in thirty minutes at my apartment. No way was I going straight to Finn's place from The Scene. I'm wearing a wig *and* a wig cap, and neither are sexy to take off.

As the driver maneuvers past a double-parked cab and onto Seventh Avenue, she glances in the rearview mirror, wide brown eyes meeting mine. "How was your night?" She asks it with mild interest, perhaps eager to fill the silence of a boring drive.

Words flash through my mind like reviews on Times Square marquees, bright and brilliant.

Wild. Amazing. Shocking. Exciting. Dangerous.

Yes, my night so far has been all of those things, but none of those words are big enough.

A handful of words fit better—*only the beginning.* "It was really good." For once, I don't try to hide my enthusiasm.

"Oh yeah?" She wiggles a brow in the mirror, then gives me an eager, "Elaborate."

Tell a stranger? No problem. "Well, let's just say it's not over yet."

"I'm jealous. Let me know if you need a ride to your next stop," she says.

"I would, but he's sending me a car," I say, and it's so easy to drop these racy little details with her.

It's fun too.

Soon enough, we're at my place in Chelsea, and I thank her then rush inside, tipping her on the app as I greet the doorman on my way to my apartment.

Once inside, I lean against the door, catching my breath even though I haven't done anything to make it speed up. Still, my heart is beating so fast.

I can't believe I'm going to do this. This is so wrong. This is so risky. This is so...*exciting.*

I lock the door, drawing a deep inhale of the lavender bouquet I picked up earlier in the week, then get moving on my to-do list. I need to fix my hair, since it's flat as a pancake under this wig, and take a quick shower since, well, playing piano for three hours makes me a little hot and sweaty.

I'm *not* going to let him undress me unless I feel good about what's under the clothes.

After unzipping my dress and kicking off my shoes, I turn my phone back on, too, just in case Finn texted with info about the car he's sending. Guys I dated in college never sent town cars. They barely sent texts longer than *sup* or *hey*.

And yes, the newest text is from him. But I freeze before I open it, dread prickling at me. What if he's canceling? He probably changed his mind when he returned home, and the weight of his choice hit him. Guilt is a powerful downer. Expecting disappointment, I click open the text.

> Finn: Do you like champagne, whiskey, wine, or something without liquor? Whatever you want, I'll make it happen.

I grin stupidly. *Anything,* I want to say. But that's a boring answer. So far, Finn seems to think I'm sexy. He likes when I'm naughty. I like being this girl with him. And there's one drink that lets him know I'm so ready.

> Jules: Just water, Mr. Adams. I'm very, very thirsty.

Seconds later, a reply lands.

> Finn: I'm hungry. I know what I want to eat. I thought about it all day at the office when you were bringing me contracts to sign, bending over my desk.

I gasp. He's doing it. He's really doing it. And so am I.

> Jules: Funny, I thought you were thinking about my tits then.

> Finn: Watch that dirty mouth, or I'll bend you over the table.

> Jules: Like you wanted to bend me over your desk earlier today. Or maybe you wanted to spread me out on your desk?

> Finn: Make that starving. You'd better get here very, very soon. I'm not a patient man, Miss Marley.

> Jules: But I'll be worth it.

With a delicious sigh, I clutch my phone. I want to linger in this heady moment where I'm aching for him. Only there's too much to do, so I set my phone down on the bureau, but a text from my father from earlier blinks up at me.

Like a pair of eyes, watching.

He'd hate me even more if he knew what I was

about to do. I spin around and ignore it, yanking off my wig and the wig cap. A minute later, I'm under the stream of water, scrubbing, washing, rinsing.

I'm out of the shower in no time, lotioning up, then swiping on lipstick and mascara.

Nothing more.

I grab a canvas bag and toss in a pair of panties, a tank top and leggings, then a toothbrush. He invited me to spend the night, so presumably, he wants to kiss me in the morning, but morning breath is real. I don't like being dirty (except the good kind of dirty), and there's no way I'm asking a guy I don't know to borrow a toothbrush.

It's just best to be prepared.

I want to be prepared to play our roles, too, so I dress the part, zipping up a black pencil skirt, buttoning a tight white blouse, and sliding into heels.

I twist up my hair, and even though I still have my contacts in, I grab a pair of costume glasses. They feel like armor.

I check the time. The car will be here in ten minutes, so I unlock my safe and take out my journal, reading the quote on the card. Then I answer the question Willa asked me every night when we were kids. *What did you do today?* Every night, I told her. I still tell her, but now I do it in a veiled way because I have to.

Stars on my ankle. A fist against the wall. Jay Gatsby, obsessed with me. A late-night invitation. A dangerous choice.

I close the book, lock it up, then grab my phone. A new message flashes on the screen.

Finn: You smell incredible.

I read it twice because that's what it takes to absorb his meaning. Heat washes over me. What the hell am I getting myself into with this dominating, dirty man?

No idea, but I can't wait to find out.

But as I race down the steps of my building, I keep thinking about my dad's text. I should open it. I should write back. He'll worry I'm dead.

I stop on the landing, closing my eyes briefly, breathing past the flash of terrible images from years ago.

I open my eyes and click on the text. He sent me an article about the best mutual funds, along with a reminder: *We need to talk about your retirement planning soon. You started an account, right?*

Um, no, Dad. I'm focused a tiny bit more on that little thing known as rent.

As I head toward the foyer, I dictate a reply. *Working on it!*

He replies immediately. *We can talk about it in the morning. Do a Zoom call after I run, and I'll share my screen and we can look at options.*

Dude, I am not zooming with you in the morning.

Surely, I'm an asshole as I reply. *Too busy with script reading tomorrow! Gotta work on that track record. Maybe Sunday.*

My stomach twists as I reread my lie. But it's the cost of a cover-up.

There's a text from my mom from earlier too. She sent me a social clip of a fashion designer making a Regency ball gown, one of those sped-up videos that shows the arduous process in fifteen seconds. *Saw this and thought of you! What are you up to this weekend? I'm at a wine festival and it's fabulous!*

Without answering, I head to the street, feeling like I'm sixteen again and sneaking out with Willa. But I don't want to think about my family. I don't want to think about *me* either. I don't want to think terrible, annoying, awful thoughts.

I just want to...*feel* all the pleasure I've denied myself for the last few years.

I push open the front door of my building and dart down the steps, scanning for the black town car Finn's sending—when I walk right into a man.

Oof.

I blink, then shake my head, relieved. "Oh. Hi."

It's Ethan. He's one of Layla and Harlow's besties, and over the last few years, he's become a good friend of mine too.

I set a hand on my chest, where my pulse is still racing. "Thank god it's you. I thought it was my parents," I say, which sounds ridiculous to say out loud, especially at eleven-thirty on a Friday night.

"Sounds like you're up to no good," he says, busting me just like that.

But one look at his stylish jeans, cuffed twice at the ankles, and tight shirt, clearly meant for a hot date, gives me playful ammunition. "I could say the same about you."

He shrugs, smiling. "Just finished a gig. I'm heading to my girlfriend's place for the night."

"Say hi to Tessa for me." She's a drummer in another band that's all the rage in the city—though his band, Outrageous Record, is pretty hot too.

"I will." He takes a beat, giving an *I'm waiting* look. "I told you where I'm going. Your turn."

Giving up secrets is so dangerous. They can slice your heart. Before I speak, I weigh this one.

I'm not going to tell him who Finn is or how we're connected. But maybe I can say a little something. It felt good to share with the girls at poker the other week. I also *want* to tell my friends. It makes this clandestine fling feel more real—and more daring too. I like being naughty Jules, racing off to a sex-cursion.

"I'm going to a sleepover as well," I begin.

His hazel eyes twinkle. "With a man?"

I laugh, half shy, half thrilled. "Yes."

"Well, well. Virgin Society no more, I take it?"

That's the name Harlow, Layla, and Ethan gave themselves a few years ago when they all carried V-cards. "Seems that way."

"And who is this masked man?"

Ethan can't know how close he's come to the truth of how I met Finn. Still, I feel seen with this comment. Safely seen. Maybe because I can answer truthfully enough. "I met him at a party. He's sometimes a gentleman and sometimes not."

Ethan's smile turns wicked. "The best kind of man."

I laugh. "I'd have to agree."

"And is there something more going on with him?"

"No. It's just a one-time thing."

"Nothing wrong with that, but he better treat you like a queen in bed," he says, like a protective guy friend should.

"I think that's at the top of his agenda," I whisper salaciously.

"Smart man."

The sound of a car parking has us both turning our heads toward the curb.

Ethan whistles at the sleek town car. "I like his style already."

I'm giddy at the sight of the vehicle. But I'm really giddy at what it represents—Finn whisking me away to lavish me with pleasure in his bedroom.

When Ethan meets my eyes again, his brows lift with concern. "Should this stay between you and me?"

I love that he asks. That he's conscious about what I would share with others and what he's privy to thanks to a coincidental encounter. But this conversation has already given me a taste of what I've been missing for years—confessions with friends. "You can tell them," I say, a little buzzed at the possibility.

Ethan pumps a fist, then leans in to kiss my cheek. "Get it, girl. Get it good."

I say goodbye, then duck into the backseat of the car.

Not two minutes later, my phone lights up like a Vegas slot machine with message after message.

Harlow: Jules! You and your secret life! I want details.

Layla: I want dirty details.

Harlow: And I want to know how long you've been holding out on us, you bad girl.

Layla: Sounds like you're going to be very bad tonight.

Harlow: The best kind of bad. Now, TALK. What are you wearing?

Layla: Um, my pet, the point is she won't be wearing much of anything.

Harlow: I meant like right now.

Jules: I promise to share the dirtiest of details tomorrow night. That is, if I can walk.

I spend most of the quick ride texting with them. Each time we connect like this—like we did over poker, like we're doing now—makes me hungrier for more friendship.

But when I reach Jane Street, I put my friends behind me. I thank the driver, get out, then stare up at the gorgeous brownstone.

Finn's on the balcony on the third floor, watching me, a tumbler in his hand. He's wearing a dress shirt and a tie, loosened. Playing the part. From down here, though, I can see the desire in his heated gaze.

I vow to put everything else out of my head for the rest of tonight.

10

WHAT HE REALLY WANTS

Jules

Before I knock on Finn's door, I take a deep breath, needing a moment to ground myself. The June night air is warm. Music plays from a bar around the corner. There's a faint scent of honeysuckle somewhere nearby.

And in front of me is...the wild unknown.

Am I ready to step into it?

Butterflies flap in my chest, but they're saying yes too. I lift my hand and rap on the door. The white wood paneling gleams in the glow from the lights on this quiet street in the West Village. Footsteps approach from inside, and I swallow hard, my heart racing.

Seconds later, the man with the chiseled cheekbones and piercing eyes opens the door, but he's not smiling. He's staring fiercely at me, his jaw ticking. "You're here at last. We have lots to accomplish, Miss

Marley," he growls, playing the hard-ass boss as he tugs me inside and kicks the door closed.

The man moves like a sex superhero, and in no time, I'm up against the door, wrists above my head, clasped in his hands.

My pulse gallops with excitement.

He dips his face to my neck, drawing a deep inhale. "I'm going to keep you very busy tonight," he says, his voice low and velvety as he runs his nose along my skin.

My cheeks heat. "With what kind of work?" I ask, a little wobbly but eager—like a foal standing for the first time.

"It's a special project. Something I've had in mind for you for the last two weeks." His eyes roam over my work costume approvingly, then he takes my hand and guides me through the foyer, past his living room. His home is sparse but warm, with white walls and wooden furniture. He leads me into a spacious kitchen. It's large by New York standards, but it's neat, with hardly anything on the clean white counters except a mixer, a kettle, and a box of cheddar bunnies. The crackers seem incongruous, but I'm not here to think about cracker snacks now. I set my bag on a stool beside the island.

Finn lifts a scotch glass, knocks back some amber liquid, then beckons me to him with one languid finger. Heat pulses through me, and I step closer to the man with the silver in his beard and the after-dark secrets in his heart. He sets down his tumbler, then pours me a glass of water from a pitcher on the counter. "Take a drink, Miss Marley. Or your throat will be parched when you scream my name and beg me to let you come."

Did he really just say that?

Pretty sure my panties are useless now. He picks up the glass and hands it to me, his fingers brushing against mine. My body hums at his touch, craving more contact with him.

I take a thirsty sip, then put it down again.

"I couldn't get anything done at the office today. Do you know why?" he says, his eyes narrowed and his tone stern, just the way I like.

"Why?" I ask, trembling.

"You're all I think about, and it drives me insane," he says, annoyed and aroused.

I touch my throat like I'm confirming the source of his madness. "I am?"

"You are. You make it impossible to concentrate on deals and contracts. Do you know what that means?" he asks, stalking closer so there's only an inch between us.

My heart pounds mercilessly in my chest. "Tell me, Mr. Adams."

I don't know exactly what I expected when I came to his home, but this is the stuff of fiery fantasies. He crowds me against the counter and brushes a strand of hair from my face. His touch is anything but gentle; it's rough, possessive, and thoroughly mesmerizing. "It means I need to punish you," he says.

While there's nothing wrong with his kink, nothing at all, I just don't think that's *my* kink. I swallow uncomfortably. Now I have to say the hard thing. "Finn," I say, breaking character.

His expression shifts to tender concern. "What is it, Jules?"

Our real names signal the change from role-play to real. "I don't think I want to be punished."

He dips his face, smiling, then shakes his head. "Shit."

Shit is right. We're not compatible. I bite my lip, feeling awful. "I'm sorry."

When he looks up, his eyes are apologetic. "Don't be sorry. It's my mistake." He drags a hand through his thick hair. "It's been a while."

He sounds pissed at himself.

But I'm just disappointed, and my heart weighs two tons.

I don't know what to say either, but he's faster and communicates without words. He touches my cheek tenderly, then cups my chin in his big hand. "But I didn't mean punish with pain," he says.

He didn't? I'm completely confused, then. "What did you mean?"

He inhales deeply. "I don't want to lead you astray. Role-play is fine. I like it enough," he says, and I see shades of my past, of my ex mocking me for my desires, twisting them, using them against me.

I can't go through this again. "I'm going to leave."

I turn away, but he grabs my arm, urgency in his voice as he says, "I'm doing this wrong." He sounds like he's beating himself up. "Let me explain."

Shaking my head, I try to pull back from him. "This

was a mistake," I say as I search for my bag, my back to him.

He wraps his arms around me tightly, resting his face against my ear as his warm breath fans across my skin. "Jules, I want to torture you exquisitely with orgasms. I want to edge you all night. I want to punish you with pleasure." After a weighty pause, he adds, "That's my kink. More than role-play."

I can't move.

I can't speak.

I can't think, and it's the most freeing feeling in the world. He wants to *give* to me. I don't even know what to say. My knees are weak. My skin is hot. And I ache for him.

There's one thing that nags at me, though, and against my better judgment, the voice telling me to shut up, I speak out. "But you let me suck you off that first night. And it was hot, don't get me wrong. I loved it. But that seems more vanilla." What if he's just fooling with me tonight? What if he's playing a cruel mind game?

"I'm rusty," he admits. "Like I said, it's been a while. And I did want to fuck this pretty mouth so much." He spins me around and runs his thumb along my lower lip. "I *took* that night. But tonight, I want to *give*," he says, roaming his fingers down my arm. As he touches me, I catch the scent of his cologne, that leather and fire mix chased with orchids. Something about this man's cologne, the way he wears it, not too much, not too little, says he's not lazy. Says he knows how to make a choice. And Finn's choice is so *fine*. Everything about him is strong, masculine, and somehow warm too.

"Tonight is about you. Just you." He holds my gaze with so much lust and need in his eyes—it's like he can't contain either one. Same here.

I choose to trust he's not playing mind games. Still, though, I ask, "You want to just give me orgasms all night?"

Well, it's important to make sure I heard the sex superhero right.

His face remains serious as he gives the simplest answer. "Yes. Now the question is—do you want to stay or go, Miss Marley?"

The name and the return to our roles makes me warm all over, like liquid gold flows through my veins. I feel both relaxed and turned on as he gives me my wishes while reaching for his own.

And while there's still one big reason to go—there will always be a reason to go—tonight, I'm ignoring our forbidden connection, including the years between us. "I want to stay, Mr. Adams," I say.

"Good. Now take another drink of water—you're going to need it for this...*project*."

Project Multiple Orgasms, here I come. I take another sip, then set the glass down.

He points to a staircase at the edge of the kitchen. "Go to my room on the third floor. It's a bedroom suite. Sit on the bed. I'll be there in a minute. I want to watch your ass as you walk up the stairs."

My pulse soars to the sky as I turn toward the stairs and ascend.

I don't look back, but I can feel the heat of his gaze with every click of my heels.

I go up the first flight then round a landing, barely paying attention to my surroundings as I focus on my sexy destination. I head up to the next floor, then find what must be Finn's bedroom door. It's open. As his footsteps grow louder on the stairs, I step inside his spacious room. Like his brownstone, this bed is huge, bigger than a regular king-size.

The bedspread is striped navy and white, utterly masculine. But the pillows are warm yellow. A nice touch. The click of his wingtips tells me he's near, so after I take off my glasses and put them on the nightstand, I follow his order, perching on the edge of the bed. A few seconds later, he enters the room, tugging on his tie, unknotting it, and stalking over to me.

"You're such a good girl," he says, brushing a strand of hair from my face, his touch gentle. "And you look absolutely beautiful." His voice is low and intimate.

I don't know what game we're playing anymore—if I'm his secretary or if I'm just me. It makes me nervous. Makes me think too much. "Are we playing or are we…"

He cups my chin, possessively. His grip is strong, demanding, but desperate too. "Tell me what you want, Jules. We have one night. I want to give you *everything*."

He's unreal, and I hardly know where to start. I want it all.

I want to take everything he'll give. "I don't want to think. I want to feel," I confess, baring a little bit of my naked soul to him. But I have a hunch he'll not only understand me—he'll want to deliver.

His smug smile says *oh yes, I will deliver*.

He drops his lips to mine and claims me in a

hungry kiss. When he lets go, he says, "Good. Then know this—I'm in charge. I'm going to focus on you. Just you, Jules. Just fucking you."

My pulse races. The role-play is over, but the night is just beginning. "Thank you," I say, grateful he's taken the lead. I don't want to at all.

He brushes his thumb along my cheekbone. "No, thank you," he corrects, then steps back and drops to his knees.

Wow. Just wow.

I shudder.

This handsome, stern, older man is on his knees before me, pushing up my skirt, spreading my thighs and roaming his hands along my legs. "I need to see how much you want me." He pauses to lock eyes with me. "Show me."

I gulp, but it's from the thrill of his command. I widen my legs a little more.

He shakes his head. "Don't be shy. Hike up your skirt. Put your hands on your thighs and spread them for me."

I comply, tugging up the stretchy material, then parting my thighs.

My reward is the animalistic groan that rips from his throat. "Fuck, honey, you're so wet for me."

"I am," I say breathily as he stares at my soaked panties.

He presses a kiss to my knee then journeys languidly up my flesh. Is he going to start his orgasm marathon by going down on me? I don't think I'd object.

But he stops when he reaches the middle of my thigh. He looks up, stands, and offers me a hand.

I don't know what we're doing. And I don't know if I trust any man, but I might trust him a little since his want is so clear. His actions spell out his wishes. He's dirty and honest, and the combo is heady.

He cups my face, rough again like he was at The Scene. "I've wanted to worship your body since I met you."

I tremble. "Really?"

"Yes. This is what I've wanted to do since that first night."

It seems so impossible. "You did?" I sound doubtful. I know I do. But I don't know how to sound any other way.

His eyes hold mine fiercely. "When you walked into the mansion, I could tell things about you instantly," he says, dipping his face, kissing my neck, adoring my throat, making me melt.

"Like what?" I ask in between his caresses.

"You're sensual. You're in tune with your body."

Me? In tune with my body? He has it all wrong. "I don't know if that's true," I say, skeptical.

He nods, firm and decisive, as he meets my eyes again. "I see it in the way you play piano with your whole being. The way you dress, like you're becoming the character. I knew you were the kind of woman who craved pleasure even if you didn't know it."

I'm warm everywhere. I'm...adored. I'm understood. After years of being shut down, I'm a flower opening to the sun, my petals spreading.

"That's what you like? Giving pleasure?" I ask, still stunned that his kink isn't role-play. It's...making me come. This is like answering the job interview question *what's your biggest weakness* with *I work too hard.*

He answers with a carnal *yes*, then says, "Let me show you."

I'm woozy already. As he unbuttons my shirt, my mouth waters.

As he unzips my bunched-up skirt, my skin sizzles.

As I step out of my clothes, I feel like I'm coming alive.

And then, for one terrible moment, I think about where I am, who I'm with, and how this will never last.

It's not supposed to last. Just enjoy your illicit one-night affair.

This man wants nothing but to make me feel good, so I take it, lying back on his bed as he slides off my heels.

Slowly, setting the pace, he undoes his shirt as I watch. He's strong, with defined abs, muscular arms, and a smattering of chest hair. Plus, that happy trail makes me very happy.

Quickly, he takes off his socks and shoes. With only slacks on, he joins me on the bed, turning me toward him and dropping his mouth to mine. His hand is on my face, and I feel like I'm melting into this heady, lust-drunk world as he kisses the corner of my mouth then flicks his tongue across my lips. His kisses are sensual and lingering. They're brushes of his mouth, teases of his lips, a lovely promise of incandescent pleasure.

He doesn't break the kiss, even as he lets go of my

face. His hand travels down my body, over my breasts, across my belly to my panties. His fingers slide inside the lace, and he groans as he touches my wetness. I'm slick and hot for him.

Outrageously aroused.

He strokes me while kissing me, but he's in no rush. He takes his sweet time but doesn't try to finger fuck me. He just caresses my clit with nimble fingers, drawing dizzying circles that make me pant and moan. He's somehow controlling me with his mouth, lavishing me with druggy, heady kisses that send me spinning with lust. I arch my hips, seeking out his hand, rubbing shamelessly against him.

"Yes, fucking yes," he says, his voice husky as I grind against his hand.

I'm panting, and I swear my orgasm is coming into view when he stops, ending the kiss abruptly too.

What?

I whimper. "I was so close. Why did you...?" I stop, coming to my senses. This is his MO—edging.

And I'm squirming.

The fucker.

He takes my hand, brings it to his slacks, and presses it against his straining cock. "This is what you did to me that night. You're too fucking tempting. This is what you do to me every goddamn night," he adds like he's angry at me for being alluring. I like this angry energy. *A lot.* "I've been jerking off to you every night."

God, the images. The fantastic images of his hand shuttling along his cock. Am I having an out-of-body experience? It sure feels like it. "You have?"

"Yes," he says, then brings his fingers to his lips and sucks them off one at a time, moaning with each deliberate lick. "Fuck, you're sweet."

I'm also empty. I want his hand. His tongue. His cock. But should I say that?

I wait for him to go next. I don't know the rules of one-night stands.

With mischief in his eyes, he asks, "You wanted to come so badly just now, didn't you?"

I nod, speaking truthfully. "I did."

"You were so close." He sounds diabolical.

"I was," I murmur, wishing he would let me.

He reaches for my right breast, squeezing it through the lace, making me gasp. "But I bet you'd like coming on my face," he says, then quickly unhooks my bra.

I shudder. "I bet I would too."

He moves like lightning between my legs, grabbing at my lace panties and sliding them off. "Fuck," he says, staring at my pussy. "You're so pretty."

All I can do is nod. I can't speak. My throat is parched with want.

"So wet for me," he says, spreading me open.

"I am," I say, and I'm in a sex trance.

Seems he is, too, gazing wantonly at me. But not for long. Sliding his hands under my ass, he pulls me close to his face and blows out a hot breath on me. I'm so vulnerable here, naked in the arms of a man I hardly know. But I like not knowing him. I like that we have no history. We have only our shared desires, comprised solely of lust as his lips press hungrily against my wetness.

"Oh, god."

"Fuck my face," he urges, scooping me closer, tugging me against his stubbled jaw and devouring me.

He's not gentle. He's not sweet. He's voracious as he kisses me like he's starving. I am his meal as he licks and flicks and eats, drawing my greedy clit into his mouth then sucking, driving me wild with pleasure. I grind and rock like he commanded me to do.

I'm so wet, it's obscene. I'm so aroused, I should be embarrassed.

But I'm not because he's so turned on. His noises are raw and primal—greedy moans paired with hungry hands as he squeezes my ample ass and worships my wetness.

In seconds, I'm close again, cresting again. Waves of bliss crash over me, and I cry out, reaching for the edge. "I'm close," I say, arching against him, hunting for pleasure.

But then, the devil—the fucking devil—stops. He sits up on his knees, and I howl. "I wanted to come."

With a smirk, he grabs my wrists and mirrors his move from earlier, climbing over me and pinning them above my head.

"I know you did." He smirks. "Tell me I'm a dick."

"You're a dick. You denied me," I say, and those aren't words I ever thought I'd say to a man in the heat of the moment. But I feel strangely free to voice them. To sass him. To give him a hard time. Maybe because he's been so forthright with me, I can be direct with him.

He shoots me a crooked grin. "Your sweet pussy is aching for me, isn't it?"

"Finn!" I'm half shocked I have the nerve to beg but mostly helpless to do anything else. "You're terrible!"

He sighs, seeming so damn pleased. "Beg for it. Beg for me."

I don't know if he means with his cock or his mouth or his tongue. But I truly don't care. "Make me come," I plead.

He reaches into the drawer of his nightstand and takes out a tiny black vibrator. "Bought this the other night. Just for you," he says.

Are you kidding me? He bought me a vibrator? My entire sex life for the last several months has consisted of quality time with vibrators. Bring it on.

"Now," I demand.

He slides the vibrating toy across my aching center, then comes close to my face. Only, he doesn't kiss my mouth. He kisses my neck while he glides the vibrating bullet across my clit.

I'm burning up with the need to climax. My back arches. My toes curl.

He didn't lie. He is obsessed with my pleasure, and I think I am too. But I'm also clawing at the sheets, overcome with the chase. I'm begging, thrashing. "Please, please, please."

It's exhilarating and excruciating all at once.

Especially when he turns off the vibrator, leaving me wailing. "Finn," I cry.

And this is strange too. This weird comfort I feel

with him. This freedom to beg, to plead, to ask for what I want.

But I don't have to ask. Because he's got a plan, and it involves his magic mouth.

He slides back between my legs and looks up at me, that glint returning to his eye.

"Come now." He eats me. I rock against his face, shouting *yes, yes, yes*. Pleasure whips through me in a wild frenzy, a burst of color and lights and incomparable bliss.

I shake with ecstasy, and he groans like nothing in his life is better than my climax.

When I open my eyes, he's standing, stripping to nothing. He's chiseled everywhere. Arms, legs, abs. And cock.

I push up on my elbows, shameless as I stare at his dick pointing at me. He's thick, pulsing. It's a little terrifying though. After all these years of not wanting sex, is it possible to want it too much?

I am just one sweet ache right now.

The weight of all this desire presses on me as he reaches for his cock and strokes it, showing me how ludicrously turned on he is. "How do you want me?"

I hesitate, unsure how to answer. Everyone says first times are better when the woman is on top. When she's in control. But I've spent far too many waking hours trying to control my own thoughts. In bed, I want to be dominated. To be taken. To be owned.

"Just. Like. This," I say, looking down at my body, spread out before him.

"Good. Because I want to look at your beautiful

face, your gorgeous tits, and your incredible mouth while I fuck you," he says, then grabs a condom from the nightstand and rolls it on. He positions himself between my thighs. But he stops, freezing in place. When his eyes lock with mine, and I see...guilt.

We've not only crossed lines; we've willfully vaulted over them. We're complicit in a crime.

We hold each other's gazes, knowing that terrible truth without needing to say it. Knowing we're wrong to come together.

And doing it anyway.

I take my fate in my hands as I sit up, cup his cheeks, and make him look at me. "Have me," I say firmly. "I'm begging you."

He shuts his eyes, squeezing them as he grits his teeth. But when he opens his eyes, any resignation is long gone. He's all fire and need as he rubs the head of his dick against my wetness, then pushes in.

I freeze. It hurts, and it hurts a little more as he goes deeper. "Jules." He's so tender. "Are you okay?"

Am I?

Of course I am.

I close my eyes. *This is just temporary. It will pass. The pain will float away.*

When I open my eyes, the ache is already ebbing. "I'm good," I say, meaning it.

He growls, arching a doubtful brow. "Are you sure?"

"Please don't stop," I say.

He gives a slow thrust, since he can't seem to resist my request. In one hour, I've learned that basic truth about him. He wants to smother me in pleasure, and I want to be blanketed.

He pauses, and I breathe deeply, then shudder past the fullness, the intensity, and just revel in the goodness. "I love this," I say, my voice trembling.

"Yeah?"

"I do," I gasp out.

I'm so aroused, so strung out on bliss. He braces himself on his palms and stares down at me, never breaking his gaze as he swivels his hips and takes me apart thrust by delicious thrust as I run my hands over his chest, twist my fingers in his hair.

It's intense, the look in his green eyes, the way he owns me, how he dominates me. "Look at you. You're taking my cock like such a good dirty girl," he praises.

Well, that's true.

And taking his dick feels incredible. He never looks away from me as he pumps those trim hips. He fucks me powerfully and passionately, following my cues and speeding up as my breath races, and slowing down as I moan long and low.

Then, when I'm babbling incoherently, he slides a hand between my thighs and rubs delicious circles on my clit. "Give me another."

"Don't deny me this time," I say, desperately.

"I won't. Need to feel your pussy clenching my cock."

His mouth, his filth, his unbridled lust, make me feel unhinged. Like I could say something dangerous, something dirty.

And...I can.

Holy shit.

I *can* say what's in my head. "Fuck me hard till I come," I blurt out, feeling wild and daring.

He complies, thrusting deeper and playing with my clit till I'm reduced to nothing but heat and sweat and desire.

One deep thrust. A few fast flicks, and I'm breaking into beautiful pieces. He roars, "Yes, fucking yes," and he follows me there.

* * *

A few minutes later, he's lying next to me, looking spent, and I'm feeling dazed.

Totally unsure too.

What do I do now? What do we say? But before I can linger in doubt, he takes my hand, slowly brushing his thumb over each of my knuckles. "I've wanted this ever since we met at the first party," he murmurs against my neck, sending shivers down my spine.

"But do you still think I'm a good girl?" I ask playfully.

He grins and drops a lingering kiss onto my lips before pulling back with a satisfied smirk. "No. Tonight you're my very naughty girl."

My cheeks heat up. "I don't want to be good with you."

His hand slides up my thigh, sending sparks of electricity through me again. This man can command my body. "You're a little defiant. You didn't obey me earlier though. With the panties."

I can't help but smile. "And you liked my defiance."

"I couldn't stop smelling you." He nuzzles my neck, whispering in my ear, "And I need to taste you again before tomorrow. Many more times."

Tomorrow—when this stolen night comes to its inevitable end and we go back to our lives. Returning to our other roles—the good daughter and the good friend who'll act like nothing ever happened one night in this city of secrets.

11

READ MY MIND

Jules

My heart is settled, but my mind is busy. What's next? Part of me wants to bolt. I'm lying in bed with my father's best friend, after all.

I should go.

Clean up, get dressed, and say *thank you*. Then call a Lyft home. He can't really want me to spend the night. What are we even supposed to do now? *Talk?*

I'm too wired to sleep.

Isn't sex supposed to make you tired? It's having the opposite effect on me. My cells are buzzing.

Finn's hand grazing along my arm breaks me out of my reverie. "Are you hungry? There's a great Korean place that's still open. A twenty-four-hour diner. And I also have leftovers from last night. If you like pizza, that is."

A laugh bursts from my chest at the absurd question. I turn to him, giggling in spite of how weird I feel lying in bed with this man—this man with hair mussed up from me tugging on it when he fucked me. A burst of possessiveness fills me—I made him look that way. And he's made me laugh. "If I like pizza? How is that a question?"

"Because of the *if,* I suspect," he says dryly.

"Fine. But seriously, who doesn't like pizza? That's illogical. That's like not liking pajamas or sunshine."

He rakes his gaze over me. "You're not wearing pajamas. And I like you."

My breath catches. While I know what he means—he's not an eleven-year-old boy giving me a construction paper heart—those three words still do stupid things to my heart.

Stupid, dangerous things.

I sit up, searching around for my bra. "I should get dressed. For the pizza, that is," I say.

"You're right. Eating pizza naked is weird," he deadpans.

There he goes again, saying things that disarm me. "It is," I say playfully, trying to keep the mood light.

Light is better.

I tip my chin toward the bathroom door. "Your bathroom is right there?"

He used it a few minutes ago to ditch the condom. But it feels presumptuous to just go in there without permission.

"Yes. Take your time," he says, then swings his legs out of bed and pads toward the walk-in closet. The view of him naked is hard to look away from. He's all long and muscular. His ass is spectacular. Firm and strong. Am I an ass woman? I just might be.

But then a terrible reminder of why his ass is so terrific lodges in my brain. He's a triathlete. He works out with my father.

On that unpleasant reminder, I head to the bathroom and shut the door.

A few minutes later, I emerge, still naked and a little sore, but no longer sex-disheveled. Finn's lying in bed, reading on a tablet, and wearing pajama pants.

Hello, view.

I'd like to whistle my appreciation. Those navy-blue pants are low-slung and sexy as hell. I stare. I can't not.

"Liar," I tease. "You do like pajamas."

As he sets down the tablet on the nightstand, he meets my gaze. "So do you." He's busted me for ogling him.

"I told you I did," I say, but I'm thinking I should have brought my bag up here so I wouldn't have to walk downstairs naked to get dressed.

Awkward.

But Finn's already up and out of bed, grabbing the shirt he wore earlier tonight. "Wear this to sleep in," he says, and my belly flips from the sexy offer.

He closes the distance between us and hands me the shirt. I take it and slide my arms into it. It's big on me, so I cuff the sleeves twice, then reach for the buttons to do them up. But he sets a hand over mine, stopping me. "Jules," he says, like a low warning.

"Yes?"

"You look incredible in my shirt," he says, then tugs

on the panels, letting out another hungry sigh. "So fucking good."

This man makes me feel like a goddess, especially as he buttons the shirt for me, stopping midway. He leaves it open at my cleavage, then runs a hand possessively over the tops of my breasts. "Perfect. These are perfect pajamas for you."

My heart flutters. He makes me feel so wanted, especially when he curls a hand through my hair to draw me in for another kiss.

When he breaks it, I follow him downstairs, passing the landing on the second floor.

I stop for a second.

There's a toy truck on a small table in the corner of the landing. I missed that on the way up.

When we reach the main level, and he flicks on the living room lights, my gaze lands on a framed photo on an end table. It's a picture of a little boy scrambling up a jungle gym.

Immediately, I flash back to the box of cheddar bunnies on the kitchen counter, putting the clues together. "You have a kid?" My voice pitches up.

I had no idea Finn was a dad. But I didn't know Finn was a dominating pleasure-giver either. So, there's that.

He looks back at me, smiling in a whole new way. "I do. That's Zach," he says, pride in his tone as his eyes linger on the frame. "He's seven now."

Which means Finn had him when he was...I don't even know his age.

And I'm curious. But I'm more curious about this

new side of the man I'm spending one sordid night with. Finn's a flirt, he's a tease, and he's a dirty talker. He's a giver. He's a friend. And he's a doting father.

Which makes me strangely sad for a few seconds. So much separates us. Even if my dad weren't between us, we're far apart in our lives. I'm just starting my career. He's at the pinnacle. He's parenting. I don't even have a cat, and don't get me started on plants. My thumb is one hundred percent black.

I try to shake off the differences.

Obviously Zach isn't here tonight. I'm curious where he is, but I don't think it's appropriate to ask. Besides, he's probably with Finn's ex-wife.

"He's with his grandparents," Finn adds, as if reading my thoughts, something he's becoming scarily good at.

"Oh, it's nice that they're close," I say. But I'm not sure I want to spend too much time on the topic of family. We might get too close to *my* family.

"Actually, I share custody with them," he adds as we reach the kitchen.

My brow knits. Sharing custody with grandparents is unusual. But I do my best not to pry since I wouldn't like it if he did it to me. "He seems like a happy kid."

"He is. I'm very lucky," Finn says, beaming like he's glowing inside. "I've been getting to know him for the last eight months. I didn't know I had a kid until then, so it's been an adjustment. But a damn good one."

That's huge, and now I'm dying to know more, maybe over pizza. Finn opens the fridge, takes out a red and white box, and says, "This is from Zach's favorite place. But his eyes are bigger than his stomach, so there's plenty for any ridiculously sexy pizza lovers in the kitchen right now."

But when Finn opens the box of half-eaten pizza, I wince. There's sausage on it. I suppose I can just pick around it though. "Looks good," I say, upbeat.

Finn tilts his head, studying my expression. "You don't sound sure."

"No, it's fine. It's great," I say with false brightness. It just seems so rude to turn the food down after I went on about my love of pizza.

"Ah," he says, realization dawning. "You don't eat meat." The man is too intuitive when it comes to me, and the weird part is I don't mind. I kind of like when he figures me out. When I don't have to spell out my wishes. I don't know what to make of that feeling though, so I try to set it aside.

"I don't. But I can pick it off. It's a vegetarian life hack," I say, making light of it. "It's no big deal."

He scoffs, then shuts the box, saying goodbye to the pizza. "A better life hack is getting you what you want. I want you to have a meal. Not something that you have to...reassemble."

It's just food. But I like his insistence. "I like Asian cuisine. Noodles and tofu and veggies and anything with spice."

That earns me a sly grin. "You like it hot?"

I'll take that innuendo and run with it. "The hotter the better."

He groans, then steps closer. "It's strange that I find

your love of spicy food attractive. But..." he says, holding my chin, "I do."

I shiver, torn between wanting to get to know him more, to ask questions about his son, and wanting a kiss. But he's shifted gears, so maybe he doesn't want to talk about family anymore. I part my lips, letting a kiss win. He sweeps one across my mouth, making me gasp before letting go.

He turns away, and as he orders food from his phone, I notice an open window letting in that tempting smell of honeysuckle. With a deep inhale, I savor the scent as he keeps busy on the screen. Does he have a garden past the kitchen? Does Zach play in it? Does my father hang out with Finn and his son right here in this house? Has he been in this kitchen? Cracked open a beer? Eaten a meal?

I rub my temple, trying to scrub away the thoughts that don't go with honeysuckle as Finn puts down the phone. "Should be here in twenty," he says, studying me. "What are you thinking?"

You don't want to know.

I flash my *all is good here* smile. "Nothing," I lie.

His expression darkens and he looks at me skeptically. "I don't believe you."

It's impossible to dance around the truth with him, so I exhale heavily, then ask, "Are you running on Sunday with my dad? I heard you two talking about it in his office." Maybe acknowledging this discomfort will defuse it. Let me move past it, at least for the rest of the night.

But his expression falters, turning somber, and I've

ruined this moment. This perfect night that's happening out of time, outside of consequences.

"Yes. That's the plan," he says.

"Will that be hard for you?"

"I don't like lying. Lying eats away at you," he says, and he's clearly speaking from experience, but whether he was the liar or the lied to, I don't know.

"It can," I say, tentatively. I don't think I want to know more. It's too heavy for a one-time thing.

"But I can't find it in me to feel an ounce of regret over fucking you," he says, holding my gaze, his eyes intense. "Do you? Regret tonight?"

How could I? I've wanted him since the first masquerade. And I'd much rather talk about us than about my dad, as it turns out. "No. I've been thinking of you too. Ever since I summoned you at the piano," I say, enjoying admitting that.

"I had a feeling you were calling me over," he says, lips curved up. "Now, tell me, Jules. Are you now as much of a fan of sex as you are of jammies?"

I smile, warming to his change of topic, my cheeks flushing. My stomach swoops as he wraps an arm around my waist. "It was better than my fantasies," I admit.

"I bet you have very elaborate fantasies," he says.

"I do."

"Are you *sure* it was better?" He doesn't sound uncertain—more like he's playing with me. Like he's flirting us right into our next bedroom liaison.

I wriggle against his hard frame. "I don't know. Try again later and see."

"Mmm," he says, then nuzzles my neck. "Worth it." He draws a deeper breath. "You wore Summer Day."

"Well, you like it just a little," I deadpan.

"I'm obsessed with the way you smell," he adds. "And the way you look." He fiddles with a button on my shirt. "In *my* clothes."

I strike a pose, enjoying my...after-sex costume. "I do like this shirt," I say coyly.

"So much you should wear it home," he says.

"Like a sex trophy?"

"Exactly, Jules," he says, and it turns out I do like getting to know him as much as I enjoy kissing him.

So much that I have to satisfy my curiosity. "Do you have a thing for honeysuckle? I smell it outside the window. I noticed it when I arrived."

"There's a shrub in the little yard. It was there when I moved in several months ago. Do you like it?"

"It's pretty. It reminds me of..."

But am I really going to say it reminds me of my first teenage fantasies? To tell him it makes me think of an afternoon tryst on a hot day, the kind I used to daydream about when I first thought about sex, when I first craved a man's touch, and now already it reminds me of you?

That's *a lot* for a one-night stand.

"What does it remind you of?" he prompts. He's not going to let me get away without answering.

But maybe I can say *a little*.

"Wanting," I say, and that seems like more than enough. "It reminds me of wanting."

Finn lets out a low rumble. "Then now it will

remind me of you." He holds my gaze with a particular intensity that emboldens me.

"How old are you?" I ask.

He smiles softly, perhaps a little embarrassed. "Forty." There's a pause, like he's waiting for a reaction from me. Shock? Surprise? But that's not what I'm feeling. I'm feeling like forty is the sexiest age ever.

And I'm getting the sense he wants to know I think that. "A very sexy forty," I add.

"And you are...?"

"A no-longer-virginal twenty-five," I say.

His eyes gleam with possession and pride.

"And I got to be the one," he says, and I love that he seems as pleased by that as I am.

*　*　*

Soon, the food arrives, and after he pays and thanks the guy, he gestures to the stairs. "Want to eat on the balcony? It's my go-to dining room on warm nights. I call it my outdoor café."

No fucking way.

But I don't want Finn to read this part of me. I absolutely don't want to admit to him that I have OCD. So I try my hardest to put on an easy smile. "Kitchen is fine," I say, breezily. "I mean, I'm half-naked."

Like that matters. But maybe it'll distract him from asking more.

Something flashes in his eyes, though, as he opens

the fridge. Something like understanding. "I should have remembered. You don't like heights?" he asks, grabbing a jar of chili flakes.

Oh.

Wow.

He remembers the rooftop, and how I said no to it. I cycle through my options—I could deny, or I could make light of it. But he's been open when I've asked questions about his son and about his best friend.

I want to give him a morsel of honesty in return. "You're right. I really don't like heights." That's a true thing. I won't share the scope of my dislike. That's part of the side of me that goes to therapy, the side my family doesn't even know about.

"That must be really challenging," he says thoughtfully as he sets the flakes on the counter. How is this guy a sex master *and* super understanding?

"They make me really uncomfortable," I admit. Apparently he has truth serum powers too. "They kind of freak me out."

Wow. That was...sort of cathartic. I didn't know I'd needed to say those words.

Irrational fears are so embarrassing. So hard to admit. But a tiny weight's been lifted now.

"Is it just heights outdoors? Or was my third-floor bedroom uncomfortable for you too?" he asks, and I rush to reassure him.

"Bedrooms are fine. Indoors is fine. It's just things like balconies, bridges, and rooftops."

"I get that. I do. Everyone has fears. We all have things we try to avoid just because...And it works just as well to eat here," he says with kind eyes and a welcoming smile.

That's not at all how he looked at me when he was seducing me. That's not how he looked at me when he fucked me either.

It's a new look, and it makes my heart speed up. How is it possible that in a few short encounters, I've glimpsed so many of his sides? His determined side, his hungry side, his dominating side, his loyal side, and then his guilty pleasure side that said *fuck the world, I want her more.*

Now I'm seeing another side, and I bet this is the man he is with his son. Kind, thoughtful, big-hearted, and accepting.

"I guess that'll be our secret too. My fear of balconies," I say, and I'm sure this one is as safe with him as the others.

"I'll keep them all, Jules. Every single one," he says, and there's resignation in his voice.

In my heart too.

He hands me a plate, and I scoop some noodles onto it, but when I open the jar of chili flakes, I arch a brow, then show it to him. "Empty."

He peers inside. "Then these noodles better be spicy on their own."

They are, and we rate them a five out of five for spice.

* * *

Later, we're back in bed and it's past two, but I don't feel anxious about the rest of the night. I'm not playing out scenarios or worried about what I'll say. Here, in bed, I feel like I can speak my mind, and do it safely. "Kiss me," I say softly.

He covers me with his body, kissing me deeply till I'm arching, writhing, and asking for more. I whisper his name, savoring how it feels on my tongue, like the last bite of a fine dessert.

His scent envelopes me, but it's like another version of his cologne mixed with notes of sex and me, the fading embers of a fire, and the last lingering hints of orchids before the flowers crumble.

Darkness wraps its arms around the city, the moon sealing up our stolen night, racing too fast to dawn.

12

THE MORNING AFTER PINEAPPLE

Finn

No meat. No problem.

An Adams man knows how to improvise. On Saturday morning, I bound up the steps to my brownstone with the bag of groceries from my early morning run to the store around the block. I punch in the entry code, and once the door closes behind me, I listen for the sound of Jules. It's early, not even seven-thirty. I don't know a ton about the habits of twenty-five-year-olds in the city anymore, but when I was that age, no fucking way was I awake this early on a Saturday morning.

Bet she's still sound asleep, chestnut hair fanned out on my pillow, eyes fluttering, like they were when I left a little while ago. She looked like she belonged in my bed maybe another morning too.

I entertain that thought for a few dangerous

seconds before my chest tightens like a belt has been cinched around it. The idea is foolish for many reasons. First, there is no *another morning* with my best friend's daughter.

You crossed a line, man. Don't even think about crossing it again.

Second, there is no next time with *anyone* right now.

My goal is to be the best father I can be. To give Zach all my love, all my attention. Even if Jules weren't connected to my life in a twisted way, I wouldn't be able to strike up anything more than sex with her.

Romance is a lie.

A year ago, Marilyn and I were in couples therapy for fuck's sake—arguing about everything. We'd stopped sleeping together. Stopped going on dates. Stopped having meaningful conversations.

We'd already argued about whether she'd ever want to have a family. She'd wanted one when we met, she'd talked about kids just after we'd married, but it was all a lie. A cold, cruel lie. She married me for money, not for love, and not for family. Pretty sure she only *stayed* in the marriage for her own financial gain.

I grind my teeth, and that dark cloud tormenting me turns blacker and colder as I head to the kitchen. I've got to get her out of my mind.

I've got to remember, too, that great sex is just that —great sex.

Nothing more.

Doing my best to shove my ex-wife far away from my one and only morning with Jules, I empty the bag, setting a pineapple, a container of blueberries, and a carton of granola on the counter. Then, I wash my hands. When I hear footsteps approaching, my heart lightens and my lips curve into a smile.

Great sex, buddy. That's all.

Jules turns into the living room, meeting my gaze from across the space, she's dressed in a tank top and leggings, her hair twisted into a messy bun, her face fresh. But there's a bag on her shoulder and a *ready to bolt* look in her eyes.

"Hey," I say, arching a brow. "Going somewhere?"

She gestures to the window behind me in the kitchen, bright morning light streaking through it. "Well, the sun is up. I think I turned into a pumpkin hours ago."

She's trying to make light of her departure, but I don't think that's why she's up so early. "Did you think I just...left?"

"No. It's your place. Why would I think that?" But her tone says she's lying.

I move around the island counter, stopping a foot away from her. "You woke up, saw me gone, and thought I, what, went out for a run?"

She sighs. "I didn't know what to think. I don't know you. And I didn't want to overstay my welcome."

"I should have left you a note letting you know I ran out to the store. Like I said, I'm rusty."

She laughs softly, shaking her head with some embarrassment. "This stuff is new to me too."

God, what I want to do with all her newness. But

that's not in the cards. Breakfast is though. "I promised you breakfast. I went out to get it," I say.

"You don't have to make me food."

"I want to." Does no one do nice things for this woman? She's probably not used to much from men. Virgin and all. Well, she *was.*

"What are you smiling about?" she asks curiously.

Oh, I guess a grin took over. "I was thinking about how much I like doing nice things for you. I was wondering if anyone else had. Then I figured you've probably met a lot of jackasses."

"Actually, I haven't really dated much," she says.

Huh. I figured she'd dated jerks. "Really?"

"Dating is...complicated."

"Yeah. I get that," I say. Marriage is too. Mine came with promises that the woman I loved didn't keep. I exhale, trying to shake off that thought. "But you know what's not complicated?"

"What?"

I head back to the spread. "Breakfast where you don't have to pick a thing off it. There's no bacon," I say.

Her grin is immediate and electric. "Yay."

I crack up. "I've never known anyone to cheer the absence of bacon."

"Well, first time for everything. You gave me my first," she says, patting her chest. "I'm giving you one." I enjoy this sardonic side of her so much.

"There are no eggs in this breakfast either." I scrunch my brow. "I wasn't sure if you ate eggs."

"I do. As long as they aren't hard-boiled, soft-boiled,

Benedict, runny, over easy or in egg salad," she says with a shudder. "Egg salad is the scourge."

"Of the food world?"

"Of the whole world," she says, emphatic.

"Well then. Let me wow you with some...fruit."

She smiles. "You showed me your sex moves last night. Now, show me your breakfast moves."

Yeah, that's the woman I met at The Scene. The one who challenged me in the library. The one who came over and demanded I make her come. That's my daring girl.

"You're on," I say.

"Do I get to help?"

"Not a fucking chance," I say.

She sits on a stool, huffing. "Fine. Mister Bossy."

"You like it when I'm bossy."

"I don't know. Do I?" she taunts.

She's got a little brat in her, and the things I could do with it. I move behind her and grab her hands, pulling them tight. She shudders. "If you taunt me, I might not let you come next time," I whisper harshly in her ear.

At those words, she tenses, maybe wondering if I've forgotten this is a one-time thing. I've not forgotten at all.

"By next time, I mean...after I feed you," I add. But my jaw tightens and I wish I could spend another night with her.

Just a night.

That's all.

I let go, move to the counter, and set the pineapple on the cutting board.

"A pineapple? You really want to impress me, don't you?"

"Orgasms and pineapple? Is that the way to your heart and soul?"

She taps her chin. "I mean, pineapple *is* pretty good."

I smile. That's new too. Smiling with a woman. Getting along with a woman.

It's the first date effect, you dick. Of course it feels like fucking magic. It did with Marilyn too.

I try again to shake off thoughts of my ex. There's no room for her in a world of pineapples and orgasms. Grabbing a knife from the wooden holder, I cut and slice the fruit, then set it in a bowl. I find a fork and offer Jules a bite. She parts her lips, letting me feed her.

I happily comply, enjoying her moans of culinary appreciation. I offer her another bite and she takes it, then murmurs "More" in a too seductive voice.

God, that word. "Be careful when you say that," I warn.

She tilts her head, dropping the act. "Why?"

"You don't want to know what it does to me," I say, sternly.

A smile teases the corner of her lips. "But maybe I do."

"Jules," I caution.

Her brown eyes gleam with mischief. "More," she murmurs.

I stalk around the kitchen counter. I grab her hips

roughly, staring down at her. "Say that to a guy like me and it pretty much makes me want to fuck. Right. Now."

She shudders then parts her legs. "A guy like you," she says, then tilts her face. "You mean someone who likes to punish me with pleasure?"

"Yes. That's exactly what I mean."

"So when I say *more* you want to give me more. You want to fuck?"

I grip her hips harder, digging my fingers into her flesh. "Yes, and by fuck, I mean...make you come."

She licks her lips, slow and tantalizing. "More, Finn. More."

That's it. I lift her off the stool, yank down her leggings, then help her quickly step out of them. Once they're off, I'm not gentle at all. I rip off her pink panties. "Turn around. Hands on the counter, ass up."

She gets in position.

I grip her hair in my fist, slide a hand between those thighs, and sweep my finger across her sweet, wet pussy. She shudders, dropping her head, her hair spilling around her. Like that, I stroke and play. Whispering dirty words of praise in her ear. "So beautiful. You obey so well. You deserve all the orgasms."

She grows wetter. Arches more. Moves faster against my hand. She's so free like this, so responsive, and it revs my engine. I fuck her with my fingers till she's gasping, begging, and shattering.

All before eight a.m.

She's still shaking from the orgasm, and I let go of her hair, lick off her sweetness, then head to the sink to wash my hands. "Want more pineapple now?"

She looks woozy. "Yeah, I do. It's my favorite fruit."

"Mine too."

I serve her breakfast, savoring her post-climax look even more than she seems to be savoring the fruit.

* * *

An hour and another handful of orgasms for her and one more for me later, she slings her bag on her shoulder, leaving my bedroom.

Such a shame. Jules looked so good in my bedroom. Like she belonged there.

She heads downstairs a few steps ahead of me when her gaze strays to the toy truck on the table in the corner of the landing. Last night, she seemed to want to ask more about Zach, but I wasn't sure what to share so soon into the night. She's the first woman I've been with since my ex-wife, and I don't know the rules or timelines. But overnight and over breakfast, Jules and I have talked about her fears and my friendships and the way we like to touch. All of those are intimate topics.

So when she says, "Cute truck," I grab the opportunity.

"That's mine," I say dryly.

She stops, turns around. "You like trucks, Finn?"

"Actually, you know what I really like?" I test the waters.

She lifts an inquiring brow. "Besides my ass?"

I laugh. "Yes, besides that," I say, then just go for it.

"I really like building things. Do you want to see a tree house?"

As far as lines go, it hardly counts. I have no idea how she'll take this suggestion, but I'm compelled to show this fascinating, complicated woman who I am.

The reward? A smile like magic. "I would love to see a tree house."

I lead her down the steps and out the side door off the kitchen, then sweep out a hand. "It's the tiniest yard in the city."

She stares, slack-jawed, at the courtyard-slash-fenced-in-patch-of-grass. Stones line one side of the small space, still covered in lava from our volcano experiment. At the edge, a mere ten feet away, is a tall wood fence. Then, in the corner is the tree, with the Lilliputian house in it.

"This has to be one of the Seven Wonders of New York City," she says. "Are there even any other tree houses in Manhattan?"

I scratch my jaw. "Good question. I haven't studied the prevalence of tree houses, but maybe I'll have my assistant look into it."

She rolls her eyes as she heads to the tree, then pats the blocks of wood that serve as the ladder up the trunk. "And I thought your bedroom skills were impressive. But this is next level. Did your son..."

She stops as if she thinks it's against the rules to ask about Zach.

"My kid asked for one, so I built it," I say, answering her unfinished question.

A laugh bursts from her. "That's it? That's all it took?"

"Pretty much," I admit sheepishly. "I might be a pushover dad."

She shakes her head. "Nah. I think that's sweet." She hesitates for a second, then asks, "Does he love it?"

"He does. I just want him to have a normal childhood. Losing his mom couldn't have been easy."

This would be heavy for a one-night stand, if Jules felt like a one-night stand. She seems genuinely interested, not just idly curious, and it's hard for me to *not* talk about my kid. I don't want to keep him a secret. Hell, I hate secrets.

"I'm sorry to hear that, Finn," she says, sympathetic despite understandable confusion about the details.

"My ex-wife isn't his mom," I explain quickly, then back up the story, giving her a little more of it, and more of myself in the process. "I met his mother eight years ago while I was in Rome on a work trip. She was American. We spent one night together and never exchanged last names." I sigh, full of regret. If only I'd given Nina my name and number. If only we hadn't played what seemed like a sexy game of no concrete details. Then I'd have known Zach for his whole life. "Anyway, when she died a few years ago, her parents made it a mission to find me. And I'm so glad they did."

"Me too. Because I can tell how happy you are being his dad."

I duck my head, shielding my expression. "It's obvious?"

She pats the tree. "Well, you built him a tree house."

"Yeah, I'm definitely a pushover," I confirm. But maybe I'm an over-sharer too. Fuck, that's bad. "That was a lot, wasn't it?"

Jules might be new to sex, but I feel new to...sharing.

"No. It wasn't." She goes quiet, but it's clear the gears are turning in her head. "I was curious last night about your son, but I didn't want to push. People share things in their own time. And sometimes not at all."

"It's hard for me to keep him a secret," I say.

"You shouldn't have to. And I'm glad you didn't," she adds, and there's something wistful in her voice. Like she's wishing this thing could turn into something more. Another night. Another time. Another moment here in the yard.

We've jammed so much into less than twenty-four hours. Shared more than most people do over a half-dozen dates.

This was a one-night stand in name only.

If we were other people, I'd take her hand and tug her into a corner by the door, far away from the neighbors, hardly visible, and kiss her against the side of my home. I'd claim her outside by the honeysuckle so we could both inhale the scent of wanting as we fucked.

Then I'd invite her over again.

But that's not what last night was. This morning and this closeness, this easy connection—they're scrambling my brain.

"Thanks for listening, Jules."

She closes the distance between us and sets a hand

on my chest, gently grabbing the fabric of my shirt. "Anytime."

That word feels like a promise we can't keep, but I wish we could.

* * *

The car service texts that they're pulling up just as we go inside. I haul Jules against me one more time, then sniff her neck. "Mmm. Your morning scent is good too. You're like a sexy garden," I tell her, but I've got to stop with the praise. No more compliments. No more kisses. I need to let her go. I clear my throat and step back. "Bye, Jules."

"Bye...Finn." She stops, like she's going to say *see you around.*

But really, we probably won't. Just in case though, I add, "If I see you when you're with—"

She holds up a hand, stopping me. "—I know. Nothing happened."

When she pulls away, I'm filled with a bittersweet ache, but soon it'll fade.

She sets her hand on the doorknob and...fuck. I can't let her leave on the thought that this was nothing. I spin her around, cup her cheek, and meet her eyes. "Thank you. For last night. For this morning. For letting me have you."

"I'm glad it was you."

"You have no idea how glad I am too."

She shrugs, coyly. "Actually, I think I do."

She leaves, heading off into the light of day. I turn

back into my home where there's a text blinking up at me from my phone on the counter.

> Tate: Five miles. Fastest time ever. See you tomorrow, sloth.

Guilt swells inside me. But I'll have to find a way to live with it when I see my friend tomorrow morning.

For now, I walk through my kitchen, and it feels empty without his daughter.

13

MORE THAN ONE WAY TO TELL A STORY

Jules

I'm pretty sure my little apartment isn't even technically a one-bedroom. The broker dubbed it a "junior" one-bedroom when I rented it. But that's just real estate slang for "there's a corner somewhere in here that lets us call it an alcove."

That evening, four women jam into my alcove, including me.

Well, I am the keeper of the wigs, so we're getting ready here for tonight's karaoke and dancing.

"Check me out," Layla says, adjusting a blunt purple wig that gives her serious anime vibes.

"You look like a fairy," Harlow declares.

"A badass fairy," Layla corrects, tapping Harlow's nose.

"But of course," Harlow seconds, flicking a few strands of hair in her long, curly cherry-red wig. "And now I'll learn if redheads really do have more fun."

Camden clears her throat while twirling a strand of her natural hair, all copper and shiny "Oh they do, honey. They definitely do," she says.

I roll my eyes. "Right, Cam. Right."

"Or maybe brunettes do, Jules," Cam says with a hint of *I know what you did last night.*

Since, well, she does.

We worked out together earlier, on side-by-side ellipticals at the gym, and I told her pretty much everything. I'm not sure if I'll say anything to Harlow and Layla, but only because I don't want to overshare. I don't want to blab either. If I said something, would it come back to hurt Finn? Or me?

No idea. But for now, I just want to have fun with the girls, trying on wigs before we head out.

The distraction helps too. I need it, badly. I've been thinking about Finn pretty much nonstop since I left his home eleven hours ago and wishing I could see him again. I knew the boundaries when I went over to his place, but my brain is wired to overthink. A few more days and I probably won't think about him again. Until then, I'll keep extra busy.

I wedge past Layla to look for just the right style for tonight.

"Where's Billie Eilish?" Camden demands as she hunts through my wigs too.

"Top shelf. Right side," I answer as I grab Lady Gaga from her Styrofoam head.

"Wait. The wigs have names?" Layla cuts in, clearly delighted. "Who's mine?"

"Katy Perry," I say, as I grab my electric blue wig, then tug it on over the wig cap I'm wearing.

"And who does Harlow have on?"

"Pink. Cam named that one." As I adjust Lady Gaga, my phone buzzes with a text.

Might be my dad confirming our mutual fund discussion time tomorrow. Gee, I just can't wait. But I also have to deal with it, so once my wig is on, I pull my phone from my pocket.

It's Hank, the doorman, letting me know there's a delivery for me and he'll bring it up since he needs to take something to my neighbor too. Huh. I'm not expecting anything. It might be chocolate from my mom, or maybe even a wine she's had overnighted from the festival she's at. She's been known to do things like that.

"I'll be right back," I say, and when I open the door, Hank hands me a pink bag with black stripes.

"Here you go, Miss Marley."

It's from You Look Pretty Today, and I know it's definitely not from my mother.

I turn around, bag in hand. There's no hiding this gift. My skin prickles both with excitement and worry.

What will they say? More importantly, what will I say? Words bubble up my throat, tempting my tongue. *The man I spent the night with is a pleasure Dom. How many orgasms do you think you could handle till you begged a guy to stop? I'm desperate to find out, to test my limits, to explore the edge with him.*

All my friends' eyes are on me as I clutch the pink

and black bag in both hands. My fingers itch to open this unexpected gift. I feel both stuck and excited.

"Who's it from?" Harlow asks, her eyes wide with curiosity.

"Is it your birthday and you didn't tell us? You're in trouble," Layla teases.

I swing my gaze from Harlow to Layla to Camden, debating my words. Finn's *nothing happened* echoes in my mind. In public, I need to stick to that.

"Or," Camden puts in, "did you just send yourself something?"

I could kiss her. She gives me a small, supportive nod, permission to spin a white lie into a way out of this awkwardness. But do I want that?

Yes, I want to protect Finn. But I think back to those moments in the town car before I got to his place, to texting my friends, and to how wonderful it felt to share my excitement.

Even if he's sent me a gift, Finn's out of my life. But I want these women in my life. Fine, they don't know all of me. They don't know about my OCD, my manipulative ex, or the way my family pointed fingers after the night Willa drowned.

But this bag in my hands simply contains a pretty gift, not the secrets of my soul. And there's more than one way to tell a story.

"While I'm a big fan of self-gifting," I begin, laughing nervously, "it's not from me this time."

Harlow grins my way mischievously. "So, Jules, I guess last night was *gooood*." She stretches the last word into ten syllables, inviting me to tell them more.

My chest swells with a strange sort of hope. The hope for friendship that lasts.

"Really, really good," Layla adds.

Their voices are kind. They're interested, hopeful that I'll say more.

I'm the bold one, I'm the bold one. I'm the bold one.

I square my shoulders, flick back a strand of blue hair, then own my right to tell the story of my first time.

"Well, girls, let's see what the man from last night sent me," I begin with a sly grin. I set the bag on the counter and open it, unfolding the soft, pale pink tissue paper. Then I stifle a gasp. I knew it was lingerie because I know the store, but wow. These are gorgeous. I reach inside and gently pull out a pair of bright, beautiful pink undies. They're low-waisted, with a tiny bow and soft, delicate lace. They're almost identical to the pair Finn ripped off me this morning and I blush fiercely at the memory.

"Girlfriend. Details. They are gorgeous!" Layla coos.

"And I want to know why he sent them," Harlow says, tapping her toe playfully.

Before I say more, I read the note attached. *If I saw you in these, I'd probably rip them off too.*

The blush? I feel it everywhere, including deep in my body. That dirty, flirty man. He's a clever man too. He didn't sign the note, so I do something really daring. I read it out loud to my friends.

When I finish, Layla howls with delight. Harlow thrusts her arms in the air. Camden fans herself. I flop down on the bed, giddy. I feel a little like champagne, all bubbly. "More, I want more," Harlow says.

Sitting up, I unspool some of last night. "He's very, very giving."

Harlow wiggles a brow. "I do love a giving man."

"Like borderline obsessed," I say. "He did things to me I'd only read about."

"Like?" Layla asks.

I bite my lip, getting lost in the memory. "He kept me up late with orgasms. And he made sure I would never forget it."

My apartment is quiet for a moment until Harlow sighs with envy. "That's hot," she says finally.

And it is hot. It was an intense night of pleasure, and, surprisingly, trust.

Trust that we would keep each other's secrets.

Still riding that wave, I look around at my friends and breathe in their acceptance and understanding. In this moment, I'm not just the bold one, the one who plans the nights out, the one who has the killer poker face.

I'm one of them. Like I've wanted to be.

"He made me beg for orgasms. And he spent his sweet time drawing them out of me," I say, getting into the details a little more. "What did you call him earlier, Cam?"

With a proud smile, she says, "The King of Edging."

Layla whistles. "Damn, girl."

"He's the one from the private party?" Harlow asks, remembering what I told them two weeks ago.

I can say that, right? Surely, they don't know Finn frequents a kink club, of sorts. "Yes."

"So," Layla says, twirling a strand of hair, "will you see him again?"

My heart sags. "It's complicated, but I don't think so."

Layla's brow knits. "Why the hell not? He sent you panties. A man doesn't send an after-sex gift unless he wants to see you again."

Oh, god. Oh, fuck. Why didn't I anticipate this part of the confession? The pressing. The questions. The *why not*.

But I don't have to explain the specifics. Sometimes, maybe most of the time, romance doesn't last anyway. "It was just a one-time thing. We're both busy with our lives. Maybe it's for the best," I say. I glance around at their sympathetic faces and...fuck it.

"I don't really trust that easily. My college ex read my journals and used all the details in them against me for weeks."

"What?" Layla's upper lip curls with disgust.

"He did," I confirm. "So, it's not like I'm dying to have a boyfriend." I pop up from the bed and make my way to my closet. "But I am dying to go out."

That's true too. I'm grateful I got that out so they'll know and understand me, but mostly, I'm ready to have some fun.

* * *

Later that night, when I'm alone again in my home, the scent of lavender calming me and the stars my only companions, I take out my journal. The card slips out, and I look at the front—an image of stars in a blue sky —then the words inside. I've memorized them. I've known them for a long time, but still, I read them. It always brings me a sense of peace, this quote from *The Little Prince*.

Then, I tell Willa what I did tonight.

When I re-read my secret language to her, I want to shake this record of my thoughts at Brandon. Shake it with a satisfied sneer. *You'd never be able to figure me out now.*

Never.

Then I lock it up.

I don't ever want anyone to read my private thoughts again.

14

BEFORE HIM

Finn

As I head to meet Tate on Sunday morning, I feel like I'm putting on a mask.

It's not something I want to do with my friend. I detest lying, but there's no getting around it. When my brother hid his relationship with Layla from his son, back when they were first dating, I advised Nick to stop sneaking around. But this weekend, I was the one sneaking around. But this weekend is over. It's behind me.

I need to get into the exercise zone ASAP. I spot Tate stretching his quads next to the bench by the entrance to the High Line and jog over to him.

He looks up, business as usual, and gives a curt nod.

I act like nothing has changed since Thursday. Which, I suppose, it hasn't.

"Surprised you showed up," he says gruffly. He does nearly everything gruffly, except write airtight contracts. That's why I like him. He's straightforward in life and diligent in business.

"Because I'm usually such a no-show," I deadpan.

He clears his throat, a reminder that I bailed in advance yesterday.

Yeah, I'm not going there. I nod to the running path, which at seven a.m. is already teeming with weekend warriors. "I stretched at home. Let's do this, old man," I say.

He rolls his eyes. "Fuck you."

It's an easy target, but I take it. When your buddy is eight years older than you, you can always rib him for being old.

The trash talk covers up my guilt and so does the exercise.

The morning air is cool, the light catching the edges of buildings, creating a golden glow. We weave through the stream of joggers, hitting a brisk pace quickly.

"So, how was your Friday night?" Tate asks. Since I didn't run yesterday, it was inevitable he'd ask. Still sucks though. "Better than it's been over the last couple of years?"

The twisting? It's a fucking knife right now in my gut.

Tate was there for me when things with Marilyn went south—there in exactly the way I needed, giving me a focus as his workout partner, finding triathlons that raised money for causes from cancer to children's hospitals, and developing a training schedule for running, biking, and swimming.

Suited his needs too. He's become addicted to our

races. He'd joined our local running club a few months after his daughter's death, and he'd once told me running was his therapy.

"I have no complaints," I say, then shift the topic. "Except that you're a fucking turtle this morning."

I peel ahead, running faster, needing distance. Maybe in a few more days it'll be easier, this...lying by omission.

But Tate's resilient. He hates losing. So he pounds the pavement relentlessly until he catches up. When he does, I make sure I take the reins of the conversation. "What about you? How's Liz doing with the new hires?"

He talks about his wife's projects at her company as we go.

This is freedom for me, outpacing other runners as we push further and further out of our comfort zones. My heart races as I outrun the recent years of heartache, maybe even the other night of pleasure too. My lungs burn and my quads scream, but with each passing mile, the unease in me lessens, like I've burned off the emotions.

Soon enough, we slow down, nearing the end of our run.

"Big week ahead," Tate says, his breath coming fast as we veer to an exit on the path. "The paperwork is all done. I'm seriously fucking proud of this deal."

I clap his shoulder, proud of him too. "You should be," I say, slowing to a light jog. "You made it all happen."

A rare smile shifts his lips. The man is stoic so much of the time, rarely letting an emotion through. I understand why. He's been through hell and doesn't want to feel pain like that again.

We slow to a walk and head to our usual coffee cart, just off the running path. "Thanks for taking a chance on this old cop," Tate says, earnestly.

I laugh. "Easiest decision ever."

"No, I mean it," he says, sounding more vulnerable. "You were my first client. You took a big chance. I want to do right by you, Finn."

Ah, hell.

The knife goes deeper, digs farther. "You have, man. You have," I say, focusing only on this deal.

I don't want to linger on Friday night, and why I invited Tate's daughter over. Or why I didn't cancel before she arrived. I don't even have a "heat of the moment" excuse. My night with Jules was one hundred percent premeditated.

I know why I invited her, why I didn't cancel —*because I wanted her.*

But in the light of day, that reasoning doesn't hold up. That's flimsy and trivial compared to a friendship that's real and true. Best to focus on that.

Tate came to me when he passed the bar. I took a chance on him when I ran my own venture firm, farming out smaller contracts. He proved his mettle. When Nick and I recently merged our firms into Strong Ventures, I told my brother we were now one of Tate's clients.

End of story.

He's my lawyer. He does my deals.

"Should be a busy week as we put the next steps in

motion," he says, as we reach the cart. "And hey, coffee's on me as a thanks."

Nope. That's not happening. "I got this." It's a small thing. But there is no way he's paying for the coffee after I slept with his daughter and bought her panties.

After we order, we head to a bench with our cups and review the week ahead.

We have our friendship. Our athletic goals. Our business partnership.

We don't need to discuss my after-dark affairs.

Ever.

* * *

"And then, with his trusty mutt by his side, Captain Dog and Captain Dude walked off into the sunset, having saved the city one more time," I say, reading the final page in a graphic novel Zach and I picked up this afternoon at An Open Book.

I'm glad the story is over, because it's hard reading in the cramped quarters of the tree house.

"Can I have one more story?" he asks, his young voice laced with hope. "I want to know what happens next." He sits up taller, his green eyes flickering wildly. "Or maybe we can get a dog like Captain Dude has?"

Oh fuck.

Oh hell.

What am I going to do with that request?

Nick warned me this day would come. *Someday he*

will ask for a dog, and you will be so screwed. It was months ago, when Zach was caught up in playing with a Border Collie in Central Park.

I ruffle Zach's hair, steering away from the tempting topic. I too love dogs. "How about that story, kiddo? But I'll read it to you when you're in bed." I sit up, unfolding from the pretzel shape I've been in these last few hours.

I built the tree house so Zach could have what he wants, and fine, to flex my dad muscles. But I didn't anticipate how much time he would want to spend here or how uncomfortable it would be for a grown man to wedge himself into a tiny tree house.

Already today we've made a baking-soda-powered rocket, and we've worked our way through a stack of comics. But the light is waning and bed is calling.

And my limbs are groaning as I make my way out of the tree house, Zach scrambling down after me.

Once inside the brownstone, he motors through the kitchen, racing to the fridge and yanking open the door. "I'm still hungry. Can I have more pineapple?"

I refuse to think of Jules. I have pineapple for Zach. That is what I tell myself.

"Of course, buddy," I say, then I grab the container, scoop some tropical fruit into a bowl, and join him at the counter. My thoughts don't linger on what I did at this counter yesterday morning, or on the pair of pink panties I ripped off of Jules's beautiful body, or the fact that they're in my nightstand drawer.

As Zach eats, we talk about our plans for the next few days and how much he can't wait to go camping with my dad and mom in a few weeks. They're taking him to upstate New York on a trip, along with their other grandson. Nick's son is twenty-two, but David loves the outdoors, so he's up for family camping.

"We'll need to stock up on camping supplies," I say. I'm glad that Zach has embraced my parents as his *new grandpa and new grandma*. I want him to know as much of his family as possible.

"Like graham crackers, marshmallows, and chocolate," he says after swallowing the last bite of the fruit.

"What other camping supplies are there?" I ask.

"A dog," he says with a glint in his eyes.

"I can already see you take after me in negotiation skills." I drop a kiss onto his forehead.

After we clean up, we head to the second floor and he gets ready for bed. As he slips under the covers, he peers around his room, questions in his eyes. "Dad, what did you do with this room before me?"

Before him. Sometimes it hardly seems like there was a before him—he's what I wanted for so long.

"I didn't have this place before you," I say, sitting on the side of the bed.

He tilts his head, studying me curiously. "Where did you live then?"

"In a very tall building in the Sixties. With my ex-wife."

"You got this house for me?"

"Well, yeah. You *and* me, buddy," I say, patting his leg.

He smiles, wide and wonderful. "That's pretty cool," he says. "I'm glad Grandma and Grandpa found you."

My heart swells. "Me too. You have no idea how

glad," I say, my throat tightening as I hug him. "I wish I'd known you your whole life."

But at least I have him now. He's what matters most to me in the whole world.

Parenting is funny like that. You go from not knowing someone to them being your entire heart.

I say goodnight, the house no longer so empty. I do some work in my office, then eventually head to bed and shut my door. Alone, in the dark, under the covers, I open my texts, allowing myself just one more peek.

> Jules: I'll think of you when I wear these.

My skin goes hot at the message. And I'm imagining her in them, and the things she might be doing as she thinks of me.

15

FREEDOM TO BLURT

Jules

"There. And it's opened." My father seems pleased over his end of the Zoom session. Retirement planning isn't my idea of a relaxing Sunday night, but now it's done.

"Thanks, Dad," I say, closing out the window on the mutual fund page.

He sighs, looking relieved. "I just want you to be...prepared."

That word sounds loaded. But no one could really have been prepared for what happened to Willa. Somehow, though, being prepared for my future, being practical, and being responsible is how he honors her.

At least, *I think so*. I don't know. We don't talk about it.

"It's never too early to start. I wish I'd started saving earlier," he admits.

"Sure, I get that," I say. My mutual fund has a paltry

five hundred dollars in it, but I suppose it's something. It can't hurt to think ahead, even though the future I'm most interested in is this week and the agenda Bridger said he has slated for me. My boss returns from a Los Angeles trip in a few days, and wants me to join him at some of his Webflix meetings to discuss another season of *Happy Enough*, and to talk more about *The Rendezvous*.

I don't let myself drift too long on the hope of working more on *The Rendezvous*, and instead focus on my dad and his financial advice. "I won't start too late," I say.

"Good. It's one of my biggest regrets," he adds.

One of. But it's not his biggest. We all know his biggest regret—that he wasn't home the night Willa drowned. That she sneaked out. But we don't talk about that night either.

"Well, thanks for helping me," I say.

"Anytime, sweetheart." That's rare too—the affection underlying in his tone. Then he adds, "I love you."

I feel awful. How would he feel about me if he knew I'd slept with his best friend?

But I say the words back anyway. "Love you too."

He clears his throat. "I'll, um, see you this week."

"We will?" He must mean Thursday night dinner. "Sure, on Thursday."

"Right, right," he says, then looks at his watch. "I have to go."

We end the Zoom, and I don't want to think about why he acted weird just now. I have my own reasons to act weird. Best we don't talk about those either.

* * *

Story of my life—I'm almost always afraid I'll say something I shouldn't say in public. But I never do.

That's how my particular brand of OCD works. The fear is enough to fuck me up. But the great thing about seeing a shrink for that fear is...*I can say whatever I want.*

With that freedom to share spurring me on, I walk into Shira Bergman's office for an early Monday meeting, and the second the door closes, I announce: "I slept with my father's best friend on Friday night."

She blinks at me, bug-eyed.

I sit down, grinning, a little devilishly delighted that I succeeded in stunning her. "I shocked you," I say, stating the obvious.

"You did. Do you want to talk about it?"

"I do," I say, crossing my legs and meeting her eyes. Her dark, curly hair frames her wise face, and she waits, patiently.

But she doesn't have to. I'm raring to go. I've got tea to spill. I'm not asking her for reassurance. I don't need her to tell me I'm okay. I *want* to tell her what's going on in my secret life.

I don't hold back the details. I tell her about the costumes, the sex, the orgasms, the panty gift, and the fact that I can't ever see him again, and when I'm done, she pins me with a thoughtful stare, one that says her brain is working through my Monday morning bombshell.

"Do you think this is related to what happened when you went to family therapy?"

What? My head spins. How did we go from talking about me finally having sex and enjoying it to her thinking this has to do with *the time we went to family therapy*?

"What do you mean?"

"You said it didn't go well when you went with everyone."

That's true. Mom, Dad, Liz, and I went to grief therapy together a few times to deal with all the hurt and the blame. At first, the sessions were helpful—cathartic even. But where it *went horribly wrong* was at Willa's grave the day after one of those sessions. I've never told Shira the things my father said to me when he broke down at my sister's tombstone. I've never told anyone. I *can't* tell anyone. The words hurt too much. All I've said to Shira is we didn't deal well with our grief. Lately, she's been urging me more to talk through the loss, and sometimes I do talk about my sister, but I don't want to today.

"You think I'm trying to get back at him?" I ask, fixating on that.

"That's not what I said. Is that what you heard me say?"

Pretty much. "I didn't know who Finn was that first night I met him. I didn't say yes to seeing him again because of my dad. I *wanted* to see him," I say, annoyed. My pulse spikes.

"Jules, that's not what I meant," she says, keeping calm as I spiral.

"What did you mean?" I ask, crossing my arms.

"I just wonder if you chose someone for your first time knowing that you *couldn't* have a relationship with him. Knowing that you wouldn't—your words—see him again." She leans forward. "I wonder if that has anything to do with your past. Maybe we can talk about what happened when you went to therapy with your family."

Nope.

Not going to. Don't want to revisit that terrible time. And she knows it.

"I'd rather not," I say, cooling a bit. "I have some meetings this week. My boss said he wanted to talk about *The Rendezvous*, and I'm hoping he'll assign me that show. I'd rather review our strategies for that. I really don't want to think sex thoughts during a business meeting."

Shira nods crisply, then says, "Fair enough."

We focus on mindfulness techniques and cognitive behavior skills for the rest of our session. The future is fixable. With her help, I can move forward.

I don't know why she wants me to face the past though. No amount of writing can change what happened to my sister late one summer night.

Or what I told her before she left the house.

Or what my father said to me months later.

* * *

On Wednesday, Bridger raps on my door and I look up from my laptop to greet him, adjusting my black glasses. "How were your meetings in Los Angeles?"

"Terrific," he says offhand like he'd rather discuss something else. "Do you have a second?"

Nerves fly down my spine.

He's firing me.

He's reprimanding me.

"Of course," I say, masking my worries with a smile.

"I was hoping you could join me this afternoon when I meet with some new execs at Streamer."

Oh, thank god.

I handle production coordination for a couple of our shows, but none are carried on Streamer. "Sure. But I'm curious why?"

And I'm hopeful. He's dropped breadcrumbs. But I've tried not to eat them or let them fill me up. I don't want to hope and then lose out.

"Because I'd like to add a show to your list. It'll come with a small pay raise. Would you want to handle production coordination for *The Rendezvous*?"

"I would very much like that," I say, and I don't try to contain my glee. I can't. This is the *it* show. I've been dying to work on it but figured I'm too junior.

"Fantastic," he says, then gives a sheepish smile. "That's why I had you read the scripts. I was hoping to make the move, but I just needed to be sure there was an open producer assignment and there is."

"I've been researching Paris and the neighborhoods where the show takes place. I feel like I could lead a tour through Montmartre," I say, touting myself. My dad would be proud.

"Great. I knew you'd be ready to hit the ground running. Or the cobblestones, I should say." He tugs up the cuff of his ruby-red shirt. "We'll meet the execs for lunch at noon."

"I'm there," I say.

* * *

We take a Lyft to McCoy's, a popular deal-making steakhouse in midtown. Along the way, we chat about the show, the shoot, and the fast-paced schedule, then Bridger segues to lunch. "Oh, and about McCoy's. Just wanted to reassure you they have more than steaks," Bridger says when we reach the restaurant with the emerald-green awning. "Harlow says the pasta and salads are amazing."

It's kind of him to think about the way I eat. It's one of the things I appreciate about my boss. But I don't want him to worry about me. "Sides are the best," I say as we slide out of the car.

"Harlow says the same." On the way to the door, his phone buzzes. "One second," he tells me, stopping to slide a thumb across the screen. Then glances at me. "I wasn't sure if he was going to make it or not, but your father is here."

That's odd. "He works with Streamer?" I ask, but

then again, his client list is one of the many things my dad doesn't share with me.

"He does some work for one of the execs," Bridger explains as we head into the oak-paneled eatery. The lights are low, and he scans the booths before the hostess can say hello.

"There they are." Bridger points to a far corner where he must have spotted the Streamer execs. He's very focused, always on alert and fast on the draw.

We make our way across the restaurant. My work with Shira has helped me deal with anxiety about the unexpected, but no amount of therapy could prepare me for when my gaze lands on the people we're meeting.

My father and Finn.

16

HIS TYCOON ATTITUDE

Jules

They say life is full of surprises.

This is not the kind of surprise I wanted when Bridger offered me the gig I'd been craving. Judging from the way Finn's brow furrows, he wasn't expecting to see me either. My dad probably knew, though, but couldn't say anything to me for confidentiality reasons.

Still, years of practice being the good girl kick in as I smile uber-professionally while Bridger talks. He knows my father, obviously, so with a laugh, he says, "Tate, of course you know Jules. What you might not know is she's on *The Rendezvous* production team as of" —he makes a show of looking at his watch—"three hours ago."

Excitement flickers in my dad's eyes briefly, then he rearranges his features into his cop face—all stoic and in control. But I've seen him when he's not stoic. When he's broken and falling to pieces. I've seen him on the worst days of his life. I try to erase those horrible images.

"Fantastic news," my father says. "So glad my Julia has become so invaluable." He means well, but it makes me feel like the kid at the table. I already feel that way with these three men. It's hard to miss the divide in age between them and me, as well as the divide in experience.

Bridger turns to Finn, the man I didn't think I'd see again so soon. "You must be Finn Adams. Congrats on the investment. I'm excited to see what you're going to do at Streamer."

Finn doesn't even need a moment to clear his throat. He shakes Bridger's hand and answers with, "Pleasure to meet you, too, Bridger, and I'm glad we could do this before we announce the deal tomorrow morning." He quickly explains to me, since I'm the one in the dark, that Strong Ventures just finalized an investment in Streamer for a majority stake in the upstart streaming service. "And with the buzz the show is getting, I wanted to meet the producers so my team at Strong can talk up *The Rendezvous* in the press coverage tomorrow."

"Music to my ears," Bridger says, rightfully proud of the show that hasn't even launched yet. He turns to me. "And Jules is going to be part of that team. I'm sure you know Jules."

He says it because my dad is Finn's lawyer. So naturally, Bridger assumes my dad has mentioned me to his friend and client.

Little does he know Finn knows me in plenty of other ways.

"Nice to see you," I say, taking his hand and shaking it as quickly as I can, refusing to think about how he likes to wrap those big hands around mine and pin me to the wall.

I swallow uncomfortably as we let go.

"I've been looking for an opportunity to move her over to *The Rendezvous*, and there was an opening recently," Bridger adds. "Serendipitous, isn't it?"

Finn gives a warm *isn't that a coincidence* type of grin. But inside, I bet he's thinking seren-fucking-dipitous indeed.

Because I am too.

I'm tempted to tug my father aside and ask why the hell he never mentioned that Finn was working on acquiring half of Streamer. He knows we pitch shows to Streamer on the reg. Alright, sure, my father's business deals are private, bound by NDAs. But I bet that's why he acted weird on Sunday night. Even though I hadn't been brought onto the show yet, he must have been aware that his deal tangoed close to my work life. He's big on ethics, as any lawyer should be, and on making sure his deals are buttoned up and done right.

This is going to be the most awkward lunch ever. As I sit, I smooth a hand over my pencil skirt, keeping my fingers busy like that, then move them to my glasses, adjusting them.

The server swings by with menus. I stare at the offerings for longer than I need to. There are only a few things I'd order anyway. But I study every item like I'm solving calculus equations.

Where do I look if not at my menu? What if I look at Finn the wrong way? What if I accidentally brush my Mary Jane pumps against his suit pants? What if I'm talking to my father and suddenly remember the way Finn spread me out on his bed and devoured me?

My cheeks will go red.

And...great. Just great. They already are.

I keep my face lowered, hoping the color drains quickly. This is so embarrassing, the way I blush so easily.

It'll pass. It'll pass. It will *pass.*

I stare forever at the lunchtime fare because Caesar versus chef's salad is such a fascinating dilemma.

I keep reading as the men set down their menus and make idle chitchat about the New York Comets to fill the time. It's funny because I know Bridger isn't as into sports as my dad is. Bridger's more of a theater guy. But he has mastered the art of small talk so he's able to contribute a smart comment about the team's shortstop or the winning streak they're on.

I can BS my way through sports talk, too, but I don't want to open my mouth at all.

Mercifully, the waiter arrives and tells us about the specials. Perhaps, he'll stay here the whole meal. I wish.

But no, he leaves and I'm left at the table with my boss, my father, and the man who sent me pink lace panties to replace the ones he ripped off me.

Kill me now.

Bridger tees up the next round of chitchat, asking

Finn what attracted him to Streamer. My Friday night lover leans back in his chair, cool and confident, speaking in that deep, sexy voice that turns me on. "I've been wanting Strong Ventures to make deeper inroads in the content business, and frankly, the whole media industry has been looking for an upstart streaming network to give Webflix some serious competition. I'd like to spearhead that and make Webflix squirm. Scare them a little." His careless, cocky shrug is hotter than I'd have expected.

But then, Finn's confidence attracted me the night I met him as a phantom.

His determination drew me closer the night he played Gatsby.

His intensity, coupled with surprising tenderness, sent me spinning into bliss this past weekend.

Now? His tycoon attitude is making me wet.

Damn my body.

"Let them feel the competition at their heels. Breathing down their necks," Finn continues, and holy shit, my neck is on fire. My skin blazes. "And I think a hot property like *The Rendezvous* is just the way to launch the attack."

I shiver then adjust my glasses again in case anyone noticed the way my body reacted.

Out of the corner of my eye, I see Finn's lips curve in the barest of grins. One he erases instantly.

He noticed the effect he had on me.

Of course he did. This man always notices me. He always sees me. It's eerie and alluring all at once.

I refuse to look in my father's direction.

Bridger shoots Finn a satisfied smile. "Absolutely love hearing that about an Opening Number project."

My dad clears his throat. "You must be as well, Julia. I know you've been keen on the show."

He might have gotten me the intro that led to my job, but I kept it on my own. He doesn't need to cue me to join the conversation.

"Yes, it's been wonderful that there's so much excitement around the show. I've already jumped right into some of the scheduling Tetris," I say. That's my special skill.

"That's why I put Jules on *The Rendezvous*. She's a genius with logistics," Bridger says.

"Thank you," I say.

"Glad you're on it," Finn says. His gaze locks with mine, his green eyes sharp. But even in his all-business mode, those irises still make me ache between my thighs. This is definitely not like those uncomfortable intrusive sex thoughts, this is something real. I can't stop thinking about sex with him as he sits staring across from me, especially after Friday night at his home. Nothing about these thoughts are uncomfortable, at all.

Which is another problem entirely.

"And we have big plans at Strong on how to compete with Webflix and gain new customers." Finn pauses before he goes on. "When my brother and I devised our plan to invest, it was contingent on a clear growth strategy for Streamer. To that end, I'll personally take an active role in the next few months in meetings with marketers, sponsors, and partners. When the show starts filming in a few weeks, my son will be off on a camping trip with his grandparents," Finn says, and even in that brief mention of Zach, his delight and pride comes through. "So I'll be going to Paris that first week and meeting with marketers and distribution partners myself."

Bridger smiles. "That's fantastic. Because I'm sending Jules to oversee the first week of shooting. Your trips should align."

I blink.

Then swallow.

"Oh? You are?" I hope my voice didn't squeak in shock.

"Yes. It only makes sense to have my right-hand woman there on the ground," Bridger says.

Across the table, my father beams. He couldn't be more thrilled with this work accomplishment of mine. "I'm glad the two of you will be able to work together. You'll learn so much from Finn," my father says about his best friend.

Little does he know.

This is the most uncomfortable lunch in the history of time.

Finn, to his credit, doesn't move a telling muscle. His is the true poker face. "Paris is wonderful," he says. He could be talking about a steak or a bottle of wine, not the city famous for enchanting lovers.

Somehow I make it through the rest of the meal, all while another loop is running through my head. *I'm going to be in Paris for a week with my father's best friend. The man who fucked me to countless orgasms the other night. The man who wants to punish me with pleasure.*

When the check comes, Finn pays the bill with no questions asked. As Finn waits for his credit card, Bridger asks, "Besides the camping, how's your son keeping himself busy this summer?"

"He has a pretty full calendar—conducting science experiments, climbing trees, and trying to devour the entire *Captain Dude* comic collection," he says.

I hide a smile at the way Finn talks about his son, with such pride and affection, like he did in the yard on the weekend.

"He's a reader, then," Bridger says with a smile.

"Definitely. Balanced with running fast and talking a million miles a minute," Finn says, then pauses. "I take it you were a big reader as a kid?"

"I pretty much grew up at the library," Bridger says, then gestures to me. "Though no one's as fast at reading as Jules. I've given her scripts at noon and she's had them finished by twelve-thirty."

I blush from the compliment.

"Speed reader?" Finn asks me, and it's strange to have this conversation with him in front of everyone when it feels like one we could have in private, in his home, his bedroom, his courtyard.

"The faster I read, the more books I can devour," I say.

"She's always been like that," my dad weighs in, and I wish he wouldn't. "That was her motto as a kid."

Kid. Thanks, Dad.

"And now I guess I know what to read next. *Captain*

Dude," I say, wrestling back some of the conversational control from my dad.

My father looks at his watch. "I have another meeting, so I'd better take off. But I'm glad this is working out for everyone."

Except my libido.

"I have to head uptown to meet with CTM," Bridger says, turning to me. "But I'll see you back at the office later, and we'll hammer out the details."

That's his meeting with the talent agency we work with a lot. I'm not needed there. I am needed back at my desk, where I should dive into all things related to *The Rendezvous.*

But when we all leave the restaurant, and Bridger and my dad take off, I'm not feeling the desire to flee quite so much.

I want to stay because I'm standing with Finn outside the restaurant on a warm summer day in Manhattan, and he's staring at me like I'm a puzzle he wants to solve.

17

DESIRE DÉTENTE

Finn

"You wear glasses," I say, stating the obvious. But I mean something else entirely.

You look stunning.

Jules lifts a hand to touch the black frames self-consciously. "Contacts most of the time. But at work, I usually wear glasses."

I bet they're a shield. A layer she keeps between herself and others. There's so much she holds inside. So much she clearly keeps to herself.

Even if she needs them, the glasses seem like...work role-play.

"I remember you had on glasses the first time I met you. A year or so ago," I say.

She tucks a strand of hair behind her ear. "I probably came from the office. To dinner."

"These are real?"

She nods. "The ones I wore the other night weren't," she says. I figured as much. She took off those glasses at my home and didn't seem to need them.

I hold her gaze as Midtown traffic chugs by and New Yorkers in suits and sweats march past us, phones glued to ears, destinations and deadlines in their eyes, and I know neither of us is talking about eyewear. We're talking about each other. The things we notice. The details we're cataloging.

She nods toward my green tie. "And you're wearing a tie." It's more than an observation. It means *I like the way you look in a suit.*

I should be talking about the meeting we just had. I really should. But I only want to ask her questions. Why do you put up barriers? What's behind those soulful eyes? Whose secrets are you keeping?

I can *feel* her reserve. She holds back in public. But in private, when I touch her, she's almost a different person.

No, that's not quite right. In bed, she seems free. A let-loose version of herself. She's the sexy librarian, taking off her glasses and letting down her hair.

For me.

Mmm. I'd like to play that scene next time with Jules. I get a little lost in the image of her in a pencil skirt, with pouty red lips, tugging a book down from a shelf as she gives me a seductive, come-hither look. I'd return all my books late to get a library fine from this woman.

"What is it?" she asks, breaking my dirty daydream.

Oh, I was just imagining the start of a filthy scenario with you.

And fuck it. "You look like a librarian," I say, my gaze raking over her. I mean, that skirt. That tight fucking skirt.

She laughs softly but with something like relief. Maybe she was restrained during that whole meal—understandable—and now she doesn't entirely have to be.

But I shouldn't get caught up in her. I'm drawn to her and that's dangerous. This isn't how I like to do life. I like to be in control in the bedroom and in the boardroom.

Too bad I like that blush on her cheeks. I crave her Summer Day scent too. It drifts teasingly toward me. I steal an inhale, and my head swims with longing.

Must. Focus.

"I didn't know you were eager to work on the show. We never talked about work," I say, both an excuse and a wry observation about our time together.

The corner of her lips curves up for a fraction of a second. "I guess we had other things going on."

I've got to stay in control now that we'll be working together closely. "I knew you worked at Opening Number because your father had mentioned it," I say, hating the twist in my gut at those words—*your father*. I should not have to mention the father of a woman I want. "But of course neither of us knew you'd be moving to a Streamer show."

With wide eyes, she says, "I can ask them to move me to a different one."

Are you fucking kidding me? It was crystal clear at lunch that *The Rendezvous* is a huge opportunity for her. Clear, too, she's eager to take it on.

"It would be easier," she says, offering kindly, like she wants to help me.

"No," I say, brooking no argument. "You tried to protect me before by avoiding me at that second party. You're not going to do it again."

She nibbles on the corner of her lips, perhaps liking my stern tone too much. "Maybe I'm protective," she says, a little feathery, like she was at The Scene, like she was at my home.

Like she *is* with me.

I step closer, drawn to her, needing just another hit of her perfume. One inhale and I'll get through the rest of the day, I swear. "Do you want to switch?"

She's quiet, but there's reluctance in her brown eyes. It's enough to make my chest ache. I want her dreams to come true. "Don't, Jules," I say before she can answer, my voice low but firm. "Don't switch. You need to work on the show. I can tell you want to, and the show needs you."

She huffs but shakes her head, a little amused. "Stop reading my thoughts," she says softly. Despite the situation, I manage a small smile at her response.

"Am I? Reading your thoughts?" I don't know why that idea excites me. It's a wicked thrill to be able to understand this woman so easily.

"It's scary how you see me," she murmurs.

Well, that's not helping me forget about her. "I like

it," I say, and it's as if it's just us, and nothing else matters.

"Same here." She seems caught up too, floating on this buzz.

Buzzed. Yes, that's how I feel with her, but what the fuck am I doing? Why the hell am I admitting this? Yes, I like being able to understand her easily, to read her closely, to sense what's going on behind those eyes with their hints of hopefulness and loneliness.

But there's no room in my life for her. More importantly, there's no *chance* in my life for her.

I try to focus on what's next. "And because I can see you so well, I know this show is important to you," I say, my tone professional.

Finally.

"I'm not the only one," she counters, keeping me on my toes. "Everything you said at lunch made it clear how much you want this deal to work. You have big ambitions."

I'm not used to a woman I care for listening closely to me and absorbing the words and meaning so deeply. It's...unnerving. And ridiculously appealing. She might be younger than me by more than a decade, and she might defer to me at times, but she listens. She pays attention. She's an equal. "You're right. We both have our dreams. I want you to reach yours," I say.

"Well, guess what?" she asks playfully.

"What?"

"I want the same for you," she says, laying it on the line, vulnerable and genuine.

My heart thumps annoyingly. But I fight off the threat of emotions. "We'll travel together to Paris. We'll work together as much as we have to on the show. It's just a week. It's not like we're going to be running into each other every day on the production. I have meetings with marketers and sponsors, and you'll be on location. We can handle it."

"We can."

She extends a hand. I laugh but then I take it, shaking like we've achieved some sort of understanding or a détente.

A détente from what though? Desire?

Maybe.

But the second I wrap my hand around hers, desire flares.

One simple touch electrifies my body. My skin sizzles. I want to haul her close, pin her against the brick wall of McCoy's, and kiss the fuck out of her until she's arching and begging for more.

My vision tunnels. The cars and the cabs and even the carriages across the street fade out of view. The midday spotlight's only on her, sweet and seductive. She's all I see.

With our hands clasped together, I run my thumb across her palm in circles, stroking her skin.

Her lips part and a soft breath seems to ghost past those gorgeous lips. I run my thumb over her fingers, and she shudders. A tease of a touch and it's melting her on a New York street.

My eyes don't leave her. "I want to see you in that lingerie," I rasp out as lust takes me hostage.

"How much?"

"So much it's driving me crazy."

She licks her lips, mischief in those eyes. "Too bad I'm not wearing them right now." Her eyes dart to the door of the restaurant. "Oh, you know what? I forgot something in the ladies' room."

She drops my hand and retreats into the restaurant. I know an opportunity when I see it, and I follow her there.

18

ABOUT TIRAMISU

Finn

I shouldn't do this. I really shouldn't.

But the second I shut the bathroom door and lock it, I forget how much I hate lying. Nothing matters but touching her. In no time, I've got her up against the wall, and she's gazing at me with heat in her eyes.

I run a hand down her hip. "What are you wearing then?"

She bites the corner of her lips. "Gee, I don't remember."

God, the way she plays. "I'd hate for you to forget."

"Me too."

I roam my hand over the fabric of her skirt. "Tell me something."

"Yes?"

"Did you think of me when you put them on this morning?"

"Yes," she says, her voice feathery.

"Did you play with your perfect pussy before you went to work?"

She gives a fast, needy nod. "Yes."

I stare at her, unable to look away from those lush lips, those dreamy eyes. "Did you picture my cock? My tongue? Or my fingers?"

She lifts her chin a little defiantly and answers like a woman who owns her pleasure. "I pictured you coming on me. On my tits."

Oh, fuck me. She's so deliciously dirty. I slam my mouth onto hers and take a hot, savage kiss, breaking it to say, "You're such a filthy girl. With a filthy mouth."

She pulls apart from me. "What do you want to do with my mouth?"

"Jules," I warn.

"Finn," she counters, holding her own.

I narrow my eyes. "I came in here to remind you who's in charge of your orgasms."

"And how are you going to do that?" she challenges.

I grab her hip, jerk her against me. "I can make you come in one minute."

"I dare you."

She has no idea who she's dealing with. "Pull up your skirt. Turn around and lift your ass."

She obeys beautifully, multitasking by tugging up her skirt as she spins.

Yes, she's wearing a beautiful pair of white lace

panties. With her face to the door, she slides her arms up the wood then pops out her ass, showing them off.

"Ah, too bad they're not the pair I sent you," I say.

"Such a shame."

"But *this*." I cup her center briefly. "This is too good."

She moans, wriggling against me.

But I don't touch her right away. She's a cautious woman about some things I've noticed, and it's only fucking respectful to touch a woman with clean hands. "My fingers are going to be deep inside you, fucking you hard in a few seconds," I say as I go to the sink and wash them.

She smiles, like I read her mind. "I like your dirty mouth and mind though."

"I know," I say, returning to her. "Now tell me, Jules," I say, praising her as I curl a hand over one gorgeous globe, plucking at the edge of the white lace. "Tell me who owns your orgasms," I demand.

"You do," she gasps, wriggling against my hand.

"That's right," I say, then crowd her, kiss her neck, and slide my hand around to the front of her panties and under them. She's so slick and ready. "I knew you'd be soaked."

"I am," she whispers. "I want you."

"You want me to make you come, don't you?" I ask, rubbing a soft circle on her hard clit.

She shudders. "Please."

I kiss the back of her neck, line my body up against her, and nip on her earlobe as I stroke. "Count," I command.

"Sixty," she says.

Another stroke, another kiss, another shudder.

She counts down from sixty, quickly losing track, as I kiss her neck and fuck her with my fingers till she's writhing, and moaning, and dangerously close to letting the restaurant know that no one can fuck her like I can—and in under a minute. "Quiet," I warn her.

"I'm trying," she whimpers.

"I'll help you," I say, then cover her mouth with my free hand as I play with her sweet clit. "Give it to me. Come on my hand."

Seconds later, she's trembling and flying over the edge. And there's nothing better in the world than her pleasure. As she shudders, I lick my fingers, then turn her around, kissing that beautiful mouth. She grabs onto the lapels of my jacket, then gazes up at me. "I want your dick, Finn. Please let me suck you."

I groan, then run a finger over her top lip. She nips at my finger, and draws it into her lush mouth, sucking, letting me know with words and deeds what she wants. "Let me," she says, when she releases my finger.

"You're such a beautiful beggar," I tell her. "A beautiful beggar with a dirty mouth."

"Please," she says in a needy whisper. "Please, let me suck you off."

"Beg for it," I demand.

She answers in action, parting her lips in a lingering *O*, thrusting out her chest, showing off those tits. "I'm begging you for your cock. Please let me taste it. I want to swallow your come. Want to feel it sliding down my throat. Want to walk out of here after you've shoved your dick in my mouth."

My chest is a furnace. My body is on fire as I shed my jacket and then she's kneeling on it, unzipping me, and dragging my dick to the back of her throat.

The pleasure is unholy. The clock is ticking. Someone will knock soon. And I don't fucking care.

She's too perfect to resist.

I thread my fingers through her chestnut locks. "Look at you. Needing my dick."

She trembles, clearly loving the praise as she draws me impossibly farther into her warm mouth.

I shake with lust. "That's right. You take me so fucking well."

She looks up with eager eyes as she shows off, letting her throat relax so my cock can slide a little deeper. I grip her hair tighter. Hot pulses of electricity jolt my legs. "You want to choke on my cock, don't you?"

Another savage nod. A fierce yes in her eyes. I curl my hands around her skull, thrusting deeper down her throat. She gags but doesn't relent, just mercilessly pursues my release. She sucks me until my thighs shake and my balls tighten. My vision blurs and I spill down her throat with a bitten-off groan.

I'm still shaking from the aftereffects as she stands, slams her sexy body against me, and shoves her hand up her skirt. She's fucking her fingers, chasing another orgasm in this tiny bathroom.

"Mine," I growl. "That pussy belongs to me."

"Then shut up and make me come," she demands, and wow.

That's hot.

"I'll give the orders," I say, "and the orgasms. And you better be quiet this time." I bat her hand away from her glistening pussy, then stroke her until she's shivering and coming again, pressing her lips together to seal in her scream of ecstasy. I watch her the whole time, her face twisted in exquisite, stolen pleasure after a business lunch in the middle of Manhattan.

When she's done, she pants, and moans, and sags against me. It's breathtaking, and I want to take her to my office, set her on my desk, and eat her pussy till she comes so many times she begs me to stop.

For now, I let go of her, and we straighten up. Once I've dried my hands, I hold out a palm. "You know what to do. Give them to me."

With a delighted smirk—she takes orders so damn well—she reaches under her skirt, shimmies off her white panties, and hands them to me. I ball them up and put them in my pocket. After I sling my jacket over my shoulder, I kiss her. It's short but passionate, chased by a needy groan.

I wish I could see her again. And I wish I could quit her too. She's so bad for me.

When I break the kiss, she's the first to say, "We can't do this again."

She's right. We can't. "We won't do this again," I add, and I've got to keep my promise this time.

* * *

That evening, after I leave the office, I swing by the shop I now know she likes. You Look Pretty Today is a feminine wonderland, with pink divans and faint notes of lilac perfume drifting through the store, an olfactory complement to the soft music that plays overhead. The whole vibe is subtly seductive.

Everywhere is lace and satin, embroidered flowers and raised butterflies, and lipstick hearts on black teddies. It's like Christmas morning and a winning hand in Vegas all at once. I feel seduced, lured deeper into an after-dark garden of sensual delights.

I can't have her again. I just can't keep crossing lines. But I can give her a little something. She deserves to be showered in gifts.

As I swing my gaze from shelf to shelf, display to display, my head swims with images of Jules in this black bra, in that white teddy, in...anything and everything.

I picture her lounging on a pink divan, stretching out her legs, posing for the camera.

I bet she'd let me take pictures of her with shadows playing across her round ass, her full breasts, and with lace covering only some of her soft flesh. She'd run a hand down her hip and give me the poutiest look.

An invitation to come and get her.

I'd say yes and give her relentless orgasm after relentless orgasm.

"Can I help you find something?"

The shopkeeper's voice snaps me back to reality. I'm

here to shop. Not to daydream of a woman I should not have touched today.

A woman I need to stop touching.

A woman whose panties are in my pocket. I'm a fucking pervert and a panty thief. What is wrong with me?

You want a woman you absolutely can't have, jackass.

I face the friendly sales associate, a woman with a freckled nose and a welcoming smile. I hold out my hands and ask blatantly for her help. "I need something that says *I can't stop thinking about you...but I should.*"

Her smile is kind but a little wistful too. I'm not the first man to make this request, and I won't be the last. "Let me show you."

She takes me around the store, and I follow, saying yes to everything. I'm unstoppable. I can't help myself. I am *consumed* and if I can't have her, I want her to have all these pretty things.

Fifteen minutes later, the associate finishes wrapping up an entire set of lingerie. There are several pairs of lace panties, along with a white lace panty and bra set embroidered with red tulips.

I write out a note.

I'll do better in Paris. I promise.

And I will. When I see her there, I'll be friendly and professional. I won't drag her into a dark corner and tear off her clothes. I won't tell her to choke on my cock. And I won't demand she come for me again and again.

I swear.

With that done, I pick up Zach from a friend's

home, a kid named Arjun who has a dog named Donut, a friendly, sparky little mutt who barks and scampers.

I'm so screwed.

As Zach says goodbye, I brace myself for the inevitable pooch request, but as we leave, he instead asks, "Can we go to the bookstore? There's an old *Captain Dude* that I've never read, and I want to read it before the new one comes out."

Well, that's much more manageable. "Let's get it."

We go to An Open Book, a few blocks away, and the second he slides past the door, Zach is off and running. I catch up in two long strides, grabbing his shirt collar. "Indoor feet," I admonish.

Chastened, he frowns. "Sorry, Dad."

He heads to the kids section and grabs the graphic novel. "Can I get some other books too? Daveed's mom works for a publisher, and she was telling us about all these other cool books."

"Get whatever you want." I'm indulging him, and I know it.

But as far as I'm concerned, books are one indulgence that should never be curtailed.

He stocks up, then we head to meet my brother and his son at Neon Diner.

Nick's kid gives Zach a fist bump. "What did you get at the store, Z?"

"Check this out." Zach beckons David closer, but he doesn't show him his haul from the store. He whispers something in his cousin's ear.

David's grin spreads across his face. No. That's wrong. It takes over the city.

"Sure," David says, and the two cousins slide into a booth together, looking like little stinkers.

Nick turns to me, shaking his head in amusement. "They're up to something."

"Yeah, they remind me of a couple of shitheads I once knew," I whisper, as we slide in across from them.

"They sure do."

Halfway through the meal, David clears his throat. "Uncle Finn. It's time you get Zach a dog. I know all the rescues in the city, and I can help."

Nick barks out a laugh then claps my back. "You're so screwed."

Yes. Yes, I am.

But I'm not a negotiator for nothing. "I still travel for work," I remind my son. "I won't be home all the time to take care of a dog."

David nods, his expression serious. "But I don't travel for work. Tiramisu can stay with Cynthia and me."

I blink, confused for a hot second, then ridiculously impressed. "You already named a dog we don't have?"

Zach sits up straighter. "It's your favorite dessert, Dad."

Nick covers his mouth but can't hide the sound of his cackling. When my brother finally shuts up, I get a word in edgewise. "I have to go to Paris in a couple weeks," I hedge.

"What I'm hearing is *after Paris* would be a great time." David turns to my kid. "Are you hearing that too, bro?"

Zach gives David a matching nod, his gaze dead serious as well. "I definitely heard that."

I drop my forehead into my palm and laugh.

Nick chuckles. "Good luck, Daddy."

I look up, dropping the smile as I lock eyes with David. "But you better send me camping pictures. Got it?" I point to the chief troublemaker—my brother's son.

David gives me a good soldier salute.

After we're done eating, and David and Zach weave to the exit ahead of us, Nick says, "Like father, like son."

"Yes. Your kid likes to stir the pot."

Nick rolls his eyes. "I meant yours."

"Yeah, that seems to be the case."

I go home with my troublemaker, and I try not to make any more trouble of my own. I've got this guy to focus on, and that's what matters.

A few days later, though, I receive a thank you note in the mail, and it makes me want to break all my promises.

The card is simple, with an illustration of a daisy on the front. Inside it says: *Thank you. I can't wait to wear them all.*

It's a miracle I don't stalk over to her apartment that instant.

19

FUNNY MEETING YOU HERE

Jules

Finn sticks to his promise over the next few weeks. I don't hear any more from him, not about panties, or planning for Paris, or anything.

I don't reach out to him either. I busy myself with work, and Krav Maga, and girls' nights in for poker, and out for dancing. One night, our crew goes to the lounge where Camden works, and she croons a sexy torch song for us—Harlow, Layla, Ethan, and Tessa, who's here with him.

"Girl, you've got pipes," Ethan says to Camden after she nails a tune about longing.

Tessa seconds her boyfriend with, "Give us more, you rock star."

Camden flicks her auburn hair, then says to the two of them into the mic, "If you insist."

She belts out another tune, mesmerizing the audience.

* * *

Camden and I walk home together after her last set. In a comfortable lull in our usual chitchat, she nudges my elbow. "So, Paris is soon. Will you do our list?"

"Obviously." How could I forget our *Someday in Europe After Graduation* list.

"Good. I might need you to add a few things." Camden taps her chin, staring at the starless Manhattan sky. "Like, have dinner with a handsome Frenchman. Or a handsome American."

"That won't happen."

She hums doubtfully. "I don't know. Seems like you two can't keep your hands off each other. Or his dick out of your mouth," she adds as we pass a martini bar, Olive and Dry, with evening crowds spilling onto the open terrace.

"Why do I tell you anything?" I faux lament.

"Because you love me," she says, batting her lashes.

"Truly, madly, and deeply." I mean that from the bottom of my weird, reserved, wounded heart. The heart that had been craving friendship—and has found it again with my crew.

"Will you take lots of pics and send me stories? Regale me with tales of Paris. Who knows if I'll ever go?"

"Oh, you'll go," I say confidently. "You'll sing on some big stage. Perform with a hot guitarist or something. And become an international sensation."

"I don't know about that. I'm pretty sure your dinner with a sexy American is more likely."

"Stop it, you enabler," I say, shushing her. "Nothing more is happening."

Even if I were to take that risk, I couldn't see Finn doing so. My father's friendship means too much to him, and already I care enough about Finn that I don't want to damage that. Friendship is precious.

Back when my sister and I were teenagers, Willa was the connective tissue for our whole big group—Taylor, Hannah, Josh, Ollie, and Emma...After she died at that pool party late one summer night, we never put ourselves back together again. We've all gone our separate ways. But Willa was my best friend—my OG bestie. She's a piece of my heart that I'll never retrieve.

I have new friends now, and I'm lucky. My dad has Finn, and I also don't want my father to hurt again.

I steer the convo back to Camden. "Did I get a vibe tonight with you and a certain *musician* in the audience?"

"He was with *his* girlfriend," she says, knowing exactly who I meant.

"And?"

"And he was with his girlfriend," she repeats.

"But he seemed to enjoy watching you."

"Because he likes music," she insists, but I stir the pot the rest of our walk. It keeps my mind off my own forbidden wishes.

* * *

But I don't talk about Finn again with any of my other friends. I don't return to The Scene, either, not even when Scarlett asks me if I want to fill in a third time. "It's a modern costume party and the theme is devils and angels," she tells me one evening on the phone as I'm heading home from the office.

I'm tempted, partly because I spotted a sexy angel costume at my favorite thrift shop recently. The skirt is so short it ought to be illegal. I'd love to wear it and pretend to be good while being very bad.

But I can't put myself in the path of temptation. And I definitely don't want to see Finn there picking up other women in shorter white skirts or tight red corsets that boost their boobs.

I grind my teeth at the awful thoughts. Those are truly awful, not just intrusively awful. "I wish," I say to Scarlett. "But I'm too busy with work." And that's true. Prepping for the production will keep me busy till I leave at the end of the month.

One afternoon in the office, Bridger and I Zoom with Solange Marina, the show's executive producer, who I'll be working with in Paris. Bridger introduces me as his rising-star producer. It's embarrassing but wonderful to hear too.

"I'm happy to help with anything," I tell her.

"I look forward to keeping you busy," she says, and she's hard to read, but she's efficient and I like that.

Over the next week, I stay busy prepping for Paris. I've researched the city countless times, planned my workdays, and mapped out what to do with my free time in the evenings.

I'm almost ready to visit the city I've always dreamed of visiting.

* * *

A few nights before my flight, I pop into An Open Book after work and peruse the new releases, hunting for a juicy memoir or a dishy tell-all for the plane. I'm flipping through the pages of a just-released celebrity biography when I startle at a voice calling, "Inside feet."

When I peer over the display, there's Finn striding across the plush, sapphire carpet. He's wearing dark blue slacks and a crisp charcoal shirt, and his hand curls over the shoulder of a little boy who looks remarkably like him—same dark hair, green eyes, and impish grin.

Finn slows his son before the boy can race down the main aisle of the store. I don't think he's seen me yet, shielded by a shelf with titles like *When I Was Young* and *Tie One On*. I feel like a spy, and it's wildly fun to see them together. A little mesmerizing too.

"Sorry, Dad. But I just want the new *Captain Dude* so badly," his kid says, insistent and eager as he stretches out the last word.

I just can't resist. I become the bold one as I step out from behind the shelves and say to Finn's back, "The new one is so good."

He stops and turns, but it takes a few seconds for

him to process seeing me here, which amuses me too. "Oh. Hey. Jules."

Are his cheeks a touch pinker than usual? I've never seen him flustered. It's borderline adorable. "I didn't know you shopped here." His kid escapes him and motors down the aisle, hellbent on his destination in kid lit.

"Or I you," I say dryly.

"Zach likes it." He gestures to the speed demon. "I should make sure he doesn't knock any shelves over in the rush to get his new book." He studies me for a beat, and I imagine the gears turning in his head. "Do you want to join us?"

That wasn't on my to-do list tonight. But checking out books with a child seems safe. "Sure," I say, and I don't hide the smile I feel. It's nice to be invited.

As we head to the children's section, Finn holds up a finger like he's pausing and rewinding something in his head. "Did you just say the new *Captain Dude* was good?"

Ah, I'd been waiting for him to catch up to my comment. "I did. I read it while I worked out this morning. On my Kindle," I add.

"You...did?" Finn asks.

I've really shocked Mister Tycoon now. This is fun. I think I'll keep doing it. "Well, I was dying to know what'd happened in Metropolisville since the last adventure," I say. "Especially after they saved the city from the runaway train. Or should I say, saved the chocolate *on* the runaway train."

"Yes!" interjects a young voice beside us. The boy

talks as fast as he moves. "I was so stoked when they got to eat the chocolate. But the dog didn't eat it. Dogs can't eat chocolate."

The mini Finn clutches the newest installment to his chest and happily inserts himself into the conversation. "But don't tell me what happens in this one, okay?"

I lift my hand like I'm taking an oath. "I solemnly swear I'll share no spoilers."

He gives a long sigh of relief. "But how do you read so fast? Can I learn?"

Finn clears his throat then sets a hand on his son's shoulder. "Zach, this is my friend Jules. She and I work together. Jules, this is Zach, my son," Finn says with such obvious pride and love that my heart thumps a little harder.

I extend a hand and Zach takes it. "Hey there, Zach. I have a very important question for you."

The kid's expression turns intensely serious. "What is it, Jules?"

"How did you feel about the cat in the last book? Did you think he should have joined forces with them?"

Zach's eyes sparkle with righteous excitement. "Yes! I kept waiting for that to happen. Why didn't that happen?"

"Some cats just like to sleep," I say with a tsk as Finn watches the two of us like we're the world's most fascinating tennis match.

"That's why I like dogs, but at least Captain Dude and Captain Dog were up to the challenge."

"They always are," Zach agrees. "No matter how hard it is." We dive into a discussion of the captains' most daring rescues, then Zach says, "We're going to get this book and get dinner. I might read it at dinner. Wanna come?"

The offer is so sweet, I grin, eager to say yes to Zach. But Finn might not want me there. "I don't want to intrude," I say when I meet Finn's eyes.

"Intrude, Jules. Please intrude," Finn says, in that commanding tone. The one he used in the restaurant bathroom a few weeks ago. The one that works on me.

Only this time, it works in an entirely different way. I'm not dropping to my knees—*obviously*. Instead, I say yes to a night I never imagined I'd want—a dinner out with Finn and his son. Talking to Zach is relaxing. Easy. Dinner with the two of them feels friendly.

"I should buy this first," I say, waggling my book, *Tie One On.*

Finn snatches it from my hand. "It's on me," he says, then we head to the counter. Zach races ahead, then slows and catches up to my side. "Have you ever made a Rube Goldberg machine?"

"No, but sometimes I feel like every day is one." Meeting Finn has been like a Rube Goldberg machine —I played the piano one night and now the dominoes won't stop falling. "But have you?" I ask, turning the question back to Zach.

"We did today in science camp," he says as we reach the counter and the clerk rings up Finn's purchases. "It's my second science camp this summer. I begged my dad to sign me up because I really wanted to make the

Rube Goldberg machine. It was pretty cool, but we're not done."

"Can I tell you a secret?"

Those green eyes flicker with *yes* and *now* and *I'm dying to know.* Finn looks on with a grin as he swipes his phone across the tap pay.

"Tell me," Zach says, practically bouncing.

"The best science experiment is still when you blow up Mentos and Diet Coke. Do you have a backyard?" I ask, feeling all kinds of subversive.

Finn laughs as he thanks the clerk and takes the books.

"I do," Zach says.

"Then I'll tell you how to do it over dinner."

Zach rushes to the door, and Finn hangs back, speaking in a low voice just for me. "You know I have a backyard, and you know I won't say no to the experiment."

With a sly grin, I just answer, "I know," then we weave through evening crowds on Madison Avenue, New Yorkers rushing toward cars and cabs, making our way to the nearby Neon Diner.

Zach goes first, and then Finn holds open the door for me. Briefly, he sets a hand on my back, and it feels...possessive.

And I like it.

Almost as much as I like sitting across from him and his son at the retro diner, with an Elvis tune playing overhead, and servers scurrying by in mint green uniforms.

After we order, Finn shifts his gaze to me across the

table, full of curiosity. "All right, how do you know every single story in *Captain Dude*?"

"Dad, duh. It's just a good series."

I laugh. "He's right." But then I give him the real answer. "You mentioned it at lunch, and since you have good taste, and since Bridger wants to produce some shows for kids, I checked it out. No one has optioned the rights, and I read the stories the next few nights. Bridger's pursuing them now," I say, then—

Oh shit. Me and my big mouth.

"I wasn't supposed to say that," I say, alarmed, and feeling so, so stupid. I'm not supposed to reveal properties we're pursuing.

"Jules," Finn says, leaning closer. "I'm not going to say a word."

My heart beats dangerously fast, a terribly anxious rhythm. "I shouldn't have said that," I say again, fiddling with my napkin.

"It's really okay," Finn reassures me. "We've got you."

I take a deep breath, trying to let my foolishness slide.

Zach frowns. "Don't worry, Jules. Captain Dude keeps secrets, and we'll do the same."

I manage a grateful smile. "Thanks."

"I promise," Finn says.

I relax a little more. I trust Finn. I trust his son already too. That's strange for me—to trust people so soon.

But Finn has proven he can keep my most important secrets. I choose to let go of my worries and enjoy the unexpected meal out with the sexy single dad and his young son.

Over my veggie burger and their regular burgers, we talk about stories and experiments and sneaking off to tree houses, and I tell Zach exactly how to make a Diet Coke Mentos fountain.

"Dad! She knows, like, everything," Zach says when we finish eating. Before I can say anything, he slides out of the booth. "Gotta go to the boys' room."

"Come straight back, okay?" Finn says, and Zach nods.

With Zach gone, Finn turns his gaze slowly back to me. "You do kind of know everything."

I wave a dismissive hand. "No. I just liked to try Internet experiments when I was a teenager. My sister and I did all that stuff." Then, I have a little fun when I press my finger to my lips. "Don't tell my dad."

Finn lowers his hand, then under the table, I feel it curling over my knee. "I told you. I'll keep your secrets."

I shiver from the touch, savoring the warmth of his fingers and the heat in his eyes. "I'm wearing your secrets," I whisper. "I have on the black lace pair."

He draws a sharp breath and closes his eyes for a few heady seconds. When he opens them, he just shakes his head and says, like a warning, "You're dangerous for me."

I didn't mean to be such a tease. "Sorry."

He clasps my knee tighter, a reassuring touch. "Don't apologize. Do you like them?"

"Very much so."

"Good. They're a gift. For you to enjoy." He holds

my gaze intently, then adds, "I wanted to take you to the angels and devils costume party, Jules."

So he did know about it. "Did you go?" I ask, crossing my fingers that he'll say no.

"Without you? Why would I? You didn't say you were going, and you're the only one I'd want to see."

That feels too good to hear. But I've got to be careful not to get caught up in this feeling. "Bet it would have been fun." Maybe because it's a big thing to invite someone out with you and your kid, or perhaps because I know how hard he's trying to be a great dad, I add, "But this is fun too. Dinner with you and your son. I like it."

I don't want him to think I only like bedroom Finn, when I'm learning single-father Finn is fascinating too.

"I'm glad you met Zach. He likes you, though that's obvious."

"The feeling is mutual," I say, a little bubbly on that fact. "He really goes with the flow, doesn't he?"

Finn smiles. It's clear he feels seen in a whole new way—seen as a father. "He lives his life *in medias res*. I have to think it's because he's had all this change. He's learned to roll with things. He very much embraces the moment."

"Good way to live," I say. I'd like to live that way myself too.

"I'm sure it's part of being seven, but I think it's also just who he is." He glances toward the restroom, looking for the little person he loves unconditionally. Someone he didn't even know a year ago.

I didn't need another reason to like the man.

But now I have one.

Great. Just great.

Later, Finn and Zach say goodbye to me on Madison Avenue, but Finn doesn't mention seeing me in Paris. I don't mention the pending trip either. It's not like we're going to make plans to meet there, to work through my European list or anything. He doesn't even know about that.

Tonight was just one night of coincidence.

20

INEVITABLE

Jules

At the airport a few days later, I can't help wondering if coincidence will win again.

Like at the Albrecht Mansion the night we met.

Like at An Open Book.

Will it go for a third time?

I look for Finn at the check-in desk. In security. A burst of adrenaline-fueled hope powers me on. I walk faster, scanning the gate just in case he's there.

But there's no sign of him.

When I board the plane to Charles de Gaulle, I still hunt, and it's half annoying, half exhilarating. I look around for him in first class, searching for his thick head of hair, his stubbled jaw, his chiseled cheekbones. His casual grin that lights me up.

Most of all, I'm searching for the eyes that seem to know me.

The first several rows are filled with women in Chanel power suits, men in joggers and backward caps, and teens in baggy jeans.

But no Finn.

I pass the curtain, leaving first class behind me.

I let out a disappointed sigh. It was foolish to think I'd see him. Besides, he's a first-class kind of guy, and I'm here in coach, sliding into row 21.

I sleep most of the flight, then grab my luggage and head, bleary-eyed, to my boutique hotel on a curvy street in Montmartre. As the taxi whips through Paris, I stare at the sights between yawns. When I reach my room, it has an obscene view of Sacré-Coeur, the basilica tall and proud against the bold, blue Parisian sky.

The bed's calling to me, but so is the city beyond that window—all the things I've never seen and never done. My limbs feel heavy, but there's too much to see in Paris, and too much to do for work tomorrow, so I wash my hands, splash cold water on my face, and change into clothes I haven't traveled in.

It's summer, so I tug on a pink crop top, and a pair of wide leg jeans. Grabbing my shades, I head out to hunt for a coffee to wake me all the way up.

A big cup I can drown my brain in, ideally.

On a yawn, I round the corner. Up ahead is a bustling square. An artist draws caricatures at an easel. Another sells silky scarves with Audrey Hepburn vibes. A string quartet plucks out a tune I don't recognize but it feels very Édith Piaf. No one wears a beret or totes baguettes, and yet the whole street feels a little like *The Rendezvous*. It's modern Paris, but with the whole vintage vibe this city is known for. The city feels both new and old—something I understand intrinsically.

At the far end of the square is a café with a red awning and, I hope, copious amounts of caffeine.

The sun is rising higher, warming my bare shoulders. I glance up at the street signs to orient myself—that's Place du Tertre—and notice someone out of the corner of my eye. Dark brown hair with silver streaks. Broad shoulders...He's walking, head bent, staring at his phone.

When he looks up, he stops. Smiles. Shakes his head in amusement. My stomach has the audacity to flip.

"Fancy meeting you here," he says, but he doesn't truly seem surprised.

"Or maybe not," I say. "Are we in the same hotel?"

"I'm at The Hotel Particulier Eighteenth. I arrived yesterday," he says, then points to the same hotel as mine. Bumping into him isn't such a coincidence then. It was inevitable. I want to ask other questions—what are you up to, how's Paris so far, what's caught your attention on your phone?

But I don't have to ask the last one because he turns the phone to me. "Check this out," he says, showing me a photo of Zach and his cousin David roasting marshmallows over a campfire. Out of nowhere, tears well in my eyes and I'm not even sure why. Maybe it's the travel. Or the jet lag. Or my need for caffeine.

Maybe it's just that it's a sweet photo of a happy kid, who does, indeed, roll with life's big changes—mom to no mom, no dad to dad.

I swallow the tears, but there's emotion in my voice when I say, "More, show me more."

Finn gives a soft smile, then flicks to the next photo. An RV.

"And they're not camping. They're glamping," I say, laughing as I accuse him.

"My mom's idea, apparently. She said she endured enough of my father's *roughing it* camping trips when Nick and I were kids. She's not doing it now."

I lean a little closer. "Confession: you'd never catch me camping."

He lifts a skeptical brow. "Never?"

I shake my head then flick my hair. "I like my flat iron, my running water, and my soft pillows far too much. Also, coffee."

"You can make coffee camping," he points out.

"Or I can get it at a café," I say as a yawn takes over.

Finn sets a hand on my back, his touch warm and confident. "Let's get you a coffee, Jules." He tips his forehead to the café with the red awning, where I was headed anyway, telling me he's wanted to try this café since he arrived.

It's just coffee. Colleagues do that all the time. "That sounds good to me," I say.

But it doesn't feel as good as his hand on my skin feels. Especially since it signals to anyone around that I belong to him.

Even though I don't.

* * *

The first cup of coffee works wonders, but it tastes awful. "I think I need to learn the French word for mud," I say, lifting the empty cup.

"The French are not known for their coffee," he says.

"You've been here before, right? Paris?" I ask, since he said the city was wonderful at that lunch. A man like him, inking deals around the globe, probably speaks French too.

We're sitting at a tiny round table on the sidewalk as fashionable Parisians stroll by. French words drift past my ears but mean nothing.

"A couple times," he says, lifting his espresso. "But always for work."

He's quick to answer, and the subtext is clear—he never came here with his ex-wife or with another woman.

Don't read anything into it.

"Do you speak French?"

He finishes his small cup, then sets it down, his green eyes sparkling. "I'll tell you a secret," he whispers.

A shiver runs down my spine. "I'm listening."

"I can bullshit my way through any restaurant or store, and that's about it," he says.

This makes me unreasonably happy. I like that he doesn't know the language. That he's brutally honest about his lack of language skills with me, but that he tries to finesse his way through it. That fits him, swaggering through life, pursuing what he wants with guts and brain and charisma.

"So, sort of like how you bullshitted your way through playing the piano," I say.

He leans back in the chair, looking smug in the best of ways. "I wanted what I wanted," he says, owning his choice to pursue me relentlessly that night.

But in retrospect, does he wish we'd been unmasked? That we'd both had all the facts before we scurried off to the library?

Maybe it's the jet lag that makes me want to ask. Or maybe it's that no one knows us here. I feel like we're in a bubble, and that bubble emboldens me. "Would you have talked to me if I wasn't wearing a costume?"

"No," he says, immediately. "I wouldn't have."

My shoulders drop. I knew that answer was coming, but I asked the question anyway.

"And I'm glad I didn't know," he adds in his bedroom voice—the one he uses when he tells me to spread my legs for him. "I wouldn't change a damn thing about the tryst in the library. The night at my home. The afternoon in the restaurant. Not a single thing." He pins me with a dark stare. "Is that clear?"

I shudder out a yes. "Crystal."

"Good. But just in case, let me add this—I'm so fucking glad I had a mask on the night you played piano. Because you are the most sensual, responsive, exciting woman I've ever known."

Known.

He didn't say *touched*.

But known. Somehow that word carries even more weight. He's not comparing me to his body count. He's putting me on a pedestal for being...well, being me.

His reassurance breaks another layer of my walls. "My ex-boyfriend in college," I begin, and he sits up straighter. "I was going to sleep with him. I didn't."

"Did he hurt you?" Finn asks, biting out the words.

"No." I shake my head. "He didn't hurt me physically. But he..." I stop, hesitate. This is harder than I'd thought it would be. Those journals I wrote in are twisted up with sex, and fantasies, and OCD, and secrets. I wasn't so good at untangling my thoughts. I didn't understand them enough to understand their separateness. And I don't want to reveal all of myself. Just a part, because it feels like he's earned it. "I used to write down what I did that day. What I thought. How I felt," I explain.

"That makes sense. A lot of people do that."

"Yeah and sometimes I had these uncomfortable thoughts," I say, because that's a safe enough way to tell him without slapping a label on myself. "Sometimes about random people. Like a professor. Or a teaching assistant."

He nods for me to keep going, making it clear he's not judging, just listening.

"And I'd write them down. Sometimes I'd mentioned a guy I had maybe gone out with once the previous year. On a date, or to a party."

"Sure. You'd tell the journal about your life."

Well, I was telling my sister. And you know what?

There's no need to keep that to myself either. "I was writing to Willa," I say softly, my voice breaking briefly.

"That must have been hard," he says, squeezing my forearm for a moment, then letting go.

"It was, but I needed it. I still need it. I tried to tell her everything in my journals. They were just mine." I draw a breath for fuel, hating what Brandon did but feeling compelled to share it anyway. "But one time when Brandon slept over, he skipped his morning class to sleep in. I went to the lecture, leaving him alone in my dorm with my journals for maybe an hour. And I didn't know it at the time, but he read them all. Every single private thought I'd written down. Whether it was one of those uncomfortable thoughts I mentioned, like about a teacher, or whether it was a recap of a date from my freshman year, or whether it was a book I read that made me want to try role-play," I say, a fresh wave of hurt washing over me. "Sometimes I even wrote the specific fantasies down."

"That's a disgusting violation," he says with vitriol.

"And then, bit by bit, day by day, he took that info and used it against me in subtle, manipulative ways. At a study sesh, he'd say *would you ever want to go into the stacks...with your bio professor.* Or he'd ask me about a guy I went out with a while ago. *Was Carson a good kisser? Are you sure you didn't think of anyone else when you kissed him*? Or even something more insidious. *Remember when you said you wanted me to handcuff you?* I didn't remember every detail I'd ever written down, but he'd stay on it, trying to trip me up."

Finn huffs an annoyed breath, like he wants to

wring Brandon's neck. "He manipulated you. He gaslit you."

I hadn't thought of it like gaslighting, but maybe it was. But it was also embarrassing. I was so fooled. "He was clever. I can't believe it took me a few weeks to puzzle together where it all came from. *From me*," I say, still ashamed he tricked me so deeply.

"Don't beat yourself up," Finn says, perhaps wanting to reassure me, or maybe to protect me from the stories I told myself about my past. "You have a good heart. You probably couldn't conceive that he would trick you like that." He sighs, scrubbing a hand across his chin. "Sometimes it takes us a while to see how we've been used."

I'm about to ask how he's been used when he adds, "What happened after?"

I need to finish my story before I ask for his. "I broke up with him. I never slept with him. And honestly, I didn't want to sleep with anyone for a long time. I shut down, Finn. I was basically dormant sexually until several months ago, after a lot of therapy and a deeper understanding of myself. That's when I realized I was truly ready. That I wanted sex a certain way. That I wanted to be...dominated. That I wanted the fantasies. And that I wanted someone who wouldn't manipulate me. Someone who'd do the opposite—who'd role-play with me, not against me."

"You found him," he says, simple and clear.

Yeah. I did.

Too bad I can't have him.

"Anyway, thanks for listening. I just wanted you to

know that when I said I was glad it was you, I'm *really* glad it was you."

He's quiet for a long beat, blowing out a breath. "Je ne regrette rien."

I don't know French, but I understand context clues. "I regret nothing," I translate.

"Oui," he says, then nods to my empty cup. "Do you need another?"

I'm grateful for the shift in mood. "I want to explore the city today, so I think I do," I say.

Finn calls the waiter over and, as promised, orders in French. When the waiter leaves, I narrow my eyes. "That was unfair."

"Why's that?"

"Because you sound sexy even ordering in your bullshit French."

He laughs. "Maybe I was trying to impress you."

"It worked." I take a moment to soak in the atmosphere, the vibe of the hilly neighborhood. Across the street is a boutique with *Les Jolies Jupes* scrolled across a window display of short dresses and trendy ankle boots. Beside that, a narrow staircase with a wrought-iron railing. Posters line the brick wall, advertising the Moulin Rouge. This was on my list too—just soaking in the ambiance.

"Have you been here before?" Finn asks.

I turn back to him, shaking my head. "First time. But I've wanted to come here. I planned out many fictional visits."

"What do you think so far? Does this compare to the trips you took in your mind?"

I pause for a few seconds, tapping my chin playfully. "I think I need to see more of the city to draw a conclusion. And I'm pretty busy the rest of the week..."

I don't want to presume he'll join me. His words were clear at McCoy's in Manhattan. His actions, too, the next time I saw him at the bookstore. Even if he held my hand minutes ago, that doesn't mean he'll spend the day with me.

The furrow in his brow and the intensity in his eyes tell me he's debating something. Then he's decided. "I'd love to show you the Luxembourg Gardens."

This man can read my soul. "I want to go there," I whisper.

"I know, Jules," he says in a throaty voice. "I know."

21

A KISS MEMORY

Jules

The lush green gardens overwhelm me as soon as we step through the gate. It's a pinwheel of nature's colors. Rich yellows, glorious oranges, ruby reds. The scent of flowers—maybe poppies, possibly petunias—wafts through the air.

This is my favorite thing, flowers and gardens, and it *should* be a wonderland here, with its paths and ponds and curves.

But right now, the tourist attraction outside the Latin Quarter is stuffed, sardine-like, with people. It's clattering with the noise of couples sprawled out on blankets on the lawn, eating cheese and drinking wine while playing music from their phones. Children shriek and chase balloons while tired parents tug on dirty hands. Tourists trudge by with phones, snapping photos and buying souvenirs from carts.

It's thoroughly lovely but completely overrun.

I'm a jerk for thinking this, so I don't say it. "Gorgeous," I say, squinting like I can block out everyone else and keep these gardens all for me. Maybe that makes me terribly selfish.

"Yes, but it'd be better if the gardens were closed just for us," Finn says, a tease of a smirk crooking his lips.

"I was thinking the same thing," I admit, relieved we're on the same page. "I wish it were quieter so I could just...enjoy it the way I want to."

"And what way is that?"

"Sniffing all the flowers. Then pretending it's my own private garden," I say.

"That's fair. And honestly, a damn good fantasy," he says.

"It feels selfish, but I was picturing it that way," I say as we weave through the midday crowds, passing a couple of boys operating remote-control sailboats in a pond.

"It's funny—I think there's this idea of certain places being perfect. Fantasy places. Paris, Rome, London, Tokyo, the Greek isles. Then you go to them and sometimes it can be disappointing."

"Are you disappointed?" I ask. I don't want him to be bored. Even if we both wished for a little more solitude, I still don't want him to wish he were someplace else.

"No. Not at all. And never with the company."

He takes a beat, those eyes journeying up and down my body then lingering on my face. "It's just...a place can be that way, don't you think?"

"A thing can be that way," I agree, soaking in the too-busy atmosphere as we wander deeper into the gardens. "You hype it up in your mind. But I'm glad I'm here. Just because something isn't perfect doesn't mean I don't want to see it."

"Good. I'm glad you're here too."

I try not to read anything more into that comment, but I do let myself enjoy its possibilities.

As we walk along a path beside a huge expanse of lawn, Finn moves closer, the faint remnants of his cologne teasing my nose.

"What's yours? Your cologne, I mean." He was so insistent to know mine, and his fire and orchids fill my mind.

"Midnight Dreams," he replies without skipping a beat.

"Mmm. Now I'll be sniffing it at department stores and thinking of you when I drift off to sleep."

"That's too alluring an image, Jules."

"It sure is."

He doesn't hold my hand or touch me, but his voice feels like sensual fingers caressing my neck when he says, "I bet we can find a place here that lives up to your dreams."

And I do read into that comment. Or, really, my body does, since I get this buzzy, lovely feeling when I'm with him. "All right, you're on. Find a place," I dare him.

He tilts his head, an appreciative grin on his lips. "You doubt me?"

"Maybe I do," I say playfully. I think he likes the challenge.

"Jules, you know that only makes me want to prove you wrong."

"Fine. Go. Prove me wrong."

"All right let's try the Medici Fountain," he says, like he just had that suggestion in his back pocket.

I nudge him with my elbow. "You tricked me. You told me you didn't know the city that well."

"Hmm. Did I say that? Or did I simply say I'd only been here for work?"

"Fine, you caught me on a technicality."

"In any case, I have only been here for work, but I read all about Paris on the flight and over the last few days. I wanted to be prepared," he says.

And damn, that's fire. That sort of preparation. "Just for the show?"

"Yes. I want to be able to speak knowledgeably about the city with my marketing partners who work here. And that means knowing Paris."

Why do smart men have to be so sexy? Oh right, because using your brain is hot. I don't really need more reasons to be attracted to this man I can't have, and yet, Finn Adams has given me another one.

"So you're traveling in first class, enjoying a glass of wine or bourbon, and just reading up on Paris on the flight, looking all classy in your tailored slacks and a dress shirt."

"You've got this complete image of what I wore on the plane," he says, clearly amused.

"Tailored business clothes are hot. What can I say? Don't ruin it and tell me that you wore sweatpants or a track suit."

He laughs lightly. "I didn't wear sweatpants or a track suit on the plane."

"Is that because you're an executive? It's probably forbidden, right?" I adopt a schoolmarm voice. "No executive shall wear casual clothes on a plane. You must maintain the image of an executive anytime you fly."

"Yes, I wore a dress shirt and tailored slacks," he says, glancing down at his jeans and polo, which is just the right amount of snug, showing off his strong arms. "This afternoon, I went casual since I didn't have any meetings," he says, but his voice is a little distant, almost coolly professional for a moment, and I'm not sure why.

Before I can think more on it, we round the bend past some tall hedges into a quieter section of the park. We've stumbled into a small garden that feels almost secret, tucked away. Just beyond the immaculately trimmed rose bushes I can hear the faint gurgling of water. I follow Finn around them till we reach a large fountain with water cascading into an emerald pool below us, like a grotto with an iron railing around it. At the base of the fountain are two carved lovers, twined together.

"The Medici Fountain. For now, we're the only ones

here. Soon we won't be. But I wanted to show you," he says, and I love that he planned this for me.

"It's so different than the rest of the gardens," I whisper. Trees canopy the fountain, giving us shade that makes the spot feel more intimate. This is not on the list Camden and I made. I'll add it myself, though, because it belongs there.

It's as if we've left the city and found the country, all alone in these secluded gardens. A sweet floral scent lingers in the air, making me feel like I'm caught in a hazy dream as the afternoon sun shines down on the pool, casting a golden glow. At last, this is the Paris in my mind. "I think even the sun wears rose-colored glasses in this garden," I say.

Finn smiles, clearly satisfied. He should be. "Did I understand the assignment, or what?"

"You did." I drink it all in, wanting to remember every detail—like the flower pots next to the statue. I point to them. "That's sort of quaint. Flower pots in the midst of this," I say as I head to them then sniff. "Pansies."

Joining me, he leans in and inhales. "You and your scents," he says then tilts his head. "What's it all about, Jules, your love of scents?"

This man pays attention. He listens, but he sees too. He notices me. "They make me happy." That simple admission is a strangely vulnerable one. But he deserves it. He's earned it. He took me here.

"Why?"

"Do I need a reason?" I toss back, but he waits patiently for me to give some kind of an answer. "I've always been drawn to scents. Maybe I just have a good nose. But there's just something about perfume and flowers and gardens that does it for me. I wish I could explain it better. But they speak to me. I close my eyes, inhale, and I feel...transported."

I draw a deep inhale, catching that fire and leather scent of him, then falling back in time. Earlier today, he must have splashed on cologne at his hotel. Closing my eyes, I see Finn in front of the mirror, freshening up. Did he think at that moment that he might run into me? Was he hoping, as he put on his cologne, to see me? A just-in-case hint of his mysterious scent?

When I open my eyes, I feel wobbly.

"Where did you go a few seconds ago? To a memory?"

Instantly, I'm rooted to the now. "I read somewhere that the sense of smell is the one most closely tied to memory. Maybe that's why I'm attracted to scents," I say, connecting the dots inside of me.

"Did you think of the past just now?"

I shake my head. "No. Just a few hours ago. It's not even my memory. It's my...imagination...You. Your room. Putting on your cologne. Setting down the glass bottle, adjusting your shirt, leaving."

His eyes darken, and his smile disappears as he stares at me like he can't look away. "You pictured it." He sounds intrigued and aroused.

"And I imagined you wanting to see me," I admit, since I want it to be true.

He glances down at his clothes. "I didn't have meetings today. That's true. But mostly I dressed like this because I hoped to see you. I knew we were staying in the same hotel." His jaw tightens for a beat before he lets go. "I chose that one because you were staying in it."

That's...obsessive. And I like it. I grab hold of the iron railing so I don't throw myself at him. "Well, it's a nice hotel too," I say dryly.

"Yeah. Nice because I wanted to run into you."

I can barely catch my breath. "Same for me."

He looks behind him, perhaps checking to see if the coast is clear. It's still just us here at the Medici Fountain. He stares at me in the way only a lover can. Intense. Passionate.

"Fuck it," he says, then he drags his thumb along my cheek and comes in for a kiss.

It's a heady, dreamy one in the middle of the gardens that makes me feel a little lost and a little found all at once.

When he breaks it, we wander through the rest of the tourist attraction as if the kiss didn't happen.

Like it's just a memory now.

22

ALL THE OTHER THINGS

Finn

The next morning, I'm sitting at a sleek black metal table in a conference room in the offices of a luxury goods marketing partner. Several stories below us, Rue Saint-Honoré bustles with shoppers and expensive cars, with the nearby Opéra Garnier just visible at the corner of the floor-to-ceiling windows.

But the city's not what's distracting me. Thoughts of a woman are.

I'm doing my damnedest to pay attention to the presentation the brand is giving my team and me about the superior quality of their luggage and the way their advertisements will reflect *The Rendezvous*.

But my mind is half here, and half on Jules.

"When we run this campaign, we can show the snippets of the characters with their luggage," Henri says, gesturing to the image projected on the wall—a mockup of one of the scenes from the show.

It'll be set in the character's flat in Le Marais. Did Jules arrange details for that flat? Did she set up the shooting schedule for that day? Is she there right now?

"So we'll integrate the travel aspect of the series into all our marketing, just as the show is slated to integrate our goods," Henri says with a professional smile, tinged with hope that this deal will come through.

And it probably will, if I sign off on these plans that were ironed out by the prior majority owners.

Plans—the things I didn't make with Jules yesterday when I took her back to the hotel. She was yawning the whole time in the car, struggling to stay awake. When we reached the lobby, her eyes fluttered closed and I said a chaste goodnight, not the words *go out with me tomorrow* that were on my lips.

But it's a good thing I resisted. I'm not in Paris to see her. I'm in Paris for business. Even though I have a marketing team who'll oversee these brand sponsorship deals, I need to make sure this flagship show launches on Streamer without a hitch. That means I need to put the finishing touches on some of the deals I inherited.

"When would you want the campaign to begin?" I ask.

"We can work on the creative as soon as we sign the contract," he says.

I shove all thoughts of the kiss I shouldn't have given Jules far, far away. "Great. But let's chat about the terms though. I have some concerns," I say, shifting firmly into negotiation mode, and out of romantic mode.

* * *

A little later, I say goodbye to Henri and to my international colleagues at Streamer, who can handle the rest of the deal.

There. I made it through that meeting without revealing that my head is elsewhere. When I leave, I'm focused on my agenda for the rest of the day, mentally reviewing my meetings and my goals as I stride by elegant artwork, pushing past the double doors out to the street.

But once I'm outside, the distractions hit me in full force.

Paris. Paris is the goddamn distraction. I could wander down a rain-soaked street with Jules, duck into a brasserie with her, kiss her under a streetlamp.

It's like she's everywhere in this city.

I check my watch. I'm free for an hour and a half, and that's annoying. My assistant built time in my schedule to get around the city, but I don't want it right now. I want something to do. Somewhere to be, so I can stop thinking about where Jules is. What she's doing. How close she is to me.

I was doing so great for the last few weeks in New York. Resisting her had become easy enough.

But one afternoon with her in Paris, and she owns my thoughts. One kiss, and I'm replaying it on a loop. It was slow and passionate yet fleeting, like it didn't even happen. That has to be why she's all I thought of last night in my hotel room. As I got into bed, I imagined spending the hours till dawn making her cry out in bliss, then taking her to breakfast, seeing the wonder in her eyes as she watched the city wake up and come to life.

When I pass the Mandarin Oriental, I tear my gaze away from the sleek hotel so I don't fixate on what I'd do with Jules in a hotel room.

When I turn toward the Tuileries Gardens, that's no better. Of course I'll think of her if I walk past another set of goddamn gardens.

I grit my teeth, trying, valiantly trying, to walk off these thoughts. But the more distance I log, the more persistent my mind becomes. We're thousands of miles from home. The distance is like a permission slip. I'd wanted to run into her yesterday. I'd known when her plane landed. I'd hoped to see her, engineered that moment.

But I can't keep seeking out chance encounters. The more time I spend with her, like I did at the diner in New York with Zach, like I did at the café and gardens yesterday, the more time I'll *want* to spend with her.

Trouble is, I have to see her this afternoon at the photo shoot and I'm more excited about her than I am about the flagship show of my new acquisition.

* * *

I arrive at the studio in Le Marais that afternoon and remind myself I'm here to make an appearance, meet the executive producer, and say hello to the cast.

That's all.

I take the stairs to the third floor then turn into a wide, concrete corridor that echoes loudly on the way to the studio. Then, it echoes in chorus as someone else turns the corner.

Two someones. One is a woman in khaki pants and a pink Oxford, clutching a phone and a tablet. I recognize her crisp businesslike appearance from photos and research—she's the show's executive producer.

The other someone? My obsession.

The producer stops and offers a closed-mouth smile before she says, "You're the new boss."

Jules answers, gesturing to me. "Solange Marina, this is Finn Adams. He runs Streamer now, as you know. And Mr. Adams, this is our EP. Solange is from Montreal and has produced a handful of award-winning shows on Webflix and LGO, including *Unfinished Business*."

I take her hand and we shake. "That show was terrific. I was glued to the ending, and Jamie made the right choice when he moved across the country with Zoe."

Solange's lips twitch, but she doesn't quite smile. Instead, she gives an approving nod. "Ah, well, I might like you now and then. *Might*."

"Now and then works just fine for me," I say. Being well-liked is not my work goal.

"Then you're welcome here as long as you don't

meddle," Solange says dryly. The comment is meant to land as a joke, but it's clear she means it. She doesn't want me to interfere.

"I only meddle in my brother's projects."

Her expression softens slightly. "Good to know." Before she can say anything more, her phone rings. She peers at it. "My daughter. I need to take this, Jules. You can handle..." She flaps a hand toward me. "Anything."

"I've got it."

The executive producer pushes on the door to the stairwell, disappearing and leaving me alone with the woman I can't stop thinking about.

Jules wears her glasses today, black pants, and a short-sleeve red blouse. The outfit is professional but trendy and young. Fitting. "She knows she's in good hands with you," I say, not surprised Jules has made such a good impression already.

"She is. And Solange is great," Jules says, and damn. That's some sexy confidence. I like that Jules knows she's good at her job.

I should let her go wherever she was heading. But I don't. "How did you sleep your first night here? Were you up in the middle of the night?" I probably shouldn't think of her in bed, but it's too late for that.

"Melatonin worked its magic, though I was up before the sun. I watched it rise from Sacré-Coeur."

I don't know what I was expecting her to say but it wasn't that. "From the steps of the basilica?"

"I was awake," she says easily, like *why would I do anything else*. "The early morning light was streaming into my window. How many times am I going to be in Paris watching the sun rise?"

I'm jealous of the church steps for getting to spend the dawn with her. "What else is on that bucket list?"

"You figured out I have a list?" she asks with a quirk in her lips that says she's impressed.

I don't need to pat myself on the back. I do need to know what she wants, what she needs. "Yes. Tell me what's on it."

"So demanding," she teases.

"Yes. I am."

"Since you're so insistent..." She checks the time on her phone, then, satisfied, she answers. "I plan to sit at a café by the Seine and read a good book, to try something I've never had before at a restaurant, to wander down a quiet street where I feel like I can get lost. Among *other things*," she adds, and I bet I'd like *other things*.

But this conversation is not helping my resolve. "You have six more days to do them," I say, but what I mean is *I can help you with the restaurant* one, and the *wander down the street* one, and *all the other things*.

"And I'm on pace. I checked one off yesterday. But I didn't even know it was on there."

I'm confused now. "What do you mean?"

Her lips curve up. "Find a hidden gem where you least expect it." She glances down the hall. "I should go."

And I should go say hello to the cast. That's why I'm here. Not to obsess over her Paris list.

* * *

But when I return to the hotel that night, I do obsess over it. And over her. I'm wondering what she's crossing off that list. What room she's in. What she wears to bed when she's alone.

And in the morning, I wonder whether I'd find her on the steps of Sacré-Coeur.

"Fucking idiot," I say, cursing myself as I get ready for the day's meetings. She's not going to do the same thing the next day, and I'm *not* going to stalk her.

Besides, I have back-to-back appointments all day, so once I'm up and out of the hotel, I refuse to look back.

If I can just make it through the next five days without bumping into her—or engineering opportunities for that to happen—that'd be great.

When the first meeting of the day ends, I tell my team I'll see them later then I take a breather to reset. Exercise has always helped me focus. When I was younger, soccer gave me tunnel vision, along with the hope that the sport would pave my way in life. Later, the triathlons I started running centered me as I grew my business. I can't go for a run along the river in my tailored slacks and button-down, so instead I drop on aviator shades and get a little lost in the city like I did yesterday, walking past boutiques, souvenir shops, and chichi restaurants, thinking about my meetings for the week—my goals for the year—when a scent stops me in my tracks.

A trace of honeysuckle tickles my nose, and I turn,

helplessly, in its direction, the open door to a perfume shop. *La Belle Vie* is written in rose-gold script on a white sign above the store.

Are you kidding me? Everything in this city is a temptation. I don't stand a chance.

I stop fighting and go inside, flashing back to the night at my home when Jules asked about the honeysuckle outside my window, a rarity in the city.

What does it remind you of? I'd asked.

Wanting. It reminds me of wanting, she'd said.

I feel the same. This sweet, heady smell reminds me of wanting. It reminds me of her.

Like a man in a trance, I walk to a nearby display of bottles, delicately carved and with old-fashioned spritzers and pumps. There are crystal ones with gold etching, purple leaves, pink and glass. It's all so feminine, so alluring. I stop at the one that's been calling to me, then read the display card next to it.

Come What May, made by a perfumer here in Paris. An American named Joy Danvers. There's a description, too, and it reads: "The smell of the first kiss and a last kiss. It is the promise that somehow, someday, we will meet again."

All at once, a pang of longing digs into my chest. I lift the bottle, bring it to my nose, and inhale, picturing Jules.

Each time I see her, she shares carefully, ever so carefully, bits and pieces of herself. Every time I talk to her, I learn a little bit more about who she is and the layers she contains, like a trunk you take your time opening so you can savor the letters, the notebooks, the photos you find inside.

She's so different than Marilyn. So very different that I'm standing in a shop here in the First Arrondissement, inhaling a perfume like a man obsessed.

Like a man wanting.

But I don't simply want another night in bed with her. I want to explore her. Understand her. *Know her.*

"Excuse me? Can I help you with something?" A soft, French voice breaks my daydream.

Can you help me get my best friend's daughter out of my every waking thought?

I don't say that. Instead, I say to the shopkeeper, "I'll take this and can you please send it to this hotel?"

Even though there's no room in my life for an obsession, I begin one anyway.

Or really, I continue one.

* * *

The perfume does the trick for a couple hours. That afternoon I'm pure focus as I meet with a European-based mobile company that we're wooing. My hope is that they'll carry our service on their phones. We want to give big shots like Webflix a run for their money, so deepening our partnerships will go a long way. I keep my blinders on during those meetings and I don't let thoughts of honeysuckle or garden kisses win.

When I say goodbye to my colleagues at the end of the day, I feel accomplished, despite my earlier distraction. I check my watch. All I need to do now is stop by the nearby set in Le Marais for a quick meeting with Solange to keep her apprised of the marketing plans. It's a few blocks away, and I head through the artsy, fashionable arrondissement.

I pass Place des Vosges, the central square filled with trees and ivy-colored buildings. Is visiting that on Jules's Paris list? No. That's too pedestrian for her. But maybe spreading out a blanket somewhere nice in the evening, sipping champagne, eating olives and cheese has made the cut.

Or maybe it's just on a new list I'm writing in my mind.

Get it together, man.

I snap my gaze to the sidewalk in front of me and keep it there till I reach a quieter street with white flats boasting planters in their windows. One of them is the location for the heroine's flat in *The Rendezvous*.

Already, there are signs of the show—some permits for shooting are plastered outside the apartment. After I check in with security, I head into the building. The crew in the lobby are finishing up their pre-production work for the day. I look past them, and then my pulse spikes annoyingly.

Jules stands at the other end of the foyer by the elevator, where the opening sequence will shoot tomorrow. Chatting with Solange, Jules looks beautiful, even in a short-sleeve black blouse, jeans, and flats. Or perhaps she's beautiful because of the simplicity of her outfit. Her chestnut hair is cinched back in a clip, with a few loose tendrils framing her face. She wears her glasses and keeps a serious expression on her face. All-business Jules is in her element. She's focused and diligent, entering details on a tablet. I feel like a stalker even though I'm supposed to be here.

I watch her closely until she turns around and makes eye contact with me.

Jules doesn't change her expression—she's a guarded woman—but a subtle sparkle lights those brown irises. I stride across the foyer, and when I reach them, Solange offers me a cautious smile before she says, "Don't give me bad news that will make me mad."

Damn, she's tough. "I only have good news."

Jules steps back. "I'll leave you to it. I need to send out some emails with call times anyway."

"Thank you," Solange says, then pats the neck of her shirt. "Merde. I must have left my glasses on the balcony in the flat."

Before she can even ask, Jules says brightly, "I'll get them."

She says it too brightly though. She'd never let on at work that she's afraid of heights.

"I'd actually love to see the flat for a minute," I say, stepping in. "Jules, would you show it to me?"

"Of course."

With Solange quickly busying herself on her phone, we head into the old elevator. As it rises, I'm so close to Jules, I could kiss her neck if I leaned in a few inches. I want to tell her there's a gift waiting for her at the hotel. Instead, I clench my fists, hold that admission back, and grit out, "How was your second day?"

"Busy. Solange is a whirlwind. But I can keep up with her."

"Of course you can. Were you up at dawn, sitting at a café?"

A tiny smile shifts her lips. "Yes. I read some of my book by the river."

Montmartre isn't near the river. "You must have been up quite early to make it to the Seine before work."

She shrugs, like *of course.* "How many times will I be able to do that?"

Many, if I have a say in it.

We reach the sixth floor and as soon as she opens the door to the flat, I set a hand on her forearm. God, her skin feels incredible. I sizzle from this small touch. "I'll get the glasses."

Without waiting for her answer, I stride through the chic flat. A red sofa, an antique armoire, and artwork that looks like it comes from an outdoor market all signal a minimalist-meets-French style that's perfect for the show's look. I step out on the balcony, grab the glasses from the ledge, then turn around in the doorway.

But she's right behind me. "Actually, it's okay."

My brow creases. "It is?"

She closes the distance between us then steps onto the balcony and peers over Le Marais. She breathes in, breathes out. I say nothing—just watch her as she checks out the view, even though I don't think she's enjoying it.

After a beat, she turns to me. "But thank you," she says softly.

I don't entirely understand her fear, but I can tell

this is important to her—this act of independence.

"Did it bother you that I wanted to help?"

"No. Not at all. I'm just not used to someone help-ing," she says like she wishes it weren't that way. "Or knowing."

Oh.

She doesn't tell people about her fear of heights. "Thanks for letting me, then. Even if I was pushy."

She takes another big breath then shakes her head. "You weren't."

I hand her the glasses, and she heads back inside, then stops in the foyer. I catch up to her, and her gaze strays briefly to the door.

Someone else from the show could come in here any second. A set designer, a costumer, another producer. But right now, we're the only ones here, and there's a charge in the air, a palpable energy.

I hold her face with my hand. "Have dinner with me tonight. I need to get to know you more. I need to learn more about you. I want to take you on a date in Paris. Is that on your list?" I ask, taking a beat to let those words land.

To watch her eyes answer with a twinkle.

Then, she says, "Yes."

* * *

When I walk into the bistro where we're meeting in Montmartre, I can tell she's here before I see her. I smell honeysuckle, and it's the scent of wanting.

23

UNCOMPLICATED

Finn

The warm night air floats down the cobblestone street, drifting seductively around us at a sidewalk table in Montmartre.

"And that's how I found out about The Scene," Jules says as she tucks a strand of brown hair behind her ear, finishing the story. "From dancing with friends at Revel House. I heard about it and I *had* to go. I mean, role-play and all."

"Do you do that a lot? Go out dancing?" I ask, gobbling up all the details I can get.

"I do." She hesitates, then adds, "That's how I became friends with Harlow...and Layla." She says it almost like she doesn't want to mention my brother's fiancée to me. Or, more likely, any of our shared connections, in case they lead to other ones.

"Our small world," I say, addressing the elephant on

the sidewalk. "Pretty sure I saw you at my nephew's engagement party several months ago. At a bowling alley."

"David's engagement party. I was there," she says, a smile coasting across her lips. She remembers it too.

"Marilyn had moved out. We were getting divorced, and I saw you a few lanes over. I didn't connect the dots that you were my friend's daughter. I just couldn't stop looking at you. You were so...captivating."

She dips her face, but not like she's embarrassed. More like she's delighted. "Really? You were checking me out?"

"Apparently, I've had a thing for you for a while," I say, and I *should* feel bad for lying by omission to my best friend. Hell, I *should* feel bad for lying period.

Yet here I am, doing it anyway.

And loving it.

I'm a bad, bad man.

Jules leans closer. "Well, I've had a thing for you since the night I met you. When we were strangers." She lowers her voice to a playful whisper. "We could pretend we're strangers again."

That's my kinky girl. "You want that tonight, don't you?"

She nibbles on the corner of her lips. "Or student and teacher. Or hotel maid and guest."

I groan, then toss my napkin on the table. "How am I going to make it through a meal with you?"

"And we haven't even had dinner yet," she says as she lifts her glass of sauvignon blanc and takes a sip, running her finger along the stem when she's done. Yes, after-dark Jules is coming out to play in Paris. The soft glow from streetlamps brings out her sexy radiance as much as the black dress that hugs her curves.

I try to picture her at a club with her friends, letting loose, moving to the music. "What do you wear when you go dancing?"

"That's specific," she says, amusement in her eyes after she sets down the glass.

"I want to picture you completely," I say. If she's going to rile me up, then she can rile me all the way up. "Set *the scene* for me."

She lifts a flirty brow, shrugs a shoulder. "Depends on my mood. Sometimes jeans, sometimes a short skirt, maybe a bustier, often a wig," she says, flicking her hair again.

"Like you had on the night we met."

"They're kind of my thing," she says with a spark that tells me she's enjoying this night as much as I am. I remember her telling me at my house that she didn't date much. That dating was complicated. That describes our situation perfectly, but maybe we can be uncomplicated for a night in Paris.

"Perfume, wigs, costumes. The Jules picture is becoming more clear."

"Is it, now?"

"You like pretty things and you like to play. You like to use your imagination."

"You get me," she says.

"I fucking do," I say confidently. I want to see her in all of those outfits. Want to watch her dress up, get ready for a night out. "So you're at this dance club, and you hear about The Scene, and you thought, *I have to go meet a well-hung man in a phantom mask.*"

She laughs, the sound carrying into the Paris night. "And when I saw you walking down the street, I knew you had to be swinging a horse cock."

It's my turn to crack up. "You were right."

"I'm so glad I estimated correctly," she says as candlelight flickers across her face. She looks different tonight—all dressed up and yet completely relaxed. Almost like how she was at dinner with Zach and me. At ease. Minus the cock comment. "So when my bartender friend asked me to fill in at The Scene," she adds, circling back, "I basically said *yes, now,* and *I'll be there.*"

"And that's how we met," I say as fairy lights in the sidewalk's trees flicker above us.

She lifts a brow. "I like that version better."

Translation: better than meeting over dinner with her father.

"It'll be our new story," I say, and it feels real enough. I'm acutely aware that our time here is make-believe. But if this is all we can have, I want it to matter. "Do you like your job? You seemed excited to work with Solange."

Her face is a mix of emotions—intensity and passion. "I don't want to show it in front of her, but yes. I'd love to be an EP someday. Honestly, it's all I've ever wanted to do."

My gaze drifts briefly to a gift bag at my feet. Something I picked up for her earlier and want to give to her later. Assured it's there and safe, I look to her again and ask, "Young Jules imagined being a TV producer? What drew you to it?"

Her brow furrows, like she's contemplating whether she wants to crack open this topic, but then she must decide she does. "I wasn't allowed to watch TV when I was younger."

Oh. Right, Tate is strict. "Your father," I say, wishing I didn't have to acknowledge *that* shared connection, but hating lies more.

"He said the world was violent enough, and we didn't need to see more of it. Ironic, because Willa and I never wanted to watch shows like that."

I sit up straighter. She doesn't say much about her sister, but I've sensed they were close. "And once you watched TV you were hooked?"

"No turning back," she says, laughing, then she leans closer, like she's sharing a naughty secret. "I love stories. Especially visual ones. They just grab me and draw me in, and him keeping TV from me only made it more alluring."

"Ironic," I say.

"Yes, because we'd sneak out to friend's houses...to watch TV."

I laugh. "That's hilarious."

"Most of the time that's what we did," she says in a quieter voice, then her expression darkens, and like an echo, she adds, "*Most*."

"You miss her a lot."

"I do." She shifts gears abruptly. "And you get to work with your brother. That must be great."

She doesn't want to stay on the topic of her sister, so

I go with her switch. "I do. We're very competitive, and we prank each other constantly, but it's a great partnership. And he's been immensely helpful with advice and such since Zach came into my life."

"Speaking of my Captain Dude friend, any new pics?" She wiggles her fingers, beckoning for my phone.

"Don't you just know the way to my heart," I say, grabbing the cell from my pocket, ready to share. "This one came in today."

I show her a picture of David and Zach jumping into the lake off a dock.

She sighs appreciatively as she studies it. "Do you wish you were there? I bet you do."

That's a tough question. "I do, and yet this is exactly where I want to be," I say, meeting her pretty eyes as I answer.

"Me too," she says softly, and moments later, the waiter brings our dishes. He sets a plate of herb-crusted salmon with sautéed asparagus in front of me. For Jules, a cauliflower steak. "From my list. Since I've never tried this before," she says, slicing into the vegetable that's been seasoned to look like steak.

She takes a bite and I ask, "How is it? Does it meet your expectations?"

"It exceeds them. And it's extra spicy. Speaking of, do you still need to replace your chili flakes?"

I laugh, remembering that I've still forgotten. "I do. I will. I swear."

She shifts gears, asking, "You said Zach came into your life several months ago, but did you always want to be a father?"

This is not first-date terrain, but we're clearly well past small talk. Even though this thing between us can't go anywhere, I'm already savoring how very different talking with Jules is from talking to my ex. She's open, she's real, she's honest. "I did. I thought Marilyn did too," I say, my jaw ticking as the memories of my marriage slam into me. "But I was wrong."

"She didn't want to after all?"

Setting down my fork, I bite off the bitter truth. "We both wanted to have kids a few years ago. Or so I thought. She told me she was off the pill for all those years."

Jules turns pale, clearly knowing what's coming.

"But," I say, tightly, "she was actually on it the entire time we tried to have kids."

"That's terrible." She clenches her fist on the table. "I hate that she did that to you."

I love her fierceness. Briefly, I picture her being that way with Zach, protective and passionate. It's a fantastic thought, but there's absolutely no room for it in my life, so I shove it away. "But, on the other hand, I'm glad I didn't have children with her. I just wish I had seen through her lies sooner."

"It's not your fault. People should be honest with each other," she says.

"They should." Even though I know I shouldn't act like this is more than a first date, I'm a little helpless with Jules. This is not what I'd expected when I walked into The Scene a month ago, pretending I was someone else. Now I'm letting her see more of me, and wanting that. Fucking craving it.

This is bad, but still I say, "That's why I wanted you to know."

My heart is beating faster for her, and I don't even know what to do with this swell of emotion.

"You know what else was on my list?" she asks.

"Tell me."

"Have dinner with a handsome...Frenchman or American," she adds with a sexy smile.

Narrowing my eyes, I growl my disapproval. "You don't belong with a Frenchman."

Her lips curve up. "I don't?"

"Not. At. All."

Her smile deepens, turning more playful. "Are you sure?"

"You're having dinner with this American. And *only* this American."

"If you say so."

"I do. That's the item on your list. Dinner with me," I say.

"Well, you *are* handsome and you *are* American, so it fits...But maybe I should add *a bossy* American?"

"Yes. You should." Because I love that list and I want to do all the things on it with her.

When we finish eating, she's quiet for a beat before she says, in a soft, sensual voice, "I brought something you gave me to Paris."

Without hesitation, I say, "Let's go."

I pay, then we're out of there.

24

APPROPRIATELY INAPPROPRIATE

Jules

I slick on some red lipstick then press my lips together, giving myself a once-over in the hotel room mirror. There, ready.

Well, I brought my stilettos. Guess I'm a hopeful girl.

I turn around, squaring my shoulders, letting my own love of dancing drive me as I step out of the bathroom, then stand in the doorway, arm sliding up the frame, hip cocked out, lips pouty.

Eyes on him.

A slow, sultry song fills my small room, and with the lamp dimmed, it feels like a smoky lounge in here.

And I feel like a different version of me. I'm the me in Paris. The me who goes clubbing. The me who doggedly chases opportunities.

I'm not the girl who hurt her family.

I left her in New York.

Finn's parked in a burgundy chair across the room, legs spread, one arm slung across the back. The other hand holds a tumbler of amber liquid. His gaze is powerful as it locks on mine, eyes a dark emerald, full lips a hard ruler. He lifts that glass of scotch, taking his time, assessing my body, his confident pose making it clear he's in charge as he studies me in the doorway.

Then, he gives the barest of nods. He's the high-end customer in my exotic dance club, I head to him, taking my sweet time. My hips sway from side to side, seductively teasing him with every step. His eyes travel up and down my body as he takes in my costume.

It's simple. A short skirt, schoolgirl style, and a tight white blouse. But the gift he gave me peeks out, since I unbuttoned the top just enough to reveal the white lace demi-cup bra with red tulips embroidered on the cups. The panties are low-cut, and they match.

"Hey there, handsome," I say as I reach him, stopping a foot away to leave some space, create some anticipation. "Can I interest you in a dance tonight?"

"Maybe," he says, a little aloof. He lifts the tumbler and knocks some back before setting it down on the oak table next to the gift bag he's had with him all night. He hasn't opened it yet. My curiosity is piqued, but I push it aside when he asks, "What kind of dance?"

I finger the top of my blouse, giving him a peek at my cleavage. "The kind with rules."

"Yeah? You think I like to play by the rules?" he asks, his tone brusque, his deep voice sending a spark through me.

I roam my gaze up and down him, the man who's playing the part of the uncaring businessman out for a night at a gentlemen's club. He's good at pretend, but the vein in his neck pulses, giving him away and giving me my power. "I think you won't let me walk away."

I spin on my black heels, the stripper ready to leave.

"I'll play by your rules," he grumbles.

I whirl around, lean closer, and run a finger over the collar of his shirt. "I had a feeling you would." I tap dance my fingers along his neck. "Here's the first one. You can look, but only I can touch."

"Fine. What else?"

"No touching, no kissing, and you have to keep your clothes on." I lick the corner of my cherry-red lips, waiting for his yes. "What'll it be?"

He reaches for his glass, swallows more, then sets it down, his eyes flickering with dirty thoughts. "Guess I just bought a tease."

My smile spreads, slow and sensual. "Yes. Yes, you did, handsome."

As the song slides into a low beat, a pulsing baseline of longing, I step a few feet back, playing with the buttons on my blouse. Fiddling with the top one, I reveal more skin. With each button I undo, his jaw tightens, his breathing sharpens.

Good. A charge rushes through me and once my shirt is undone, I glide a hand down the valley of my breasts, over my stomach, stopping at my skirt. "Just a little torment for the customer," I whisper.

"Gimme more," he says. "That's my rule."

"That's a very good rule, handsome. I'd hate to

break it." I come closer, enough that my thighs brush against his knees. I set my hands on the arms of his chair, giving him a dance.

Finn draws a sharp inhale through his nose. A man coming undone.

Biting the corner of my lips, I move away, shaking my ass in time with the music. I can't see him, but I can feel his eyes tracing my curves. I run my palms over my ass, sticking it out, letting him enjoy the view.

"Yes," he rasps.

I smile privately then turn around, letting my shirt fall to the floor. I return to him, standing as I slide one thigh of his between mine. He grips the arms of the chair, and I grind down on his strong muscle so he can feel my desire in my wet panties.

He grunts. "More."

I feel powerful, like a goddess. Like I'm in charge of my own fate, like I've made no mistakes.

I grind and I touch, my hands covering his chest as we move together. The line between fantasy and reality blurs. We're dancer and customer. We're two strangers. We're lovers in Paris. We're us, making up our own rules, and bending all of them.

As his breathing turns labored, and my skin grows hot, I tear myself away, walking slowly across the room, unzipping the skirt, and stepping out of it.

One spin, and I'm a wicked woman as I stand before him in white lace, black heels, and flushed skin.

He's fully clothed, and his erection is tenting his slacks obscenely.

Finn grits his teeth as I sashay my way back to him,

shaking my tits, my hips, my ass. All the curves he loves. When I reach him, I turn once more so I can lower my butt to his thighs and grind down on him, my hair spilling over his chest.

His harsh breath fills my ears, the sound of a man's restraint crumbling. His fingers twitch, and then as I rub my ass against his hard-on, he breaks, one big hand coming down on my thigh, squeezing possessively.

I shake my head, then peel off his hand. "Don't break the rules," I purr.

His lips coast along the back of my neck. "Fuck rules," he warns me.

Heat sparks down my spine, heading straight for my core, but I try to stay in character. "Rules are rules, handsome."

He drags his nose along my neck. "My rule is I want you. *Now*."

I go up in a white-hot blaze of sex and lust. I can literally feel my panties dampen. He can, too, since he grabs my hips and presses me harder, more urgently down on him.

I should stay in character. Truly I should, but I'm melting under his strong hands, his commanding voice, and his unchecked lust.

I'm still amazed he feels this way for me.

Me.

A woman who for years didn't want sex. Who abandoned all interest in it until she started thinking of it again in the most inappropriate of ways.

Now, here I am being appropriately inappropriate. Touching, teasing, toying with a man I shouldn't have.

High on this feeling of power and sex, I push my luck. I step away, walking toward the bed, each click of my heels on the hardwood a punctuation mark. I wheel around, unhook my bra, and toss it at him.

"Stay there," I say, before he can devour me. I hold up a stop-sign hand. "Don't break the rules, handsome."

Finn says nothing, just seethes with desire, huffing like an animal. I return to him, straddling his lap, wrapping my arms around his neck, then dry fucking him. Rock, grind, thrust. Rinse, lather, repeat, until I fire the starting shot. "Break them," I order.

A racehorse at the gates, he's up, hoisting me over his shoulder, carrying me to the bed, tossing me down.

As he toes off his shoes, he says, "Leave your shoes on."

My inhibitions are out the window. He slides next to me and thrusts an eager hand inside my panties, and I arch shamelessly.

"My rules now," he growls as he glides those talented fingers over me, and I writhe.

"What are they?" I gasp out. "Your rules?"

He stares down at me with eyes dark with lust. "You come till you can't take it anymore. Understood?"

I shudder. "Okay," I say, breathless as I rock into those long fingers.

"No, it's not fucking okay," he says gruffly. "Say you want it."

He takes his fingers away from my pussy, and I whimper. "I want it."

He brings them to his mouth, licks off my taste, then turns me to my side so we're face-to-face. "Say it."

"Make me come till I can't take it."

My reward is a hot kiss. Fingers between my thighs. A relentless mouth questing across my neck, and a tense, tantalizing pulse in my core.

He rubs a mesmerizing circle on my clit till I'm arching, gasping, then clawing at the sheets.

"Give it to me," he growls, but I'm already there, coming on his hand.

Before I can even catch my breath, he's grabbed the gift bag and returned to the bed. After he yanks off my panties, he reaches into the bag, then wields a toy, a small peach-colored vibrator, with a tiny hole in it.

He turns it on, grazes it over my clit, and I shout. "God. Yes. What is that?"

"I went shopping for you this evening. When in Paris," he says, then rubs the toy over my clit where it pulses and vibrates with air.

"This is crazy," I say, moaning.

He looks mad, wild with pleasure as he kneels between my legs, demanding, "Spread them wider. Need to see your pretty pussy."

I let my legs fall open, wanton and shameless under his determined hands. The man bought a vibrator for me before dinner. This is next level sex. This is why older men rock. No one will ever compare after this kind of relentless attention. This devotion to my pleasure and...oh, god.

He's just turned up the speed, and I'm one long nerve, fraying with desire. "I'm close," I pant.

"Good. Then follow my rules, Jules," he says, going a little faster, then faster still, till my mind is spinning and my body is almost tipping over.

"Rules," I murmur, barely focusing as bliss comes into view.

"Yes. This rule. Don't fucking come." In a cruel heartbeat, he turns it off, leaving me aching.

"Asshole," I mutter. I was on the edge.

He laughs as he flips me over so I'm on my stomach, naked with only shoes on.

"Jerk," I grumble.

But then he straddles me and pushes my hair to the side, leaning down to dust a kiss over my neck.

Oh. That's nice. So nice.

My shoulders now.

His lips travel down my back, reverently kissing me, adoring my skin as he goes. His caresses light me up. I ignite again, hot and bothered and so turned on as he journeys down to the top of my ass.

He kisses one cheek. All over.

I squirm, feeling out of control and wanting less and less control. He moves to the other cheek, layering kisses all over my ass, then sliding his tongue along the crease.

I tense for a second. Is he going to go *there*? Do I want him to? I don't know, but he stops and grabs me roughly, manhandling me in the way he's learned I like.

He hauls me up to my knees. "Ass up. Keep your arms stretched out."

"I will. I am," I say, though it feels like a plea as I give in to his every demand to please me.

Then, he reaches into the bag once more, comes around the top of the bed, and dangles a long swatch of black silk in front of me. "My rules. Your blindfold."

He waits, asking for permission. "Yes," I say, granting it.

"Good." In seconds, everything's dark and black and silky as he ties the fabric around my head. "Okay?"

"So okay," I gasp, then I feel the mattress press down and hear a buzzing. One hand's on the top of my ass while the other returns to my spread thighs with the vibrator. Thank god. "Yes, please make me come," I beg, desperately seeking sweet relief.

Doesn't take me long. Soon, I'm shamelessly fucking the toy and shattering, breaking apart under the powerful force of a second orgasm. It's still rocketing through me when Finn turns me over, spreads me out, and buries his face in my pussy.

"So fucking good. So fucking sweet," he praises, then slides his hands under my ass and devours me while I'm still coming down from the last orgasm.

It's almost too much. I'm so sensitive already, but he's merciless, licking me ferociously, sucking on my clit till my belly coils with the delicious threat of more pleasure. I'm close, so damn close. This can't be happening. I can't be coming again.

But impossibly, I am, grabbing his head, drawing him nearer and coming like a woman drunk on orgasms.

While I'm still crying out, he unties the blindfold then unbuttons his shirt, giving me a view of his broad, toned chest. He stares down at me while he strips. His eyes spark with desire. He's more turned on than I've ever seen him. My throat is dry. My voice is hoarse, but I lift a hand, reaching for the ridge of his erection through his pants. "Your cock. Gimme your cock," I beg.

He shakes his head. "Not enough, honey. You haven't come enough," he says, then he tugs me off the mattress. I feel loose and noodle-y, and I'm not even sure I can stand, but he bends me over the bed, then unzips his pants. I crane my neck as he takes out his cock and rubs it against my ass, teasing me with what I want most, but not giving it to me.

Instead, he gives me his hand again, sliding those determined fingers between my thighs, rubbing his cock against my ass. I'm wrung out, panting, sweating, and crying from the intensity.

I come again, then once more with the vibrator, collapsing onto the bed, boneless. I feel like my body isn't mine. It's his to play with, his to take, his to cherish.

I can't stand all this pleasure. "It's too much. Just fuck me now," I gasp as I stare up at him while I finally kick off those damn heels.

His smile is so damn satisfied. "All you had to do was ask," he teases as he sheds his pants and boxer briefs at last, then reaches for his wallet, no doubt for a condom.

I sit up, setting a hand on his arm. "I'm on the pill and safe."

He groans. "I'm safe too," he says, then climbs onto the bed, settling between my thighs. He spreads me open. "Mine," he says, and I shudder. "Want to see your sweet pussy. Want to feel it bare. Want you to come on my cock till you can't take it anymore."

I'm not sure I can take his brand of domination. But I *am* sure I want it. And him. I loop my hands around his neck. "Fuck me into tomorrow."

His sigh is carnal, and needy as he slides into me. "Jules," he grunts. "My fucking Jules."

My.

Sometime tonight, I became his.

* * *

In the morning, I'm still buzzed. I'm pretty sure now that being sex drunk is a real thing. Or maybe I'm intoxicated on honesty. Finn's someone who takes me as I am. He doesn't try to trick me. He doesn't try to twist my wishes. He meets them openly, then exceeds them.

With him, I feel a newfound confidence that comes from embracing my personal after dark. From feeling comfortable in my own skin.

With that in my mind, we get dressed, then head out together into the Montmartre morning, a summer breeze wafting through the air as the city wakes up. We head down a curving, hilly street with Sacré-Coeur watching over us, and no one knowing who we are.

We were secret lovers for a night, and I want more of that. We haven't talked about the rest of the time here in Paris and whether we'll spend it together. But that's okay. I know this fling can't last, so I'm rolling with it, living life like Finn said his son does—in medias res.

"Let's do your list," he says after we grab coffee and croissants. "You said wandering down a quiet street was on it. Montmartre is full of quiet streets where you can get lost. I don't have a meeting for a couple hours. When are you due on set?"

"Two hours," I say.

We go. I've checked off a handful of items already with him, so the list feels like it belongs to both of us now as we turn on a cobblestone street with no cars allowed.

It's quiet, like I've stepped into Paris in the Belle Époque. We walk past historical-looking buildings with doors painted purple, bright green, and sunshine yellow, and with window boxes lining each story. As we wander, I take photos and send them to Camden with little captions.

"Let me take a picture of you," Finn says.

That tone makes me comply, but so does the emotion in his voice, the clear sense that he needs this picture to remember this day when it's long gone. When all that's left is the memory.

I stand by an orange doorway, but I don't smile because I don't think that's what he wants. I think he just wants to remember me here. I brush a strand of hair from my face and I know that's what he's capturing.

When he looks at his phone, he murmurs, "Perfect."

Then he gazes up at the building, probably six stories high. Each flat has a balcony.

You could tell him.

Just as that thought lands, my mind says it again. *You could tell him.* And I think I'd be okay if I did.

I practice it silently a few times, but he's faster. When he looks at me, he asks, "Jules, is there something more to the balcony thing?"

25

YOU ARE THE LIST

Jules

There is no judgment in his question. All my long-held impulses to hide and deny, to cover up and keep secrets, have vanished here with him in Paris.

Where I'm far away, and where I suppose I feel safe.

"I have OCD," I admit. "I haven't told anyone besides Camden." It's easier to say than I'd ever expected. Maybe because he asked his question so genuinely.

Or maybe it's because I've been doing the work. Facing the thoughts when I need to. Trying to understand myself more. Perhaps, I don't need to hide behind an *everything is fine* poker face.

Finn nods slowly, processing but not judging. "I don't know much about OCD. Except for what you see on TV or in the movies. Handwashing, stove-checking," he says. "But I don't know if that's part of it for you?"

I shake my head. "I don't have those compulsions, though I do understand them." That's what most people think OCD is. Yes, some people practice those rituals. But that's not how my anxiety manifests. "But I have these...intrusive thoughts," I say, sharing that secret, shameful part of me out loud for perhaps only the third time—I've shared it with Camden, Shira, and now, this man.

I'm grateful for the quiet street. Grateful for the anonymity of Paris. But mostly, I'm grateful I don't have to keep the secret from him anymore. "When I'm on a balcony or a rooftop or a bridge, or even a subway plat-form, I sometimes think terrible things," I say, then I take a fueling breath. "Like that I could throw myself off the balcony. I could jump off a bridge. I could step in front of the train," I say, my voice wobbly, my throat tight. "Or even at your home, when you sliced the pineapple. I just think...well, I hate knives. They make me think too much. About uncomfortable things. But I'm not suicidal. I swear I'm not," I say, imploring him.

His gaze is caring as he keeps it locked on me. "I understand. I get it. You don't want to, but the idea takes hold."

"Yes," I say, desperately relieved he's following. "I think these things when I'm there. I think that I could hurt myself, and it makes me really uncomfortable, and I feel awful, but I have to try to talk back to my brain and remind myself the thoughts will float away... I think other awful things too," I say, the words piling up, and I'm blurting them all out now, but I want to blurt out all these words, to say them to someone else.

"Sometimes when I'm in work meetings, I start thinking about sex, and I don't want to think that because I don't have those feelings about anybody I'm in a meeting with. They just come to my head, and I hate them, but now that I understand where they're coming from, I try to let them float by, accept them so they can eventually go away. I think that's one of the reasons, besides my ex, that I didn't have sex for so long."

He pauses, seeming to quietly take that in. A bird chirps a couple floors above us as I study his thoughtful expression, wishing I knew what he was thinking. Have I scared him? Is he disgusted?

"What do you do about the OCD?" He asks in a kind tone that says he isn't afraid. "It sounds like you're treating it? If that's the right word."

"I see a therapist who specializes in it. She's helped me learn some skills. Some things that I can focus on instead. Things that I can say to myself when I have the thoughts so I know that they aren't who I really am or what I want. I tell myself *I'm the reader of my thoughts, not the writer*. And that helps. They're part of my brain but not part of a true desire. Do you know what I mean?"

He nods passionately, reassuringly as he steps closer to me. "That must be hard for you. Even if you know where these fears come from, they're still real."

"Yes," I say, my voice pitching up. "They are. But I can't avoid them all the time. I have to face them. That's why the other day, I went out to the balcony too. And I stayed there for a bit. My therapist encouraged me to have exposure around some of these things instead of avoiding them."

"I sensed that was important to you. I'm sorry I plowed ahead."

"Don't be," I say. "It was kind. But I had to do it too, you know?"

He nods. "I do. I get that. I'm glad you felt comfortable joining me there."

"I did. I feel better telling you too. So you...get it," I say.

All at once, I feel lighter. I wasn't looking for this understanding from him but now that I have it, I don't want to let it go.

His soulful green eyes meet mine, holding my gaze with his own vulnerability. "If there's anything I can do...if there's anything that you think would help me understand it and you, would you let me know?"

I could cry. Those aren't the words of a man who just wants to fuck me. Those are the words of a man who cares about me. Just like I care about him. I feel safe with him. I feel like myself with him.

"Honestly, you did that just now. And the other day, too, on the balcony. Just that kind of quiet encouragement helps. But mostly, thank you for listening." But that's not all. I'm so glad he asked. I didn't know I'd want that till it happened. But I feel seen, and understood.

Finn holds my face gently. "That can't have been easy. Thank you for letting me in."

I close my eyes, taking his comfort, needing it. That was hard, but it feels so good. This wasn't on the Paris list—telling my father's best friend the truth about my mental health. But I've done it and somehow it makes me feel even better about all of the sex that we've had.

When I let go, I take his hand, and we walk until it's time for work.

* * *

We make plans again for dinner that evening. As the twilight darkens the sky, we duck into a bistro with a back patio, hemmed in by tall hedges. "No one can find us here," I say.

"Where?" he deadpans.

"Exactly."

"It's just us," he says as we settle in at a small green table in the corner.

It sure feels that way all through drinks and dinner. After the server clears our plates, Finn's phone rings with a FaceTime call from his son.

"Mind if I answer?"

"Not at all," I say, glad he's not thinking twice about talking to Zach around me.

Finn chats with him at the table, then adds, "Jules is here. Got any burning *Captain Dude* questions?"

My heart skips a beat that Finn's so easily bringing me into the conversation.

"No, but I want to tell her something else," Zach says, then Finn adjusts the screen so I can see his kid.

Zach's hair is a wild mess. He's unkempt and probably unwashed, but he's lit up with excitement as he tells us about making a dam with David, then asks me if I've ever made one, then says he and David are going to try the Diet Coke and Mentos experiment at home. "Can you come over and join us?"

For a few delirious seconds, I feel like I can say yes.

Like saying yes would be part of the *just us* deal his dad and I made an hour ago.

But I can't. That's the rose-colored glasses of Paris making me feel like anything's possible. Instead I say, "Thanks for the invite."

I won't be able to accept, but I'm lucky to have received it.

* * *

The next day, Finn and I meet as soon as the workday ends, heading to a brasserie on Île de la Cité, a little island in the middle of the river. It feels like an escape within an escape, like we're tunneling farther into this make-believe dream of us.

As we eat at a sidewalk table, Finn tells me about his family, how he was raised, all the things he wished for as a kid. They grew up with little, and he wasn't even sure he'd be able to afford college. "I put all my focus into soccer and went on a scholarship," he tells me over wine, then he shrugs. "But I wasn't so good that I could make a living at that. So, the business degree helped."

"I'll say. And now you own the world."

He laughs. "Not quite. Not yet. But at least I don't have to worry about taking care of myself or my family."

His expression turns serious. "That was important to me."

His drive is sexy. "And you've done it. So what will you conquer now? Streamer?"

"Well," he says, a little sheepish, "the deal is a big one, don't get me wrong. I wanted to expand. To make sure I'm secure, and my family's secure." He takes a pause, drinks some wine. "But honestly, I really just want to be a good father."

My heart thumps. "That's a perfect life goal. The best one, really."

"Thanks," he says, then drags a hand through his hair. "It's hard. And it's weird, starting at age seven. But I want to give him everything."

Funny, how I don't even know if I want children. And I've never been attracted to single dads before. But then, I haven't been attracted to anyone in a long time, until Finn. Now, each detail I learn about him as a person and as a father makes me wish we could be together beyond Paris. "You are, Finn," I assure him, meaning it.

He takes my hand, runs his thumb over the top of it. "It was nice seeing you talk so easily to him in the bookstore, and at the diner, and on the phone last night," he says, and oh god. Oh hell.

This man is opening his heart to me here. I don't know what to do with it after this trip. But right now, I say, "He's great. I liked being invited."

"Do you..." He stops, shakes his head as if admonishing himself. But I *know* he was about to ask if I want kids, and I don't want the question to go unanswered. If he's asking it, or trying to, it's important to him.

"Do I want children?" I ask.

He rolls his eyes. "We don't need to talk about it. It's not..."

But he wants to know. And he listened to me discuss my hard thing. This is probably hard for him, given what he told me about his wife. "Maybe someday," I say, before he can back out.

The corner of his lips twitches in a grin. "Yeah?"

"Yeah." It's not a false promise like his ex made to him, but it's not a lie either.

After dinner, Finn takes my hand as we walk through the moonlit streets. We reach an open iron gate, and he peers past it into a courtyard, teeming with flowers, lifting a brow in a partners-in-crime invitation. I say yes, and seconds later, he's kissing me against a vine-covered brick wall under the Paris moon. If kisses were words, this one would say *I'm falling for you*.

The next night, I pick a hole-in-the-wall vegetarian café in the Latin Quarter, tucked into an alley where no one can find us. Finn doesn't even grumble about ordering a spicy eggplant sandwich. When we sit to wait for our orders, I cross my legs, but he reaches for my ankle, runs his thumb over the star anklet, and says, "This was how I knew it was you. I saw it in your father's office that day, but I didn't make the link until I went to The Scene again." He doesn't linger on uncomfortable reminders of our connection. "You wear it all the time. It must be important to you."

I fiddle with the stars on it, but I don't feel sad thinking of Willa. I don't always, or even often, feel sad when she comes up. I've had six years to adjust to life without my first best friend. Sometimes, I just want to talk about her. "My sister gave it to me for my eighteenth birthday. It was a thing we did. We used to give ankle bracelets to each other. Especially when we learned what they originally were used for."

"I have no idea what they stand for so you'd better tell me."

I picture Willa and me at sixteen and seventeen, curled up on my bed, overstuffed with pillows, a laptop on my knees as we searched out info on anklets. Then, we were rolling our eyes and giggling when we learned the ancient meanings behind them. "We read that sometimes women in olden days would wear them so men could hear them coming and not say naughty things in front of them. And then they were worn to show social status. So we'd give them to each other and say, *Now I can hear you sneaking into my room to steal my shirt*. Or, *this means I'm the favorite daughter since I did the dishes*." I glance at Finn, and his smile says *keep talking*. "But in the end, we decided that to us, they meant *fuck the patriarchy*."

A laugh bursts from him—a rich, vibrant sound that I'll miss when our time here ends. "The patriarchy should be fucked, toppled, drawn, and quartered."

I arch an appreciative brow. "I like you even more now."

He leans closer and murmurs, "It's very mutual." Then, he cups my cheek, holds my gaze, and breathes out my name: "Jules."

He says it like I'm his not only for now, but beyond Paris.

I swoon. Too much. Too far.

After we eat, we head to the hotel, but he stops under a streetlamp on a corner and kisses me, making my head swim with desire and my heart burst with hope. "Was that on your list?" he asks. "Being kissed under a streetlamp in Paris?"

You are the list, I want to say.

But that's too much. That's not part of this deal. Instead I say, "It is now. You keep adding to it every night."

There's a glint in his eyes like he's making a plan. "Good. Then I have something else to put on it."

"What is it?"

"Let me make some calls," he says.

I faux pout. "Tell me."

"It'll be worth it."

You're worth it, I want to say, but that, too, I keep to myself.

* * *

In the morning, as I'm spritzing on Come What May in my hotel room—which has become ours—he comes up behind me and wraps his arms around my waist. "I have a surprise for you on our last night."

"Will it be worth it?" I tease, calling back his words from an evening ago.

He kisses my neck, murmuring against my skin like he doesn't want to leave Paris or me. "You're worth it, Jules."

My breath catches. I feel like I'm filling up with hope. I can't stop picturing New York with him. Yes, my head knows New York will never happen. It *can't* happen. And yet, my heart wants what it wants.

Does he imagine it too? Us in the city? Us finding a way?

But that's foolish to even think about. My father would lose his mind, more than he has in the past. He'd say I'd disappointed him, that he'd expected better, that this is not the woman he'd raised me to be.

But that's nothing compared to what he'd say to Finn. My father would never forgive his friend.

And I won't destroy their friendship.

Yet I can't stop picturing all the possibilities as we drink coffee at a café by the hotel twenty minutes later, chatting about our respective workdays ahead. As I lift a cup, I say, "Mud. I'll miss our mud."

That hardly covers these feelings.

"Me too," he says, then seems like he's about to say something else. Something like *We'll have better coffee in New York. In my kitchen, in the backyard, at a coffee shop, every day.*

I swear, it's on his lips. I can't be the only one wishing for more. I can't be the only one feeling so much it hurts. It's like my heart is going to burst with all these emotions. "Maybe..." I begin, testing the word.

He smiles, soft and tender, receiving it with his own, "Maybe."

This is so wild—this floaty feeling. I had no idea anything could feel so good. This is better than dancing, than inhaling flowers, than getting lost in a story. I'm getting lost in my own story, tuning out all the noises of Paris, all the sounds, the clicking of shoes, the clatter of silverware, the rumble of cars.

I live in the make-believe a little more as the city fades away. But when I open my eyes, I'm staring at Solange, who's heading toward us, studying me like I make no sense anymore.

Like she can't believe I'm sitting at a café enjoying a romantic morning with the man who owns the network.

26

IT'S NOT WHAT YOU THINK

Jules

A surge of panic rushes through my veins. My heart pounds so loud I'm sure everyone in the café can hear it.

Like, oh, say, Solange, who's mere feet away. As she cocks her head and says, "Good morning, Jules," my skin goes hot with a blush of discomfort. Where's my poker face when I need it?

"Hi," I say, but that little word is stuck in my throat. Do I still know how to speak?

Finn rises, sticks out a hand. "Good to see you, Solange. Have you tried this café? I can't recommend the coffee in good conscience."

He offers her a smile, but it's one that says to me he's going to handle this situation. Good, because I can't.

"I don't care for coffee," she says as they shake.

"Join us for breakfast then. Jules and I were catching up on the plans for the show in New York next week," he says as he sits back down, so easily, so seamlessly that even I believe him.

"It'll be busy then too," she says, but she's assessing us, like she's not sure she's buying his cover-up. Embarrassment washes over me. Even if Finn's not my direct boss, she must think less of me for this. She must think I'd sleep my way through the business. Everything I've worked hard for is spiraling because of my dumb heart.

"It will. Our American brand partners are all set though. Like we talked about the other day," he adds.

That must have been when he came to the set, the evening he grabbed her eyeglasses.

"Yes, and I think I know how to integrate the watchmaker," she says.

"Fantastic. Did you want to chat about it now?" he asks. I have no idea how he can be so normal, but I'm glad he is because I'm not.

She looks at her own watch, a functional, waterproof-looking one that is pure Solange. "I can't now," she says crisply, then glances at our empty cups on the table.

It's just coffee. Please let that be all she thinks this is.

"But later is fine," she says, then turns to me. "When you come in, let's have a chat about the New York scenes coming up next week. Is the fountain at Lincoln Center really the best location for the breakup shot? Or should we do it on set instead?"

Changing a location from the streets of New York to the studio is easy enough. "I'm partial to Lincoln

Center, but if you think something like the office set is better, then I'll make it happen."

With a sigh, she taps her chin, clearly weighing the options. "I'll think on it."

Her words are polite, but there is a cutting edge to them.

Could I lose my job? Will she say something to Bridger? Will he say something to my dad? Finn didn't even touch me in public.

Still, I must be wearing all my thoughts on my face. *I'm falling in love with this man.*

My gaze drops to the ground as heat spreads across my cheeks.

She's a woman I respect: a sharp, no-nonsense producer. How could I have let myself get so close to Finn? What was I thinking?

But for once, I *wasn't* thinking. I was only feeling.

"You must be staying nearby," Finn says to her when she shows no signs of leaving.

"Yes. My hotel, too, is around the corner," she says, and that *too* makes me think she's been aware of us for longer than I've realized.

My stomach twists with guilt and shame. "It's a nice hotel," I say, and I sound like a chastened child. I feel like one.

"It's terrific," she says. "Well, I better go. I'll see you shortly, I trust?" The question is directed at me in a concerned tone.

"Absolutely."

"Good," she says, then spins on her heel and heads into the crowd.

She's gone, and I should feel relieved. But my throat constricts and my lungs struggle to fill with air.

"Jules," Finn says with some concern. "It's going to be okay."

"You can't know that," I say, my voice wobbly.

I've got to do something. To go. To explain. I could chase after her. Say *it's not what you think.*

But it is what she thinks. She's not stupid, and I have to fix this.

That's what I do at work—fix problems. I need to fix my own problem, right now, right here, before it gets worse.

I jump up as Finn tosses a few bills on the table. Grabbing my purse and phone, I walk, then I jog, pushing past tourists and locals.

I'm barely thinking as I rush through the streams of people till I reach the corner. I'm about to call out the producer's name when a hand wraps around my wrist.

"Jules," Finn says, firm and sharp. "Talk to me."

"I have to explain to her," I say, rushing urgently down the sidewalk.

"No. You don't." He tugs me down a quiet side street. "Breathe," he says once we stop in an alcove next to a clothing boutique. "She has no way of knowing anything."

I shake my head. He's wrong. "She's smart. How could she not suspect something was going on between us?"

"First, it's none of her damn business. Second, she didn't see anything." He tries to reassure me, trying clearly to take control of the situation. "And you're not my employee. You don't work for me. This is not an office romance."

"I know that," I bite out. "I'm not stupid."

"I didn't say that. I'd never say that. I know you aren't," he says. "I'm trying to help."

"It's too late," I say as guilt wells up inside me. "It's just too late."

"Jules, it's not," he says, emphatic.

But I'm hellbent on going. "I have to tell her it was nothing. I have to make sure she knows."

His grip tightens, and he jerks me closer. "If you need to tell her it's nothing, I won't stop you. If you need to tell her the truth, I won't hold you back either. You have to do what feels right to you," he says, staring hard at me, but his eyes are full of emotions and concern too. "Whatever you decide, I will understand. All I want right now is to be here for you. Whatever you want. Whatever you need."

My pulse starts to settle a little. This man isn't trying to save himself. He's trying to be here for me.

"I feel so stupid," I say weakly as I slump against the stone wall.

"You're not stupid. Or if you are, I'm stupid too." He shrugs helplessly. "Whatever you need, just tell me. I'll protect you. I'll follow up with her. Your father won't know. Bridger won't know." He gulps but keeps his chin up.

I hate that he has to lie. I try desperately to swallow my tears. "I should go," I say, frowning.

"Jules, I'm sorry you feel this way. Especially

because..." He pauses to draw a breath and slides his thumb along my jawline. "I'm falling for you."

My heart soars at his admission, but then crashes when my phone buzzes. I look at it. There's a note from Solange.

Can you have lunch today?

27

WATCH YOUR BACK

Jules

We're shooting on one of the bridges over the Seine. It's a pivotal scene where our heroine debates her next move with her best friend. I go through the motions like a robot, executing every request Solange makes of me till lunchtime rolls around. The harder I work, the faster I move, the more perfect I do every task, the sooner—perhaps—she'll forget what she saw this morning.

When we take a break, she tips her forehead to the ribbon of water snaking through the city where I stupidly fell in love. How cliché am I? Traveling to Paris for work and falling for an older man. He might not be emotionally unavailable, but he's unavailable all the same.

"There's a café I like a few blocks away," she says in

the crisp tone of a woman accustomed to being in charge. "We'll walk," she says.

More like *walk the plank*.

This isn't a simple work lunch to pass the time. This is a correction. Or worse.

We pace along the waterside, passing bouquinistes in green wooden stalls peddling very French-looking posters of the Moulin Rouge and the Eiffel Tower. Solange makes idle small talk about New York. "It'll be good to be back there next week. I need the faster pace of Manhattan."

"I can see that," I say, wishing she'd get to the point and dreading it at the same time.

"I like the go-go-go rhythm of New York," Solange says as a tour boat lolls by in the river, tourists snapping photos of the sights from the deck. They're so far away, I know no one can reasonably capture us. But if they did, I imagine the picture would be labeled *Before The Shoe Drops*.

"You'll be there, I presume?" she asks.

Unless you get me fired.

Is falling for someone in the business a fireable offense? I don't think it is, for all the reasons Finn pointed out, but logic doesn't stop the scenarios unfolding in my head over my office-adjacent romance.

She'll tell Bridger, and he'll be disappointed. My stomach roils at the thought. I've already been living with my father's disappointment for years—I don't know if I can stomach his too.

She'll have me removed from the production. Can she

though? Bridger's company is producing the show, but TV production hierarchy can be a tangled skein.

Solange stops at a stone parapet along the river. Quickly, I scan the scene, and I'm safe enough from my thoughts. There are too many layers of steps and staircases heading down to the river for my mind to imagine terrible things.

But my mind doesn't have to because reality supplies them.

"Jules," she says, in a sharp, clear tone. The chitchat is over.

"Yes?"

Solange stares over the water, a faraway look in her eyes. "When I was younger, probably your age, I fell in love with an older man."

Oh. That wasn't what I was expecting. I swallow past the uncomfortable knot in my throat. "Okay."

"He was in the business. A director. I didn't report to him," she says, and for the first time, she doesn't sound cool and together. She sounds like she's reminiscing. Like she's wistful. "He was..."

She shakes her head like the thought of him is too much to bear. She squeezes her eyes shut briefly, as if she's erasing the images of him, then turns to me. "He was wonderful, and I was swept away."

Clearly her love story doesn't have a happy ending. "What happened?"

I brace myself for her to say she lost her job, or he was Harvey Weinsteining.

"Nothing," she says.

I furrow my brow. "Nothing?"

"Like I said, he wasn't my boss. Just like Finn isn't yours. There are degrees of separation." Her comments are both reassuring and not. She's saying the insulation is ultimately irrelevant. "But that's not always what matters."

I say nothing. She called this meeting. I'm just waiting for the blade to drop.

"I don't want you to lose your way," she says, and now her pensive tone has vanished, replaced by a passionate one. "You're a hard worker. You're diligent. You're focused. That matters more than talent in this field."

"So I'm not a good coordinating producer?" I ask, even more confused.

"You are. A good producer is a hard worker, diligent, and focused." She sighs heavily. "But men like that? Older, confident, established, rich? They don't face risks like we do as women. They aren't building their reputations. They're untouchable. But us?" She points to herself, then me, and it's strange to be included in this sisterhood now. "We *only* have the work we do to build on."

My skin crawls. I hate that she makes so much sense.

Her eyes pin me with a newfound intensity. "You and he—you're in different places, Jules." Something in her voice says she's imparting vital knowledge to me. Woman to woman. Passing it on down the line with a plea—*don't get involved at your age with a man who's already worked his way up.*

I suppose it's one thing to fall for a guy who's young

and hungry and scrappy, and entirely another to fall for a man who's made it. Who has a family. Who might not want the relentless questing of my young heart.

But I say nothing. I don't want to reveal too much of myself to her or too much of my heart.

Solange seems undeterred by silence. She simply adds to her point, "I want you to find your own way. I don't want you to rely on a man."

"I don't rely on him," I say, defensively.

"I know. But soon, you will. I can see it in your eyes," she says. "I saw it this morning at the café. You're quite taken with him."

The knot in my throat turns into a lump, one that threatens to break.

"There are so many people out there wanting your job, wanting this opportunity you've made for yourself," she says.

I think I get it now. "You're saying *watch my back*?"

She gives a resigned smile. "Yes, I am. I don't want you to lose your focus, or for someone to steal it." She waves to indicate whoever is out there, wanting my job. Unnamed, unknown people. "You're tenacious now. Don't lose your tenacity because a man makes your life easier. I lost mine for a while, and it took me years to build it back."

"But you're in a great place now," I say.

She gives an *oh please* look. "I'm forty-seven. It's not easy." Then, after a pause, she adds, "Correction—it's especially not easy for women. Do you know what I mean?"

My skin tingles with understanding at last. She

means *fuck the patriarchy*. She means it's a man's world, and women have to work harder, fight harder, and never get complacent. "I do," I say, wishing I didn't.

She lifts a hand almost like she's going to squeeze my shoulder, but then drops her arm to her side. "Finn Adams can have anything he wants, and I don't mean women. I mean companies, businesses, and choices. All we have, women like you and me, *are* our choices."

Translation: *get my shit together and stop being a starry-eyed girl.*

"I understand," I say.

"Good. Let's have lunch."

That'll be fun.

* * *

Lunch isn't fun. But it's eye-opening as she lets me into her world, sharing behind-the-scenes tidbits on productions she's worked on, telling tales of the business. With something like the pride of a self-proclaimed mentor, she says, "I see big things for you."

The message is clear: choose work because love won't last.

She's probably right. Not for the reasons she's said, but for even more complicated ones.

Ones I shouldn't ignore any longer.

Finn and I were never destined to be real. It was only ever role-play with him.

28

MY IMPOSSIBLE WISH

Jules

Things that make me feel like I'm doing something wrong—furtively glancing behind me while I knock on the door of Finn's hotel room in the early evening.

I already texted and told him I wasn't sure if I could meet tonight, but he asked me to come by to talk in person anyway. I'm not cut out for sneaking around. I can't keep doing this.

No less than two seconds after I knock, he opens the door, his expression resigned.

I step into his room, wanting to fall into his arms but knowing that'd be a mistake. "Hi," I say heavily.

"Hey, you." His voice is like a warm hug, one I hardly deserve.

"I was such an idiot to be so public with you," I say, my shoulders falling.

"Don't say that. You're brilliant and bright. You're not an idiot."

"But I am. For thinking I could…"

Could what? What's the point of this confession? Finn and I never made any promises to each other. We never said we'd do anything but spend every night together in Paris. We were always an affair.

I draw a soldiering breath and try to put the lunchtime conversation in its proper place—it was a valuable piece of advice that I was lucky to receive from a woman who's made it. "Solange said I should focus on work, and she's right," I say, resolute.

Finn's lips straighten into a ruler, and not in a sexy way like they did the other night. His eyes turn guarded. His nod is slow as he takes this in. "Okay."

His tone is stripped of emotion. And I hate it. I just hate all this pretending. I hate all this sneaking around. I hate all this…role-play.

"Look," I say, grabbing his shirt collar. "I fell for you too. Maybe that's ridiculous and stupid. But I did. And we both know *we* can't happen. We were never supposed to be more than a one-night thing, and we kept falling into each other. Tomorrow I go back to New York and you have your son. That's your focus, and I need to think about work, and there's my father and—"

His lips crash down on mine. Hard, bruising, passionate.

He pushes me against the wall and grabs my face in his hands like I belong to him. Like no one else can ever touch me. He kisses me possessively and madly.

But like he's angry with me too.

When he breaks the kiss, he huffs, still mad. "You're so fucking perfect for me it makes me crazy."

What?

Perfect for him?

I swallow past my surprise. "What do you mean? Perfect for you?"

His touch is still rough. "I can talk to you. I can be myself with you. I can tell you things and know you're not manipulating me. You're open and honest and caring, and I can't stand how much I want you. In every way," he grits out, every word seeming to rip him apart. He shudders in a breath like he can barely control his emotions. "And the last thing in the world I want to do is hurt you."

He loosens his hard grip on my face only so he can thread his fingers gently through my hair. "Know that, Jules. I want *this*. But know, too, I don't want to be the one to hold you back. To hurt you. To ruin any...relationship."

But my relationship with my father was ruined years ago. I don't know if it can recover or if I'll just keep pretending everything is fine with him. I don't know how to move forward with Finn, either, or if I even can. Maybe I'm too broken. Or maybe Solange was right. She's certainly right that Finn and I are in different places. I don't know anything anymore.

The knot from earlier today has nothing on this new one rising up in my throat, like it's going to strangle me with all these damn feelings. "Finn," I say, choked up.

He strokes my hair. "Come on one last date with

me. I told you I had a surprise for you. And it's actually something that's on your list."

That perks me up. The intrigue is too hard to resist. "But we've done everything on it."

"Yes and no. The first day you said you wanted a garden all to yourself. So I arranged one for tonight." He pauses, steps back a few inches so he can watch my reaction, I suspect, as he says, "We can go to Monet's Garden, and it'll just be you and me."

If I wasn't already in love with him, I am now.

The town car he arranged whisks us to Giverny in just over an hour. We arrive as the sun coasts toward the horizon, pale pink and orange streaks painting the summer sky.

We go inside the big house with green doors, Finn handling the details with an older woman whose gray hair is cinched in a bun. She must be managing this icon of gardens, and Finn's *buyout* for one night.

I'm still stunned that he's made this private visit possible. Then, I'm awed to walk into the famous gardens at the height of their summer glory.

Emerald is everywhere, from the vast lawns to the trees canopying the grounds. Wildflowers pop up as we walk, rippling in the summer breeze in a riot of shimmery purples, ruby reds, and vibrant oranges. Lavender is everywhere.

With Finn's hand wrapped around my waist, we wander along a tree-lined path with a wooden fence, then deeper into the gardens, the endless peonies and poppies saying goodbye to their blooming days, as roses shoulder their way up in bold pinks, whites, and reds.

Butterflies escort us, and bumblebees hum as they flit from flower to flower. It's a dreamlike place, and tonight it belongs to us. The walled gardens and house make this moment feel even more intimate as we're surrounded by sweet and delicate scents of flowers, and even the silence is soft and lush.

It feels like a sin to speak, but I do it anyway.

"My favorite things," I say, gazing around at the flowers.

"I know." He sounds pleased. He should be.

"I've never been someplace so serene," I say in a hushed voice even though we're the only ones here. But there's a magic spell in this garden, and I don't want to break it.

"You deserve it," Finn says, pressing his hand firmly against my back.

I let his words burrow into me—*I deserve it*. Finn makes me feel that way—like I deserve good things.

But he also seems to love giving those things.

"I think your whole *let me punish you with pleasure* mantra has reached its peak," I say to the man obsessed with my bliss.

He laughs. "Let me know when you can't take it anymore."

I gaze around the vast gardens that go on endlessly. "I can definitely take it."

We wander past peonies, their sweet aroma taking

me back to younger days, when Willa and I would sneak out as kids.

Those are both my best and my worst memories. Of summers. Of days spent with friends. Of nights wanting more. Of my sister, always pushing, always wanting, always a little wild.

My heart aches even as it fills. When we reach the famous green bridge arching over a pond of water lilies, Finn lifts a brow. "This bridge is okay?"

I love that he asks. But it's only a few feet over the pond, so it's not an issue for me. "I'm good with this one."

He returns my smile with one of his own, but it falters as we stop in the middle of the bridge, with more roses on the other side. "I'll miss you, Jules."

"I'll miss you," I say.

This time, when I draw a deep inhale of the roses, the scent becomes the smell of my stepmother's perfect rose bushes just outside my window, and I fall back in time to six years ago—the summer after my freshman year of college. The summer before what would have been hers.

She was bored that Friday night, but Willa was always bored if she had no one to see. She was the ultimate social butterfly, the glue holding together Hannah, Josh, Ollie, and the whole crew from our high school and hometown. That night, she danced into my room with twist-my-sister's-arm intentions. I can remember it so perfectly, it feels like it's happening all over again.

Finn must read the longing and the missing in my

face because he says the same thing he did at the Luxembourg Gardens: "Where did you go right now?"

To a place I don't like to talk about.

But as I glance around the gardens, I feel like I'm in a dream. A good one. A safe one. Like this is a place out of time. A few days ago on a quiet street in Montmartre, I told Finn something I've never told my family. I shared the truth of my OCD with him, and it felt freeing. Like I no longer had to live all alone in a dark secret.

I no longer want to live with *this* dark secret either.

I'm tired of how much it hurts. I'm tired of carrying it with me. "The day Willa died..." I say, steady and careful. I have things to say, and I *have* to get through this. I've met somebody I trust with my secrets. This man might not be in my life the way I want, but he values honesty so deeply. He's been here for me with a willing ear, and a big heart, and the most care I've ever known.

On Monet's bridge, gazing over a pond of water lilies, I give him what he asked for—the truth.

"She wanted something to do that August night. There was a pool party I had heard about. I didn't go. But she did, and I helped her get there. Because that's what I'd always done."

"How so?" he asks with curiosity but no judgment.

"We were at my dad's house, and he was out that night with Liz, and when Willa said she wanted to go to the party at Josh's house, I said, 'You know how to sneak out and you know how to sneak back in so Dad won't know you were gone.'"

I wince but don't look away from Finn as I continue my confession. "See, I'd taught her how. I was the older sister, after all. We'd been sneaking out our whole lives. That was what we did to get away from him and his rules."

"What happened at the party, Jules?" he asks, as gentle as the summer breeze, as soft as the ripple in the pond in front of us.

"I didn't know it at the time—this was pure Willa— but she'd taken some wine from our mom's home." I can't be clinical anymore as I recount the story. Briefly, I stare at the lavender, blinking away tears as I jump ahead to the collateral damage. "Afterward, my dad blamed my mom. He said she should have locked up the liquor. My mom blamed him and said he should have paid more attention. He blamed her right back and said she shouldn't have had liquor at her house in the first place. She blamed him and said he shouldn't have been so strict that it made Willa want to sneak out." I feel emotional whiplash all over again, the blame game the two of them played.

Finn sighs sadly, running a reassuring hand down my arm. "Losing a child would be hell," he says, pain etched on every feature. "They were going through hell." But then he squeezes my arm. "But you were, too, losing your sister."

I get why they acted the way they did. "We all blamed each other. I blamed myself. I even told them as much," I admit, inching closer to that terrible day in therapy when I told them.

"Why would you blame yourself?" Finn asks with a furrowed brow, like that's the craziest notion.

"I taught her how to sneak out," I say, impressing it on him, even though I just said it. I just admitted it. "And I should have gone. But I stayed home for a dumb reason. To text my college friends. I was sitting there on my bed with my phone and reminding Willa what window to escape through. Then I told her to come back in through my room using the door that wasn't on camera because it was farthest away from Dad's," I say, both choked up and mad at myself all over again. "And while I was texting about meaningless stuff, my sister got drunk, jumped into a pool, hit her head on the side of it, and drowned." I sound dead when I say that last part because a part of me died that night. "She was my best friend. The person I was closest to in the entire world." I take a deep breath, and I push on. "And it *was* my fault."

Finn's jaw comes unhinged. His eyes darken with anger. "It was not your fault. *Who* told you that?"

I purse my lips together. I don't know if I can say it.

But Finn isn't done. "*None* of that was your fault. It was terrible and it was tragic but it was not—"

"I taught her to sneak out." I say it again so he gets it. "I was the older sister. I should have been responsible. If she hadn't snuck out, she'd still be here." Doesn't he get it?

He breathes out hard. Grips my shoulders. "No."

That's all. A firm, clear no.

My eyes sting with tears.

"No, Jules. It's not your fault," he goes on, biting out each word. "You have to know that. It's not your fault."

"But if I hadn't taught her that, she'd be here—" I insist, but more tears fall, sobs stopping my words.

His eyes flood with concern and rage. "Who told you that?" He asks again, this time more urgent. "Who made you believe this?"

I close my eyes. My throat is too tight. My head hurts too much. I don't want to say it, but I'm tired of not saying it. "My father," I say, barely audible as I give voice to the hurt I've carried for years.

"What?" Finn hisses, like I can't have just said that.

But I can and I did. I said the thing I've told no one. I take a huge breath and meet his intense gaze. "We were in therapy a few months afterward, and I told my parents that I'd taught her. They said it wasn't my fault. But the next day we went to visit her grave, my dad and me, and he was a mess, but he said, 'If you hadn't taught her to sneak out, she'd still be here.'"

Finn's eyes flicker with shock. For a few long seconds, he's simply speechless. "Fucking Tate," he mutters, then he blows out an angry breath and shakes his head vehemently. "He's wrong. He's just wrong. Things happen. Life happens. Your sister made a choice, and it was tragic. But you didn't push her. You didn't make her drink. And you should *never* have to carry that with you."

Finn lets go of my shoulders so he can cup my cheeks instead as he implores me: "Promise me, just promise me you won't carry that guilt with you anymore. I'm sorry about the loss of your sister. I'm sorry that she's not here. I wish you had your best friend. But it's not your fault. Not at all. Not one bit."

Could he be right?

I replay Finn's words, trying to hear the story through his ears, trying to see that day through a new lens.

"You've been telling yourself that for years?" he asks.

"Yes," I admit.

He half looks like he wants to punch the wall like he did the night at the Albrecht Mansion when he learned who I was, and he half looks like he wants to hold me in his arms forever. "Jules. My sweet, wounded, wonderful Jules. If it had been reversed, would you have wanted Willa to punish herself like that?"

My head swims with that unexpected question. One I've never contemplated till today. But one I know the answer to deep inside myself. "No, I wouldn't."

And saying that, something in me lifts. It rises from my heart, and maybe, just maybe, floats away into the summer breeze, carried on the scent of roses.

"Then next time you write to her, write that down. Because I know that's exactly what your sister would say to you too—it's not your fault. You need to tell yourself until you believe it to be true. Since it *is* true," he says, then presses his fingertips to my sternum. "So you can let go of this awful, terrible guilt that isn't yours to bear. You loved her, and she died. That is all."

Was it this easy after all?

Did I simply need someone else to say it to me? Yes,

I think I've always needed that. And he's the one who did.

I wrap my arms around him, rest my face on his shirt, and take what he's offering.

I stay in his arms on the bridge for a long time as the sun sets over Giverny. When twilight coasts into the gardens, finally I break the embrace. "I fell for you too," I say. I said it in the room, but I want to say it again. "Take that with you."

"I will."

He gazes at me with such tenderness, such poignancy that I want to say screw the world. I think he does too.

Instead, we kiss until night falls and it's time to go.

* * *

On the flight home the next day, I return the way I came—alone. But maybe that was the point of Paris.

Finn helped me to let go of something that had been hurting my heart for years. I showed him that two people can share honestly.

Even the ugly parts. Especially the ugly parts.

29

THE LAUGHING STARS

Jules

Two nights later, jet lag has left me, incomprehensibly, both wide awake and exhausted. "This sucks," I moan to Camden, who's camped out with me on my couch, binging a new TV show.

"It's eight. You're allowed to be up," she says.

"No, I meant the missing," I say.

She pats her shoulder. "Here. Lean on it."

With a frown and a yawn, I obey. Sighing. And thinking some more on everything that happened in France. "But I also needed it, you know." I think I mean both the Paris affair and the end of it. I'm not sure I'm ready for anything more.

She hits stop on the show. "I think you did."

Camden knows I told Finn about my intrusive thoughts. Earlier tonight, I gave her the rundown on my trip, leaving out the garden revelation in Giverny.

I figured I'd spend the flight home replaying the *it's not your fault* conversation, letting it fully soak in. Instead, I read, watched a movie, fell asleep. Maybe cracking open that close-held secret was all I needed to unburden me.

I don't *only* want to tell a man though. Solange might not have been right about everything—I'm not convinced falling for an older man would ruin my focus—but she made good points about not relying on a guy.

"There's something else," I say, ready to tell Camden.

My friend sits up straighter at my tone. "What is it?"

I rip off the Band-Aid and tell her about the night Willa died, the thing my father said at her grave, and the way I've felt for six years.

When I'm done, she wraps her arms around me. "Why didn't you ever tell me? I would have told you the same thing. *It's not your fault.*"

"It was too awful," I whisper.

"I hate that you thought that for so long."

"Me too."

She hugs me tighter, holds me closer, then lets go, eyes as sharp as her voice. "Are you going to talk to your dad?"

I wince. "Someday. Maybe."

"Yeah, sometimes that's all we can hope for. A someday. But I'm glad you told me. Because he's just wrong." She wags her finger playfully at me, narrows her eyes. "But I'm still mad you didn't tell me till now."

There's something I can share just with her. "Do you want to see this card I keep in my journals?"

"Of course I do," she says.

I grab the journal, then slide out the card. "I saw this card once in a gift shop, and I bought it. For myself." I square my shoulders. "It's, um, a sympathy card."

"That tracks. Let me see it," she says, holding out a hand.

"I haven't written on it. I just like the quote. It's from *The Little Prince.*" I read aloud, "*In one of those stars I shall be living. In one of them I shall be laughing. And so it will be as if all the stars were laughing when you look at the sky at night.*"

Camden's eyes shine. "I love that. I believe that," she says softly.

I believe it now too.

Taking the card, she studies it a little more, clearly weighing something before she speaks. "Maybe all the writing you do in your journals was what really helped you believe it wasn't your fault. And then Finn just helped you close the door on your guilt."

I give that some thought as I fiddle with the stars on my anklet, then I meet her eyes. "I think you're right."

* * *

The next night, after work, I shower and then break out my journal. I haven't written in it since I left for Paris.

But tonight, I tell Willa what I did while I was there.

I don't write a long letter. I still write in code

because it makes me feel safe. But it's not as obfuscated as it once was.

A quiet street in Montmartre. A dinner in a courtyard. A secret visit to a garden. The scent of roses. And then the words—no, no, no.

You'd have said the same to me. I should have said something sooner, but I know now. And when I look at the sky, all the stars are laughing.

* * *

A busy week of work on *The Rendezvous*, a night of filling in for Scarlett on piano at a speakeasy in Murray Hill, and on the weekend, I'm lounging on Harlow's orange couch, waiting for the rest of the women to either stay in or fold.

Layla hums as she studies her cards, then tosses them down with a harrumph. "Cards, you suck."

Harlow sighs. "I'm out," she says, folding too.

Camden shrugs, having already bowed out.

I grin like a Cheshire cat then take their money. My poker face is still good, even with this ace high. "Poker night should never end," I say.

Before we begin another round, Layla turns to me. "Paris report. Now."

Here goes. I was expecting this demand tonight. I made my decision before I walked in the door. "Well, since you asked," I say, nerves chasing me, but confidence too. I'm trying to change. Trying to let my friends in. "There's this guy."

Harlow's eyebrows lift in obvious excitement. "Two things that go together well—Paris and a guy."

"Yes." Even though there's a pang in my chest over missing Finn, I push past it, turning to Layla. "And you know him."

She blinks. "I do?"

I'm not violating his privacy here. My friends aren't going to blab about Finn to my father. "He's Nick's brother," I say, connecting the dots for them.

Layla's mouth falls open. "Finn," she whispers in shock.

"Yes," I say, and I don't tell them everything. I don't break Finn's confidence. But I tell them a little more about our time together abroad. "I fell in love with him in Paris, and he fell for me."

The sighs, the hearts, the flutters from my girls.

But then, I tell them the heartbreak. "Except it's not meant to be."

Harlow tosses up her hands. "Why not?"

"He's friends with my father and Dad's his lawyer," I point out, because hello? That's still a thing.

"So? Bridger was in business with *my* father," she says, and damn, she's not wrong. They crossed that hurdle.

Still.

"He's in a different place in life. He has a kid," I add.

Layla scoffs. "Um, Nick has a twenty-two-year-old kid. Who I used to date."

And that's fair too.

Camden just smirks. "Girl, you picked the wrong audience if you want sympathy for this dilemma."

I sigh, then try again. "Because...neither one of us said we wanted to keep going."

That shuts everyone up. Really, that's the bigger issue. I *could* have said something on our last night together. I didn't. Because there are things I need to work on—for me.

And I did one of those things tonight—I stopped hiding myself from my friends.

30

YOUR DAUGHTER

Finn

Zach's eyes flutter closed as he settles under the covers with a contented sigh. But before I turn off the lights, he pats a small spot on the bed next to him. "Right here, Dad."

"What's right there?"

Does he want me to join him? I've been back for a week, and since Candace and Michael took a trip to Maine, I've had this kiddo all to myself for the last several days.

The extra time has been great. Visiting science museums, going to the playground, debating what kind of pizza we prefer but opting for Chinese instead because a trendy new Chinese restaurant opened around the block. I get the super spicy noodles, and he doesn't, and I try not to think of Jules and how much she loves spice.

But that describes the last week—I'm trying to forget Jules. So far, I'm not winning that battle.

"This is where Tiramisu can go," Zach says.

Right. His future dog. I ruffle his hair and drop a kiss to his forehead. "Next weekend. It's on."

"Yes," he says, pumping a fist as he yawns.

I say goodnight and then head downstairs, grab my laptop, and settle in at the kitchen counter. I search out dog walkers since I'll need someone during the day when I'm at work, and dog trainers since I know nothing about how to teach a pup to sit or stay.

But I promised this kid a dog, and I'm getting him a dog. Does Jules like dogs?

I roll my eyes. Of course she likes dogs. I grab my phone and tap out a text asking that question, but before I hit send, I berate myself once more.

What are you doing, man? Sending her a text like she's your girlfriend?

Nope.

You don't need to interact with her.

But I want to. Fuck, do I want to.

Except, if something were going to happen with her, it would have happened already. I told her in my hotel room how I felt. That she was perfect for me. That I want *this*. But she didn't seem ready, so I didn't push it. I don't want to be that guy.

I click over to the dog rescue David suggested, checking the hours for next weekend. But first, there's *this* weekend. And the triathlon with Tate on Sunday.

That should be real fun. Groaning in annoyance, I drag a hand through my hair. I haven't trained with him since I returned. Don't want to face him. There are too many things I want to say to him.

I half want to cancel the event but I follow through on my commitments.

* * *

The event is in a park outside the city. As I near the finish line, I am wrung out. Twenty kilometers on a bike, and 750 meters in the water will do that to you, then add on a 5K. My muscles scream. My lungs beg me to stop moving.

Almost done.

A few more feet, then a few more. I glance behind me. I'm ahead of Tate. We weren't racing against each other, per se. Neither of us is vying for a top finish. But still, I want to beat him.

I want to beat the fuck out of him.

I always do. But today, I want it more than usual. I want it perversely.

Out of breath, I cross the finish line ahead of Tate.

Take that.

He crosses a few seconds later, sweaty and panting as he offers me a hand to high five. "Nice work," he says.

I smack back but I don't mean it. "Thanks," I mutter, the exhaustion masking my mood.

I'm still furious with him.

We walk through a sparse crowd, coming down from the high of finishing as we pass tents full of race organizers offering energy bars and electrolyte-laden drinks. I'm not ready to celebrate with him.

Or even to talk to him.

I could blame it on the grueling event, but I won't. Instead, I grab some water from a volunteer at a table full of coolers. "Thanks," I say, then glug it quickly.

When I'm done, I recycle the cup, then I swallow my annoyance with Tate. I spent far too long ignoring the problems in my marriage. I don't want to ignore a big fucking problem in my friendship.

Except I have to handle it delicately. He *can't* know. "So, I'm getting a dog next weekend. Zach wants one," I begin.

Tate laughs. "Never thought you'd get a dog. With your long hours. But the kid has your number."

Bingo. "Yeah, but you know how it goes with kids. You'd do anything for them," I say as we walk through our cooldown.

"Sure. I get that," he says.

"Wish I could have done it years ago. But that's just something I have to deal with," I say.

His eyes are full of question marks. Understandable, since I'm being deliberately unclear. "Get a dog?"

I scratch my jaw. "Get a dog. Raise a son. Face my regrets. The usual."

And he does. He's well aware that my biggest regret is time—wishing I could have had all of Zach's years. He knows I want to make the most of the ones I do have.

"Sure," Tate says, but it's curious, like he wonders where I'm going with this convo.

Yeah, me too.

I tap the gas a little more. "I don't want to have regrets. Like about things I've said. Things I've done. Know what I mean?" I toss him a glance. I'm sure he has his fair share of regrets about the night his daughter died.

"Yeah," he grumbles.

I grind my jaw but then try to let go of my irritation, since my anger at him isn't the fucking point.

The point is he needs to make things right with his daughter, but I can't let on that I know what he did.

"I remember when I first met Zach's grandparents, I was so nervous and excited about Zach, I barely acknowledged they'd lost their daughter." Maybe this is an anvil-sized clue, but maybe he needs it.

He tilts his head, studying me more closely, maybe sensing I'm onto something.

"It didn't hit me until a while later, what I'd said," I continue. "Or really, what I'd *not* said. And then I talked to them. Extended my sympathies. But I regret that, you know? I wish I'd done better sooner," I say, hoping, no, praying that my story will light a fire under him. Make him think about what he said to Jules that day in a cemetery.

His forehead crinkles. But he doesn't speak, perhaps waiting for me to go on.

As we walk off the run, heading away from the race and deeper into the park, I say, "The more I thought about it, the more I didn't want them to think I was someone who didn't acknowledge a loss. I asked how they were coping. I asked about Nina. And I listened when they talked."

I can't say *go talk to your daughter*. I just have to hope that that's what he hears.

He stops, still breathing hard from the race. "Is there a reason you're telling me this?"

Yeah. A big reason. He's not a good lawyer for nothing.

"It made me think about your daughter." I don't say which daughter. I've felt like a liar with Tate for a long time. Hell, I *am* a liar. But I don't care. If it takes lying to get him to fix things, then I'll do it. "If you ever want to talk about her, I'm here."

As angry as I am, the point of this conversation is, I want him to figure out what he did wrong and fix it.

"Thanks. I appreciate that," he says.

I nod, then turn the other way. When I leave, I'm still lying to my best friend, but I don't feel so torn up about it anymore.

* * *

When I arrive home, there's a box waiting at the door. My fingers itch to rip it open, and as soon as I'm inside, I grab a dull knife and slice the tape between the folds, then open the flaps.

I laugh.

And I smile.

And I miss.

It's a pineapple.

And there's a card attached.

I hope the race went well. You deserve a pineapple. I know they're your favorite.

It's just a pineapple. But also? It's not just a pineapple.

* * *

The next night, Zach and I return from dinner with Nick and Layla and find another package waiting on the front stoop.

"What's that?" Zach asks, scooping up the small box.

"I have no idea," I say honestly, and I hope it's not something I really shouldn't open in front of him.

For a few seconds, I picture naughty things. A photo of Jules in pink lace panties and nothing more. Silk boxers. Or even something classy and sexy, like cufflinks—but that would still require an explanation.

When Zach rattles the box, something rolls from side to side. When I see a red pepper on the side of the box, relief washes through me, along with amusement.

Inside, I open it. It's a jar of chili flakes and a note.

Five out of five.

I try to hide a smile. I swear I do. But I know, I just know there's a hidden message behind this five out of five.

"Dad, this is a boring gift. Why don't people send you a jar of chocolates or something? Or a jar of pizza?"

He makes a good point. "A jar of pizza would be a good idea."

But I like the chili flakes more. I text her when Zach goes to bed.

Finn: So, what's a five out of five, Jules?

Jules: You know.

Finn: Do I?

Jules: Yes.

Finn: Say it.

Jules: You.

That damn *You.*

That might be the best gift ever from her.

A part of me doesn't know what to do with this note, or with her, or with all these feelings that aren't going away.

But another part does.

31

IT HAPPENS

Jules

"So, it's a go?" I ask Bridger, barely able to contain my excitement after he delivers the news.

My boss leans back in his desk chair, the picture of a cool, confident executive. "We got *Captain Dude*. Thanks to you."

I'm glowing. I can't even sit down. I just pace in front of his desk because I'm bursting. "That's amazing. Totally amazing."

"You deserve the credit."

I shake my head, too overjoyed to accept his praise. I want to tell Zach. I want to tell Finn. Sure, there are no guarantees a project will get made, but securing the rights is the first step, and we have them.

"You started reading the books and you tipped me off. The author will be in town for a reading next weekend. We can meet him and talk about the project."

Bridger stands, comes around the desk, and stops near me. I can sense this is important to him so I stop pacing and meet his eyes, letting my smile disappear. This feels serious.

"When you first started working for me, you were a diligent, hard worker. That was all I knew. But over time, you've proved your knowledge and acumen. I couldn't have built Opening Number without you. The work you've done on all our shows is tremendous, from *The Rendezvous* to *Happy Enough*. And now to find a project like this," he says, shaking his head in amazement. "Just promise me this—if anyone ever tries to court you, give me a chance to make you an offer and keep you."

I'm floored. But what would he do if he knew I slept with the head of a network we pitch shows to?

"And I'd like to give you a raise and a promotion," he says.

I should jump for joy. But my shoulders fall. I can't take this if he doesn't know.

But there's nothing to know, another voice argues.

And yet, there is.

"Bridger," I begin, then I go to the door and shut it. I have to be careful. I'm not involved with Finn, and I don't want to presume I ever will be. But I don't want to cause a scandal either. I think that's the message Solange was trying to impart. *Be careful.*

She's not wrong. But sometimes being careful doesn't mean walking away. Sometimes it means walking into the fire.

This won't be comfortable in the least, but I need to say it. To ask it. It's the right thing to do.

He tilts his head, then tugs on the cuffs of his emerald-green shirt. "What is it, Jules?" he asks, taking a seat then gesturing to the one across from him.

Then, I do another hard thing. "Would it bother you if I was involved with someone in the industry? Hypothetically."

He sinks back in the chair, seeming relieved. "You scared me there."

"But I'm serious."

With a weighty sigh, he nods a few times. "Jules, I fell in love with my business partner's daughter. It happens."

Yes. Yes, it does.

Maybe there's a way for it to happen to me too. Because the thing I want most in the world right now is to tell Finn about a kids' book his son loves.

* * *

I head into Shira's office the next day with a newfound confidence. This is the first time I've walked in here when I haven't felt like a shaken bottle of soda, ready to spill.

I do plan to spill.

But I feel steadier.

Less out of control.

"How's it going today, Jules?" she asks as she takes a seat.

I flop down onto the sofa across from her then dive

right into things. "Remember that time I slept with my father's best friend?"

"I sure do. I'm guessing you're going to tell me something else about that?"

I draw a deep breath. "Yes. Like...everything."

I take her through the restaurant encounter, then the bookstore run-in, dinner at the diner, then Paris, from the café to the Luxembourg Gardens, to all our meals, and to the moment on the streets of Montmartre. "And I told him about my OCD. And about my sister."

Shira looks impressed but cautious. "And how did that go?"

I flash back to that morning in Paris. To the way I felt during, then after, then days later. For years, I've felt hidden. But I chose to be that way. "I love masks," I say, beginning in a roundabout way. "I love dressing up. Putting on a costume. But I think I loved it because I didn't want to be...me. Or maybe I wanted to deny parts of me."

She nods, absorbing that, and her expression says *keep going.*

"And then I didn't feel such a need to deny it anymore."

"Why do you think that is? Did you feel accepted?"

I take a deep breath, letting the air fill me completely. "I felt understood. It was better than a mask."

"That's progress. Sometimes we need to be open about our challenges. It helps us face them," she says with a proud smile. But it morphs quickly into a questioning look. "Is there something happening with him?"

I shake my head, wishing I could give a different answer. "No. Because I have to do something else first."

"What's that?"

I swallow what feels like a stone, but I say it anyway. "I have to deal with something my father said to me years ago."

Then, I tell Shira, and immediately she hands me a box of tissues.

When I've gone through them, she says, "And what do you think you're supposed to do now?"

The answer is finally easy.

Face it.

32

DO YOU REMEMBER

Jules

A fleet of hummingbirds flaps in my chest as I walk past the brownstones lining the narrow street in my father's Brooklyn neighborhood.

My stomach dips as I reach the stoop, with its iron railing and stairs lined with potted plants, thanks to Liz. The imposing stone facade and immaculate white-shuttered windows are thanks to my father's career shift, which has afforded him a place like this in Brooklyn, much bigger than our childhood house.

This brownstone is not home to me. But it's where I need to be right now.

I walk up the steps, hesitantly raising my hand to lift the brass knocker. A few seconds after it falls, Liz swings open the door. She's perfectly put together in pastel blue leggings and a workout top, a swingy ponytail complementing her toned look.

"Hi, Jules," she says. "So good to see you. How was Paris? I can't wait to hear all about it."

It was eye-opening, Liz. And you probably don't *want to hear all about it.*

"It was great," I say, then sigh in relief when she grabs her keys and phone from a wooden table in the foyer.

"I'm excited to hear about it sometime. I'm off to Orange Theory."

Last night when I reached out, I told my dad I needed to talk to him privately about mutual funds.

I didn't tell him I wanted to discuss something that's been weighing on me for six years. That would be cruel, to let that gnaw at him all day. The coordinating producer in me timed it around Liz's workout schedule.

My father's footsteps echo from the direction of the kitchen, coming closer. When he appears in the front hall, he's still in work clothes, but his suit jacket is gone, and his cuffs are rolled up. He looks like it's a regular day for him.

Does he have any idea what's truly on my mind?

"Hi, sweetie," he says with affection.

No, he has no idea.

"Hi, Dad," I say, and it feels strange to talk to him so casually, knowing what I came to say.

Liz drops a kiss on his cheek. "Bye, darling. See you later," she says, then trots down the steps, off to the gym.

He shuts the door behind her and gestures to the kitchen. "Want an iced tea? LaCroix? Anything else?"

He doesn't offer wine. I wouldn't take it even if he did.

"Sure," I say, distracted by thoughts of what's to come. What if I say the wrong thing? What if I tell him the truth about Paris and his best friend and me? What if I tell him where I met Finn?

Stop.

Tonight is not about Finn.

And I won't blurt out anything inappropriate.

The thoughts float out the window.

"Which one?" he asks.

"Water," I say as we head into the kitchen. He fills a glass from the tap, then grabs a bubbly water for himself from the fridge.

"I have my laptop ready and lots of spreadsheets," he says.

Oh, Dad, what I have to say won't involve rows and columns.

I take a seat at the counter next to him. Last night, I rehearsed what to say, but now that I'm here, all my practiced words fall away. Not by mistake—I am one hundred percent intentional when I skip the preamble and speak the truth. "It's not my fault."

His brow knits in confusion. "What's not?"

I am strong. I am ready. "Willa's death. It wasn't my fault. Just because I taught her to sneak out, it wasn't my fault," I say, my voice catching, my throat tightening.

His eyes widen. His voice is thick with concern as he asks, "What's going on, Julia?"

"You said it was my fault," I say, pushing past the

tears pricking the back of my eyes. "You said it at her grave."

He blinks like this doesn't add up. Like I don't add up. "I-I did?"

A plume of anger rises in me, stoked by his reaction. "You don't remember?"

My father stares off like he's rushing through his memory banks, checking the files for *that awful day*. "After the family therapy session? When you said you felt bad for teaching her to sneak out?" Each phrase is clipped, like they're hard for him to say.

Welcome to the club, Dad. Lots of things are hard for me to say.

"Yes, and the next day you were putting flowers on her grave, and you started crying." My rebellious tears fight their way out, rolling down my face as I remember my father on his knees at the grave, his face in his tear-soaked hands, and me trying to comfort him. Trying to say something. *Anything.*

"I said, *I miss her too. I miss her so much.*" I push on, needing him to do some work here. To remember the awfulness. "When I said, *I wish she were here,* do you remember what you said to me next?"

He can't miss the ache in my voice. The hurt. But he can't miss the strength in it either. I'm not leaving this stone unturned.

He's quiet at first, but his face is pained. At last, he shudders out a rough, rattling breath. "I remember that day was awful. I remember every day was awful," he says, then presses his lips together, fighting off a torrent of anguish like he did that day.

"But I try not to remember that time," he adds in a barren voice. "I try not to go there. It hurts too much."

This will hurt him even more. "You said Willa would be alive if you'd been home that night, and if Mom hadn't had that wine at her house."

He drags a hand over his chin. "Yes. I said that. I said that every night."

"But that's not all you said."

It's as if he's staring into the mirror at a monster. "What did I say?"

Somehow, I manage to get out the awful words. "You said she'd still be around if I hadn't taught her to sneak out."

He brings his hand to his mouth. "I said that?" His eyes flood with tears.

I won't let him wiggle out of this. "You did."

He covers his face again. I haven't seen him like this since that day. He's...broken.

"I'm so sorry," he mutters, then his big shoulders tremble more as he finally looks up.

"You don't even remember?" I'm a mess now too. Tears rain down my cheeks. I can't believe I've carried this for so long and he doesn't remember.

"I don't doubt I said it," he says, sounding ashamed and maybe tortured too. "But I don't remember much of that day, Julia. Or any of those days. I just remember hating myself. Hating life. Hating everything. I remember for months wishing it were me. I remember wanting to trade places with your sister," he says. "I remember wanting to die."

Oh god.

He was in such a dark place. I had no idea. "Why didn't you tell anyone?"

He shakes his head, then says quietly, "I wasn't supposed to feel that way. A man, a father, a former cop. I was supposed to look out for you, and I did a horrible job. I was so lost, I said something terrible to you, and I'm so sorry." His eyes glisten with both a fresh round of tears and the hope that I'll forgive him. "I was in so much pain, I didn't realize what I said when I was like that. When I was grieving. When I was breaking apart. But that's no excuse." He stands, comes to me, and grips my shoulders. "It was not your fault. It was never your fault. You did nothing wrong. And nothing, I repeat nothing, could make me stop loving you."

I stand and take his hug as he wraps his arms around me, pulling me close in a tear-soaked embrace that's six years overdue.

I cry. He cries. The kitchen fills with the sound of sobs and snot and years of guilt unraveling.

When I break the hug at last, I grab a nearby tissue box and wipe my tears, handing him a wad of tissues too.

He swipes his eyes. "I'm sorry, sweetheart. I've been a terrible father."

I don't want him to carry that either. "No. You're not a terrible father. I should have stood up for myself. I should have said something sooner. I let it define me."

"It doesn't define you. It just happened. It's...a tragedy." For a moment, he looks a little lost in time, like he's remembering something else. "Sometimes we don't say things when we should. Someone said that to me recently. And it's true. I should have checked in with you. I should have asked how you were doing. I should have tried harder. I regret that. Deeply. But it's not your fault."

"It's not yours either," I say simply.

He gives a resigned smile. I don't know that he'll forgive himself. But I know I forgive him for what he said to me.

He clears his throat. "Do you want to get dinner before Liz comes home?"

Dinner sounds like a fine way to start over. "Yes."

"But nothing healthy, please. I can't take it tonight."

I laugh. "French fries make everything better."

We go to a diner to eat, and it's awkward. It's hard as hell. But it's necessary.

* * *

The next day, I feel different. Yes, I forgive my father, but that's not the only burden that's lifted. I'm not beholden to him anymore.

Or really, I'm not beholden to the guilt.

It's gone, and so is my reluctance to live my own life. I'm going to do it, no matter the consequences.

After work, I take that step, and I send Finn another gift.

33

NO REGRETS

Finn

My brother and his son are locked in a who-can-make-a-bigger-cannonball contest. I'm out of the competition because I'm being chased through Nick's pool by a small dragon on a noodle.

I freestyle it through the chlorinated water, but of course the fire-breathing creature is faster, shouting "gotcha" as he topples me, dunking me under with a little hand.

I pop up, feigning breathlessness as I slide a hand over my wet head. "You win. You win," I say, begging Zach for mercy.

"Yes! I am the pool dragon!"

I'm not even sure what game we're playing. But after a few more rounds, it ends, and I climb out of the water. David and Zach will stay in till they become fish or prunes, whichever comes first.

"Need to get back to Miami so I can enjoy the outdoor pool," I say to my brother as I grab a towel and dry off. It's been a while since I made it to South Beach, and I'd like to soak in the rays there.

"Come to think of it, I wouldn't mind crashing at your place someday soon," Nick says as he flops onto a lounge chair.

"You're not taking over my house before I get to go there."

With a shrug, he says, "I might."

"Please," I scoff.

Now I really need to plan a trip there, just to beat him. But I can't picture a weekend or more in Miami without a certain person there too. The person who hasn't left my thoughts since I left Paris two weeks ago.

That someone has been sending me little gifts all week, starting with that pineapple, then the chili flakes, then a book she thought I might like, then another card 'n the mail with a daisy illustration on it. Inside, it read:

regrette rien.

'₊ time she sends me something, I text her, and
ᵗhat all night. Well, text like that.

ʰone before I sit down, in case she texts
ᵈdicted.

'ᵘck. An email notification blinks
'ᵒrk Public Library—a trio of
ᵛith the author of *Captain*

ᴖ

'll be ridiculously

' her note.

Would you and Zach like to go with me?

I smile, probably a little dopily.

I'll write back later when I can indulge in a longer conversation. Not going to lie—I look forward to her gifts each night. I think they mean something. Like she's trying to send me a message she's not ready to say out loud. Like she wants to give me things, like I gave her perfume and lingerie and a tour of the gardens.

But I don't want to push her. I said as much in Paris. The ball is in her court and she seems to be playing it, so I've been happily receiving her gifts, waiting to see what she wants.

I set the phone on the table and sit next to my brother.

"So, tomorrow is Tiramisu day," Nick muses.

"Yup." We're going to the shelter to find a dog.

Nick sighs contentedly, parking his hands behind his head as he watches our sons splash around in the pool. "You'll have a kid and a dog."

He says it like that's all I need.

But is it? Because I'm picturing Miami and Jules, Paris and Jules, New York and Jules.

And Zach and Jules.

And the library and Jules.

And all these gifts and Jules.

And then all the things I meant when I sent he gifts.

With the perfume...I can't stop thinking about yr

With the gardens...I'd do anything for you.

Suddenly, I know what she's saying.

I sit up straight. "I'm an idiot."

"No shit," Nick says with a snort.

I turn to my brother, intensely serious. "No, I really am." I can't believe it took me this long to figure it out.

His droll expression burns off, and he sits up too. "Why now?"

"Because she's been sending me gifts all week, and I've been waiting. I can't keep waiting," I say, popping up from the chair.

Nick blinks. "Whoa. Back it up. Who's she?"

I haven't told him. I haven't told a soul.

Ah, fuck it. "Tate's daughter."

Nick sputters out a "What?"

"I'm in love with her." It's easy to say and it's right to say. It shouldn't be something I have to lie about, something I have to hide. It should be something I get to enjoy every day. That we can enjoy together. I say it again because it feels so right to voice it out loud, "I'm in love with her."

"Okay," Nick says, standing too, trying to follow my train of thought then shrugging as if deciding to just catch up to where I am. "And does she know?"

"In Paris I told her I wanted more, but..."

I flash back to that moment in the hotel room when I said I want this.

When I said she was perfect for me.

When I said I wanted to be with her but I didn't want to hurt any other relationship.

That wasn't enough. At the time it felt like it, but it clearly wasn't.

"She just sent me tickets to this library event and asked if I wanted to go with her and Zach...and..."

Suddenly, I can't wait.

I can't just let her take the lead. She's been making overtures all week. And I know exactly what she's been saying with her gifts.

"What about Tate?" Nick asks.

I saw my friend as the obstacle, but all along, my regrets were the roadblock.

Regrets over my marriage and so many regrets over time I lost with Zach. How I might have had more time if I had just given Nina my info.

I don't want to lose any more chances. Like I told Tate the other morning, I don't want to have any doubts about the things I've said. Or *not* said. "There's something I have to say to the woman I love." I glance at my kid in the pool. "And I have to do it now. Can Zach stay with you for a bit?"

"He can stay the night. Go get your girl."

I say goodbye to my kid and I leave with no regrets.

34

FACE MASK

Jules

I'm stretched out on my couch, the sea clay mask on my face finally cracking—which is, incidentally, one of life's great unsung pleasures—and the newest episode of *The Dating Games* hitting peak emotions, when my phone buzzes with a text.

It's Friday night so I expect Camden with an update on her date. Eager for the news, I grab the phone, pause the show on my laptop, then click open the messages.

But it's not my bestie. It's from Hank, my doorman.

There's a delivery for you. If you're home, I can bring it up. Or them, really.

Huh. That sounds intriguing, so I call him. "Hi, Hank. Who's the delivery from?"

Hank clears his throat, then sighs, like he doesn't want to be a pawn in a game. "Um...it says it's from... Your piano teacher."

Electricity jolts through me, chased by fireworks. Then, a healthy dose of *oh shit*. I'm in sleep shorts, a tank top, and I look like mud is caked to my face.

Because mud *is caked to my face.*

Is Finn downstairs with the delivery? No idea, but I can get ready fast. "Is someone there?"

"Nope."

But he might be nearby, and no man needs to see my mud face. "Do you mind bringing it up? Or them."

"Might take a few trips, but sure I can do it."

A few trips? Did Finn bring me a palette of perfume? A dozen boxes of panties? "Okay," I say, already breathless with anticipation. "And thank you, Hank."

"Of course, Miss Marley."

I scrub the sea clay off my face at a record clip, finishing just as footsteps sound outside my door.

I'm slathering on lotion so I don't look rubbed raw, when I hear footsteps *again.*

Next comes a knocking as I'm tugging on a crop top and jeans. What did Finn send that takes multiple trips? And will my doorman hate me?

I don't have time to find out since his footsteps fade just as I reach the door and unlock it.

When I swing open the door, I gasp.

My doorway is bursting with blooms. There are boxes full of arrangements. Vases bursting with flowers. My doorway is filled with peach roses, lush delphiniums, fluffy peonies, gorgeous tulips.

My nose is in heaven. My mind is overwhelmed. And my heart is thundering as I take it all in. Easily a dozen bouquets wait for me. Tucked in one of them is a simple white card with my name on it. I pick it up, opening the flap as my pulse skyrockets.

I tug out the card, my skin tingling.

Don't let this be bad news. Don't let this be something terrible.

I take a beat, then a calming breath, letting any terrible thoughts float away.

I open the card. I don't move as I read it. I barely breathe.

Jules,

When we were in Paris in the Luxembourg Gardens, you closed your eyes, and I asked where you went. You told me that you went to a memory of my hotel room. You painted the scene from your imagination. It was vivid and vibrant and told me exactly where you were and who you are.

Now, back here in New York, when I catch the scent of honeysuckle outside my kitchen window, I picture you. I see you walking down the street, coming up my steps, dancing for me.

But then again, my thoughts always go to you.

When I go to the bookstore, I imagine you're wandering among the shelves. When I'm in the diner, you're joining me. When I turn the corner, you walk toward me.

Wherever I am, you are.

But I don't want to be lost in a memory, or caught only in a dream. I want to be wrapped in the present with you, and planning a new future together. I'd take you to Monet's

Garden to tell you this, but instead, I'm bringing the garden to you.

Can I come up and see you?

xo,

Finn

I clutch the card to my chest for several long seconds, then sway. I grab onto the doorjamb, so I don't fall under the weight of the swoon. I'm going to need a fan. I'm going to need to pinch myself.

I grab at my phone and try to slide it open, but I'm so excited I can't unlock it at first. Once I get it open, though, I stop.

I know Finn.

He's not far away.

I bet he's...

As if drawn by an invisible force, I head to the window and stare down at the street.

My heart slams against my ribs when I see him on the sidewalk, pacing, gripping his phone like it's a lifeline to me.

Waiting for me.

He's so unbearably handsome in the summer twilight, the day drifting away, the night coasting in. In tight jeans and a fitted T-shirt, he's the man showing up for me.

I fling open the window, giddy. "Yes!" I shout it without thinking.

He turns, following the sound of my voice, staring up, then smiling slowly, like his smile is filling him up.

"Come up," I add excitedly, in case it wasn't clear.

"I'm on my way," he says, then bounds up the steps.

I call Hank, tell him to let my piano teacher in, then I rush to the door, gingerly passing the flowers so I don't knock any over. I turn down the hall and head to the staircase.

Then, I run, barefoot, ready, eager. I yank open the door, right as Finn reaches the top of the steps.

My man. My love. The guy who was off-limits for the longest time, till I ripped down the barriers—the ones inside me.

"Hi," I say, bursting with hope.

"Hi," he says, then sweeps me up in his arms, lifting me in the air, bringing me close. "I miss you too much to stay away any longer. I miss you too much to be without you. I miss you too much to let another hour go by without telling you," he says, as I wrap my legs around him, thrilled to be back here, with him. "Tell me it's the same for you."

He gazes at me with such vulnerability, such passion that I wish I could capture this moment and remember it forever. The moment he declared his heart. The moment when I'm ready to do the same. I sneak a hit of him. Fire, leather, orchids. My favorites. But soap too. He just showered.

Even his hair is damp.

I eat up all these details, recording them so they become my photo albums and I never forget how I feel right here, right now. "Yes. I miss you. I want you. I need you," I say, then I swallow, taking a fortifying breath before I say three more words. "And—"

But before I can speak, he says, "I love you."

"You beat me to it," I say, laughing, my whole body singing, my mind dancing.

"As a man should," he says, then he sets me down and holds my face like he's about to come in for a kiss, but he pauses.

Sweeps his gaze up and down me. Then finally brushes his lips to mine. I sigh happily against his mouth.

It feels like both a kiss and a declaration.

We're choosing this. Choosing us. I know this in a bone-deep way. When he breaks the kiss, I take his hand and lead him out of the stairwell and down the hall, stopping at my open door.

"Want to see my place?"

"I bet it smells really good."

"Like a dream that became real," I say, unable to stop smiling.

His expression softens, his eyes gleaming as he cups my cheek. But before he hauls me in for another kiss, he lets go and gets to work.

"You brought the gardens to me," I say as I pick up a vase and a box.

"And I always will."

Another declaration, and it fills my whole soul.

A few minutes later, the flowers are in my tiny kitchen and we are too.

He takes my hands, threads his fingers through mine. "I want to be with you. In case that wasn't clear," he says, his green eyes sharp, intense.

"You can tell me again," I say.

But his smile disappears. His expression is serious. "I missed you terribly. I fell in love with you in Paris, and I did a terrible job telling you. I wasn't bold enough. Wasn't clear enough. I don't want to stop telling you now. I just love you, Jules, and all the reasons to resist this don't matter anymore. I let them go. I'd do anything for you. Even if I lose your father's friendship, I'll take that chance," he says, his tone somber, underscoring his meaning. "If you'll have this guy who's a little bit older, who has a kid, who's divorced."

He says it like those things would hold me back.

"I'm all in," I say, voice feathery as I fight off happy tears. "I've been holding back for too long. Keeping my own secrets for too long. I haven't been living. Then, you came into my life and I'm not afraid to be myself anymore. I'm not afraid to live every day of my life. And to love...deeply. I want that with you." My eyes well with the emotions rising up in me.

Finn swipes a thumb along my eyelid, wiping away the start of a tear.

But it's not a tear of sadness. I don't feel sad anymore.

"Good. Let's love deeply together."

That's our vow. One that says we're worth the obstacles. That this love is worth the challenges. He's here for me. And I'll be there for him.

"There's so much to talk about. So much to figure out. But right now, I want to show you how very, very good I will be to you," he says in that bedroom rasp that makes me want to drop my panties.

Well, they are pretty soaked.

That's just the way he likes it. Ten minutes later, his face is between my thighs, and he's lapping me up, driving me wild, and making me grab the sheets on my bed.

Good thing I closed the window, or all of Chelsea would hear me scream his name as I writhe and thrash.

I'm panting, moaning, gasping as I pull him up and grab at his shirt. "Now. Get in me now."

"Beg for it," he says carelessly.

And I do.

I slide off the bed, get down on my knees, and gaze up at him, feeling like *his*.

He runs a hand over my hair, like he cherishes me. "Do it."

He's still dressed, and I clutch his hips tight as I say, "Please fuck me. I'm begging you. I want to feel your cock deep inside me. I want you to fuck me hard and good, like I'm the only one."

"You are." His gaze is feral, and in a heartbeat, he tugs me up. I make quick work of his clothes, stripping him eagerly, savoring having my hands on him once again.

He falls to the bed and pulls me on top of him. "Ride my cock. Ride me till you come again. Use me to get off. And I won't stop till you're drenched in orgasms."

That's my man.

He holds to his promise, fucking and loving, and wringing climax after climax out of me as I ride him, as he puts me on my hands and knees, then as he lifts my arms over my head, and pins me down, so he can slowly, exquisitely take me over the edge with him.

* * *

"Do you like dogs?"

I turn to my side and arch a brow Finn's way. "Is this another trick question? Like *Do you like pizza?*"

"Well, do you?" He runs a finger down my naked hip, a few minutes post-O.

"I like pizza, pineapple, pajamas, and dogs. Now, tell me why you're asking such a ridiculous question."

"I'm adopting a dog tomorrow. I mean, we are. Zach and me," he says, and my god, he sounds so cute when he's all new daddy. "I was going to text you a week ago and ask if you liked dogs. But I didn't." He dips his face, nuzzles my neck. "I just wanted to talk to you. But I wanted to know the answer too."

"So you're really asking if I like dogs?" Pretty sure he's asking something else. I'll wait, though, for him to say it.

He lifts his face, but he's quiet, clearly thinking. After he takes a big breath, he asks, "Would you want to walk a dog with me? Come over if I have a dog? Spend time with the dog and me?"

And we're getting warmer. I smile, and it feels serene but a little playful. I'm almost positive what he's truly chipping away at. "Sure, Finn. You and a dog."

He drags a hand through his hair, gearing up for the next thing. "And my son?"

Nerves lace his voice, and I laugh, then drop a kiss

to his stubbly cheek to put him out of his misery. "Did you think I didn't know you had a kid when I agreed to all that love stuff a few minutes ago?"

"A few minutes ago? Please. That was an hour ago. Clearly, you've lost track of time with all the orgasms I gave you."

"Occupational hazard of being..." I stop on the word. But then I decide to own it. I'm the bold one, after all. "Your girlfriend."

His smile is electric, thoroughly pleased with the title I gave myself. "Yes. It is. And yes, I know you're aware I have a kid," he says, as his eyes hold mine with a particular intensity, but with some trepidation too. "I want you to be a part of my life. Of *our* life. Do you want to?"

My heart melts a little more. I run my fingers along his cheek. "Oh Finn. I do. I don't know much about kids. But I know you're a package deal. And you being a father was never something that worried me."

"Good. And yes, I want to go to the New York Public Library event with you. Zach and I would love to," he says.

"I can't wait," I say, picturing it already. The three of us. I never imagined I'd want to hang out with a single father and his young son, but I never imagined a man like Finn—bossy, dirty, loving, giving.

I want all of him, and I want to know his son too. I just do. It's that simple.

He leans over and kisses me quickly. "Are you hungry?"

"Is this a trick question?"

Thirty minutes later, we're half-dressed and eating spicy noodles on my couch. Since I've grown tired of beating around the bush, I face the big issue head-on. "What should we do about my father?"

He sighs, setting down the chopsticks. "That's the question. And honestly, I haven't felt much inclination to run or bike or swim with him."

"Because of what I told you in Giverny?" I ask, a little surprised at the rift. They seemed so close.

His eyes are hard. "Yes. Because even before you became mine, you felt like mine. I would never let anyone hurt you. Including your father." There's no question in his tone. He's chosen.

I'm floored. I didn't expect him to choose me. But he did. Maybe because of what I told him, or maybe because of how he feels for me. Either way, it's a lot to absorb. "Really?"

"Yes, really," he says, emphatic. "When we did our triathlon, I said something to him."

I flinch. "You did?"

He sits up straighter. "I would never break your trust. I didn't reveal what you told me. Instead I talked generally about regrets. About the things we say, and the things we don't say. I couldn't leave it untouched."

I breathe deep in relief. "I talked to him, Finn. Last night." I don't reveal my father's confidences either. Those aren't mine to share. But I desperately want him to know that he doesn't have to protect me here. "And... I think we're going to be okay. I forgive him, and he wanted to be forgiven."

Finn's smile is soft and sad. "Maybe it was supposed to work out this way."

Instantly, I know what he means. "You give him up? I get him back?"

Finn swallows roughly, while nodding. "Yes. Maybe this was always supposed to be our path. Our needs changed. I need you more than I need him. And you needed him back on your side."

There's a certain poetry to that. To the choices we're both making. Neither one of us was ready to make this choice before Paris. Or even after Paris. But maybe the missing over these last few weeks was enough. For me though, it was facing the past so I could move into a future I choose.

"I did need him back," I admit.

Will my father stay on my side after he learns I'm with Finn? I think so. I trust that my father's love for me runs deep. We'll weather it. We've survived something infinitely harder.

"What will we tell him? And how?" I ask, wanting to organize this talk like it's a location shoot I'm coordinating.

Finn wraps an arm around me. "I'll do whatever you need. You come first. Do you want me to tell him? Do you want to? Do you want to do it together?"

Those are good questions. "I think the answer is together."

"Name the time," he says, but then hedges. "But can we do it after we get Tiramisu?"

I blink, amused. "Is that the name of your dog?"

"And my favorite dessert," he says, like he's pleased with his dog-naming abilities.

I seriously fell in love with the best man. "Yes, we can do it after."

"Oh, and Jules, I want you to come with us when we adopt him or her tomorrow."

I say yes to that too.

A little later, Finn gets under the covers with me. Falling asleep with him feels peaceful. Waking up feels right.

We leave for breakfast, holding hands. When we hit the streets of Chelsea, all those happy, buzzy feelings vanish at the sight of my father walking toward us.

35

GOODBYE AND ALWAYS

Finn

I don't drop her hand. I hold it tighter, giving her a subtle squeeze for strength, in case she needs it. No matter how tough Jules is becoming, it's not easy facing someone you love when that person is staring at you like you no longer make sense.

Tate slows his pace as he comes closer. His normal, confident stride turns to slow-mo as he shifts his gaze from her to me, then back again. Math problems flash in his eyes, but without a solution.

"You've got this, Jules. *We've* got this," I say in a whisper.

She gives a small nod, then when we're a few feet from Tate, we stop. He stops.

I'm not sure why he's here now. But the *why* hardly matters. He is and we need to deal with it.

The three of us stand in front of a brick apartment

building in Chelsea on a Saturday morning, as week-
enders hit the sidewalk, pushing strollers, rushing to
cafés, heading to the gym. Heat rises from the concrete
as summer bears down on the city.

"Hi, Dad," Jules says. Her voice wavers, but she lifts
her chin like a warrior.

"Tate," I say. It's crisp, firm.

He squints. "What's going on?"

Said not as a friend, not as a father, but as counsel
in the courtroom hit with a surprise witness.

"Dad, I'm seeing Finn. I'm in love with Finn. We're
together," Jules says, the witness on the stand taking
the oath and sticking to the truth.

"Yes, we are. I love your daughter very much," I say,
meeting his gaze.

But when he meets mine it's with a sneer, then a
dismissive glare. He turns back to Jules. "W-when?
How?"

Tate is no longer in a courtroom. He's the father,
shocked by his daughter's choices.

I don't say a word. She doesn't either. He won't be
privy to how we met after dark.

"That...dinner?" Tate asks, like he's cycling back in
time to the night I met his daughter when I was with
Marilyn still. But he blinks that away. "Oh. Paris?"

Sure. That's close enough. "Yes," I say, since Jules
doesn't need to lie to him.

I can take that one on.

Tate huffs out a breath. "When I said I hoped you'd
learn from Finn that wasn't exactly what I'd had in
mind," he says to her dryly.

She doesn't take his sarcastic bait, even though I suspect it's coming from his own shock.

"I'm happy," she says, standing her ground. "You don't have to be happy for me, but I was going to tell you today. And this is what I want. Finn is who I want."

With a curl in his lips that I swear he tries to erase, he jerks his gaze away, drags a hand down his face, then turns back to us. "I don't know what you want me to say," he says tightly.

It's my turn to step in now. I squeeze her hand tighter. "I love Jules, and I'll take care of her. I'll look out for her. I'll be there for her."

His eyes are bullets. "We won't be running together anymore."

I knew that, but I respect that he needs to say it. "I understand," I say.

Tate blows out a long, disappointed breath. But I'm pretty sure the disappointment is for me, not her.

Jules lets go of my hand, gesturing to the end of the block. "I'll meet you at the café. Okay?"

I don't want to leave her, but I understand what she needs.

"I'll be there." I don't drop a kiss to her cheek. There's a time and place for that, and right now it'd be rubbing it in Tate's face.

Before I can go though, Tate clears his throat. "Finn, she's my *daughter*." His voice is ice and fire. "What the fuck?"

I can't fault him for his reaction. I can only own my choice. "I get that you're cutting me out of your life. Just know that I'll treat her right. That's a promise. For always."

Then I walk away from the friendship. But he catches up with me seconds later.

His jaw is so tight it looks like he's grinding his teeth, but then he grits out words. "If you hurt her—"

"I won't."

He seethes. "I mean it."

I don't break eye contact. "So do I."

Then I leave, going to the café to wait for my woman.

36

THIS THING

Jules

Sometimes it's easier to deal with logistics. "So, what brings you over here on a Saturday morning?"

"Right. That," my father says slowly, but he's still out of sorts. Understandable. "But...Julia."

He heaves a sigh, then says nothing.

I can't not fill the silence. "Are you mad at me?" I feel like a kid all over again. I guess that never goes away with your parents.

"No," he says without hesitation. "I'm just... surprised." He jams his hands into the pockets of his shorts.

"This isn't how I wanted to tell you," I say, wishing I had scanned the street first, seen him coming, something, anything. "That probably sounds trite. Like a line. But I mean it. I wanted to sit down with you and tell you what was going on."

I hope he hears the plea in my voice.

"Yeah, that would have been nice." It's not sarcastic, though, just an admission that he'd rather not have been surprised. I get that.

"As soon as we knew that this was real, that we were committed, I wanted to tell you. He did too." It's weird and uncomfortable to say all these things to my father. But I suppose I've been prepared for weird and uncomfortable for a long time. "I didn't want to just shock you with it like that," I add, flapping my hand in the direction of my apartment where we obviously came from. I don't need to spell out the rest of what we did in my apartment. *Ever.*

"I am shocked. And I'm honestly not sure what to think, Julia," he says, a little lost. He might be for a while.

And I can't make this go more smoothly. I lied by omission, so I don't have the moral high ground. I'm okay with what I've done though. "He's good to me. I promise," I say.

That word hangs in the air, fragrant like perfume. Finn's promise. My promise. I'll write about all these promises in my journal tonight when I tell Willa about my day. "I promise," I say again. I want him to feel the strength of that word deep inside him.

My father's quiet for a long beat before he nods at last. Perhaps, that's his olive branch. "Good. A man should treat you like you're the center of his world," he says.

If I was looking for acceptance, I just got it. I beam, like the sun. "He does. He really does, Dad."

Impulsively, I reach out and hug him. His arms wrap around me, and he gives me a fatherly squeeze.

When I step back, I tilt my head, refusing to let go of my first question. "So, why were you here on a Saturday morning?"

"About that." Dipping a hand into his pocket, he clears his throat, then takes something out. His fingers curl around a small cloth bag with a little ribbon cinching it closed. "I...found this a few years ago. Well, Liz found it when she was going through some—" His voice catches, but he must swallow past the pain, since he adds, "Some things. I held onto it, but I thought you might want to have it. I didn't connect the dots at the time, but after the other night and what you said, I started thinking about the past, and about things that I missed. I've been thinking about that a lot since we spoke. And then I remembered...you and Willa used to give these to each other. I don't even know why. I just know you did."

Without even looking inside the bag, I know what's there. My fingers tingle with hope. He hands it to me, and I open it and fish out the silver anklet.

Daisy charms dangle on it. Willa's favorite flowers. Wild daisies for my wild-child sister. "I'll always hear you coming now," I say quietly, a little mesmerized as I stare at the silver bracelet I gave to her.

My dad's brow knits in question. "What do you mean?"

I look up.

His eyes flicker with curiosity. He so clearly wants to know something about his other daughter—my best friend. To learn something new about her. I can give him that. I'm the *only* one who can give him that.

"It was this thing we did when we gave each other these ankle bracelets," I say, eager to share at last. "We pretended they meant different things. Like *I can hear you sneaking into my room to take my lipstick* or *I'm going to steal Mom's dark chocolate*. They were inside jokes. It was just...this thing we did."

His smile tells me he likes knowing *this thing*. "Thanks for sharing that."

Memories are all we have, and so we keep them alive in our own ways. Sometimes, we can keep them alive together.

I clutch the jewelry, this piece of Willa, tighter. "Let's keep talking about her," I say, my throat catching.

"Yes. Let's do that....Jules."

It's rare when he uses my name. It feels like starting over.

EPILOGUE: THE STARS AND THE FLOWERS

Jules

That afternoon, I go with my boyfriend to Little Friends to adopt a cute long-haired dachshund mix that Finn names Tiramisu.

In the evening, as Finn's making dinner, I hang out with Zach in the little backyard as he tries to teach the tiny girl to sit.

"Sit, Tira—" he stops, then starts again. "Sit, Tirami—"

I chuckle under my breath.

Frustrated, but not with the pooch, Zach straightens his spine, holds out a treat for her and says, "Sit...Captain Dog."

A few more attempts and the dog is sitting and she has a new name. When I go inside to help Finn, I come up behind him, and give him a kiss on the neck. "Guess what? Your son renamed the dog."

Finn gives me a look like *no way.* "He did?" He sounds crestfallen.

"Yes, way," I say, then I tap his chest. "And because you're you, you're not going to have a single issue with it."

I'm right.

Later that night, when I'm home at my apartment—there will be time later for sleepovers—Finn texts me a photo of a tuckered out pup snoozing next to an equally tired boy. It's captioned *You were right. Here's Captain Dog.*

When I see Shira that week, we talk about what's happening in my relationship and she nods, absorbing it. "It sounds like this feels like a really healthy relationship for you," she says, and that's good enough for me. "When you're ready, I still think we should talk more about what may have set your anxieties in motion. The loss of your sister."

She's right. We should talk about it. And so, I do.

A few days later, I'm in the small theater in our Opening Number offices, finishing a screening of the first episode of *The Rendezvous* with all the key players —Bridger, Solange, and several other producers. When it's over, everyone claps, but Solange quickly quiets the applause and asks for feedback in a few key areas.

I file that away—her willingness to learn. It'll come in useful for me if I'm in her position someday. Though, come to think of it, that's always a key skill—willingness to learn.

She listens as a few producers make minor suggestions, then when we're done, she catches up to me as I'm gathering my laptop and purse. Everyone else is gone. "How's everything going, Jules?"

It's a generic question, but not really. She means something very specific. "I'm doing well," I say, then we chat briefly about the show and the business. But once we're done, I add, "And thank you again for your advice in Paris. I appreciate it. I'm with Finn, but I'm definitely finding my own way."

"Oh," she says, a little thrown off, but then she recovers. "Good. That's what I hoped for." She holds my gaze for a weighty beat. "Truly it is."

"I know," I say, meaning it.

Then I leave, headed to Finn's home. "How are things with Streamer, *boss*?" I ask my guy after he gives me a chaste kiss at the door. Finn's had a busy few days finalizing a couple distribution deals. "Did you use your tycoon attitude?"

He shuts the door, then dips his voice. "I did. Is that something you'd like me to use on you soon?"

I smirk. "That'd be a yes."

"Good. Now tell me how everything's going with your projects."

As we head into the kitchen, I update him on the shows I'm working on, and the script reading I'll be doing tonight. "Most of all, I'm excited about *Captain Dude*," I say, then cross my fingers. "Maybe I can be more hands-on with it."

"I bet you will be."

He's probably right. Because I'm a damn good junior TV producer no matter who I love or how I love. Guess that's part of finding my way.

A few minutes later, Zach trots downstairs. "Are you ready, Jules?"

In medias res, indeed.

"Ready," I say, then I dip a hand into my purse and grab some Mentos.

Zach motors to the fridge and snags a bottle of Diet Coke. The three of us head to the backyard and conduct an experiment, making a very messy fountain.

When Zach goes to bed, his father pulls me close in the kitchen, and kisses me desperately. "I want to take you to my home in Miami next month. Just you and me."

I say yes.

* * *

A few days later, we walk up the steps of the New York Public Library together. I'm not holding Zach's hand. That's a little insta-family for me.

But I'm right there with them—this man who adores me, and his son who's welcomed me into his life like I'm maybe the cool aunt he's always wanted.

Like this is where my story was always meant to be.

As they go through the doors, I lag behind for a moment. I glance back at the city that's my home. My friends are scattered around Manhattan, my family over the Brooklyn Bridge.

Later, I'll look up at the stars and I'll see my sister. For now, I look down at the two anklets I wear. Mine and hers. Stars and flowers.

When I go inside, I'm so much more than happy enough.

* * *

At the end of the summer on a Saturday night, I adjust Lady Gaga in front of the mirror in my home, making sure the strands look just right. Then, I strike a pose with Harlow, wearing Miley, and Layla, dolled up as Taylor.

"Got my sparkle bodysuit, my wig, and now I'm good to go," Layla says, blowing a lipstick kiss at our reflection.

Harlow juts out a hip, showing off her strappy little black dress, looking like the honey-voiced singer in her wig. "We'll duet, baby."

"Hello! We'll be a band," Layla adds, then squeezes my shoulder. "We have Lady Gaga here at the helm."

"We'll call ourselves The Wigs Made Me Do It," I say, then we take a picture and head to Rebel Beat, a club near Gramercy Park.

Ethan's band, Outrageous Record, is playing here tonight. His band's become a bit of a *house act*, coming back, like a returning son, to the place where they broke out a few years ago.

We get our drinks, stake out a spot by the lip of the stage, and then rock out as Ethan and the crew roll through some of their most popular tunes. When they finish "Blown Away," there's barely a second for the crowd to lose its mind before Ethan says into the mic, "And now we have a special guest. This girl—you're going to say you heard her when. *Camden.*" He gestures to the wings, and my bestie joins him onstage, in her vegan leather pants, belting out a song she wrote, "Whiskey Memories," with Ethan harmonizing along.

And wow.

My girl's got pipes and stage presence.

Talk about blown away. When I meet her later offstage, I say, "I feel like I just witnessed the start of something big."

She's glowing as she crosses her fingers. "Let's hope so," she says, then she adds, "I told you it was about the music. Ethan and me."

"Fine, fine," I concede.

A few days later, a video of her performance of "Whiskey Memories" goes viral. Guess someone's about to be a rock star.

* * *

A week later, when Zach heads to Connecticut to see his grandparents for a few days, I pack up for a getaway trip. But I don't head straight to Finn's.

Instead, he sends a town car to pick me up.

I drop my suitcase in the back, and when I reach the Albrecht Mansion, I thank the driver, who'll wait for us, then slide on my mask.

Tonight, I'm an angel. A very naughty one. I give the

password to the bodyguard twins. "I'm good but not an angel," I say.

"You may go inside."

Once there, I look for a man dressed all in black, with a red mask.

We pretend we're strangers at the party. In the library. And in the car on the way back to his home.

Then he fucks me like I'm his one-night stand and the love of his life.

After my third, or sixth, who knows how many orgasms, I'm worn out in the best of ways, so Finn pours me a glass of wine, and asks me if I want to sit in the backyard and enjoy the warm night.

"No. Let's go to the balcony."

He crooks a brow. "Are you sure?"

"Positive."

I'm not cured. I'll never be cured. But I've learned from Shira that sometimes, when I'm less anxious, the uncomfortable thoughts come less frequently. And they don't have such a hold of me.

Funny thing—letting go of my guilt over my sister let go of some of my persistent stress.

So I step onto the balcony with a glass of wine and my guy. For a few seconds, it's a battle in my head. But it's one I want to face.

Because this is where I want to be. In Manhattan, with him, looking at the stars.

* * *

The next evening, we're relaxing by his pool in Miami.

"I've always wanted to take you here," he says, as he stretches out on a lounge chair while the sea breeze drifts by.

"Take me anywhere," I say.

"I will."

It's a new promise. One I know we'll keep.

ANOTHER EPILOGUE:
HONEYSUCKLE KISS

Finn

I reach for my credit card the second the lunch bill arrives.

But Tate's faster. "I'll take care of it," he says gruffly, grabbing the tray then slapping down his credit card.

I don't protest. This is clearly important to him. Just like the conversation I had with him over eggs was important to me.

He slides the tray back to the server. "Thanks so much."

"You're welcome. Be right back," the server says.

When it's just us again, my one-time closest friend glances around the café in Brooklyn, not far from his home. His eyes dart to artwork on the wall, graphic designs with kitschy sayings like *Don't talk to me before I've had my coffee.*

After perusing them longer than most people

would, he turns back to me, face still stony. It's been an uncomfortable meal, but an important one.

"Thanks again for meeting me," I say.

"Well, yeah."

"I appreciate it, Tate."

He nods. That's all.

Soon, the server returns, and we leave, pausing in front of the café, ready to go our separate ways. In the past, we'd have shot the breeze more. He'd have said something cheeky about my Friday nights. I'd have given him a hard time about his age.

We don't make those jokes anymore. We hardly see each other these days.

But today, he gave me his permission. I didn't need it, but I wanted it. I wanted to show him that I respect who he is to the woman I love.

"Thanks for everything," I say, then extend a hand.

We shake. "Don't ever break her heart, Finn," he instructs.

"I won't," I say in the easiest promise ever.

* * *

Across the ocean a week later, our town car pulls up, to a garden in Giverny.

Jules steps out of the car and reaches for my hand. We get in line. We aren't alone here today. She wanted to see Monet's Garden with people in it, enjoying the scents and sounds and colors.

That's all she thinks we're doing here today—

paying a visit to one of her favorite places while on a European vacation.

Once we leave the house and enter the gardens, she lifts her nose, inhaling the irises, poppies and pansies. "I'm like a kid in a candy store," she says, eyes sparkling.

"You should have your own garden someday," I muse as I look around at the wildflowers and the emerald lawns.

She arches a brow my way. "Isn't that what I have in your backyard?"

"*Our* backyard," I correct since she's been living with Zach and me in Manhattan. She moved in several months ago, and promptly started planting flowers outside the tree house.

Zach joins her as she works. The sight of them gardening together breaks my heart in all the best ways.

"Ours," she repeats, since she's still getting used to it.

"Yes, but a bigger one. I can see you in a home, with a huge yard, and flower beds as far as the eye can see."

She smiles as we wander. "I like that image," she says as she stops near the central alley leading away from the house, where trim green arches canopy the path. "They're covered in honeysuckle," she says, staring up at them.

"I know." I know since this is exactly where I planned to be right now.

This is why I saw her father last week.

This is why I took her here.

And she is why I get down on one knee.

When she realizes I'm no longer walking with her, she turns around. It takes a few seconds for her to process the sight, but when she does, she gasps. "Finn," she whispers.

I don't feel an ounce of nerves, only excitement over what's to come for us. "I love you madly, Jules. I never imagined I could love someone so deeply, so fiercely. Someone who'd love me the same way. You love with everything you have, and that's all I've ever wanted. I've found it in you. I want to give you love every day for the rest of our lives." I reach into my pocket and take out a blue velvet box. "Will you be my wife?"

With a smile more radiant than the sun, she says, "Yes," and drops to her knees, throws her arms around me, and kisses me madly and deeply.

When she lets go, her face is soaked with tears, and her eyes shine with happiness.

Mine probably do too. I'm going to make this woman happy for the rest of our lives.

I slide a brilliant diamond onto her finger, and then kiss her once more in a garden that feels like ours.

Want more from these characters? Download their sexy, forbidden romances for FREE in KU where you can binge the entire Virgin Society series!
The RSVP: Bridger & Harlow
The Tryst: Nick & Layla

If you've devoured this series and are ready for more sexy romance full of heat and heart, you'll love my

spicy, fake dating, lessons in seduction romance Plays Well With Others, available for FREE in KU!

Want a peek into Jules' and Finn's future together? For a look into their life over the next few years, click here for a bonus epilogue! Or scan the QR code!

AUTHOR'S NOTE

Thank you to Jill and to Amy Bowen for their insight into OCD. I am grateful to these two therapists for their keen insight into this aspect of mental health in The Tease. OCD can manifest in many ways. For this story, I chose to focus on the intrusive thoughts aspect of OCD and have done extensive research into it, and also experienced it. This story and the fine details of OCD would not be possible without Jill and Amy and their professional guidance in this area, both in the treatment and the manifestation. Everyone's experience with OCD is unique to the individual, while treatment plans and choices, ranging from varieties of therapy, like exposure and cognitive behavioral therapy, as well as medication, are unique to the individual too. If you or someone you know is struggling with OCD, anxiety, panic or any other mental health issues please reach out to your local support network. Or visit the following pages for more resources:

United   States: https://www.nimh.nih.gov/health/
find-help

International: https://findahelpline.com/

BE A LOVELY

Want to be the first to know of sales, new releases, special deals and giveaways? Sign up for my newsletter today!

Want to be part of a fun, feel-good place to talk about books and romance, and get sneak peeks of covers and advance copies of my books? Be a Lovely!

MORE BOOKS BY LAUREN

I've written more than 100 books! **All of these titles below are FREE in Kindle Unlimited!**

Double Pucked

A sexy, outrageous MFM hockey romantic comedy!

The Virgin Society Series

Meet the Virgin Society – great friends who'd do anything for each other. Indulge in these forbidden, emotionally-charged, and wildly sexy age-gap romances!

The RSVP

The Tryst

The Tease

How To Date Series (New and ongoing)

A series of standalone romantic comedies full of love, sex and meet-cute shenanigans.

My So-Called Sex Life

Plays Well With Others

The Dating Games Series

A fun, sexy romantic comedy series about friends in the city and their dating mishaps!

The Virgin Next Door

Two A Day

The Good Guy Challenge

Boyfriend Material

Four fabulous heroines. Four outrageous proposals. Four chances at love in this sexy rom-com series!

Asking For a Friend

Sex and Other Shiny Objects

One Night Stand-In

Overnight Service

Big Rock Series

My #1 New York Times Bestselling sexy as sin, irreverent, male-POV romantic comedy!

Big Rock

Mister O

Well Hung

Full Package

Joy Ride

Hard Wood

Happy Endings Series

Romance starts with a bang in this series of standalones following a group of friends seeking and avoiding love!

Come Again

Shut Up and Kiss Me

Kismet

My Single-Versary

Ballers And Babes

Sexy sports romance standalones guaranteed to make you hot!

Most Valuable Playboy

Most Likely to Score

A Wild Card Kiss

Rules of Love Series

Athlete, virgins and weddings!

The Virgin Rule Book

The Virgin Game Plan

The Virgin Replay

The Virgin Scorecard

The Extravagant Series

Bodyguards, billionaires and hoteliers in this sexy, high-stakes series of standalones!

One Night Only

One Exquisite Touch

My One-Week Husband

The Guys Who Got Away Series

Friends in New York City and California fall in love in this fun and hot rom-com series!

Birthday Suit

Dear Sexy Ex-Boyfriend

The What If Guy

Thanks for Last Night

The Dream Guy Next Door

Always Satisfied Series

A group of friends in New York City find love and laughter in this series of sexy standalones!

Satisfaction Guaranteed

Never Have I Ever

Instant Gratification

PS It's Always Been You

The Gift Series

An after dark series of standalones! Explore your fantasies!

The Engagement Gift

The Virgin Gift

The Decadent Gift

The Heartbreakers Series

Three brothers. Three rockers. Three standalone sexy romantic comedies.

Once Upon a Real Good Time

Once Upon a Sure Thing

Once Upon a Wild Fling

Sinful Men

A high-stakes, high-octane, sexy-as-sin romantic suspense series!

My Sinful Nights

My Sinful Desire

My Sinful Longing

My Sinful Love

My Sinful Temptation

From Paris With Love

Swoony, sweeping romances set in Paris!

Wanderlust

Part-Time Lover

One Love Series

A group of friends in New York falls in love one by one in this sexy rom-com series!

The Sexy One

The Hot One

The Knocked Up Plan

Come As You Are

Lucky In Love Series

A small town romance full of heat and blue collar heroes and sexy heroines!

Best Laid Plans

The Feel Good Factor

Nobody Does It Better

Unzipped

No Regrets

An angsty, sexy, emotional, new adult trilogy about one
young couple fighting to break free of their pasts!

The Start of Us

The Thrill of It

Every Second With You

The Caught Up in Love Series

A group of friends finds love!

The Pretending Plot

The Dating Proposal

The Second Chance Plan

The Private Rehearsal

Seductive Nights Series

A high heat series full of danger and spice!

Night After Night

After This Night

One More Night

A Wildly Seductive Night

Joy Delivered Duet

A high-heat, wickedly sexy series of standalones that will set
your sheets on fire!

Nights With Him

Forbidden Nights

Unbreak My Heart

A standalone second chance emotional roller coaster of a romance

The Muse

A magical realism romance set in Paris

Good Love Series of sexy rom-coms co-written with Lili Valente!

I also write MM romance under the name L. Blakely!

Hopelessly Bromantic Duet (MM)

Roomies to lovers to enemies to fake boyfriends

Hopelessly Bromantic

Here Comes My Man

Men of Summer Series (MM)

Two baseball players on the same team fall in love in a forbidden romance spanning five epic years

Scoring With Him

Winning With Him

All In With Him

MM Standalone Novels

A Guy Walks Into My Bar

The Bromance Zone

One Time Only

The Best Men (Co-written with Sarina Bowen)

Winner Takes All Series (MM)

A series of emotionally-charged and irresistibly sexy standalone MM sports romances!

The Boyfriend Comeback

Turn Me On

A Very Filthy Game

Limited Edition Husband

Manhandled

If you want a personalized recommendation, email me at laurenblakelybooks@gmail.com!

CONTACT

I love hearing from readers! You can find me on Twitter at LaurenBlakely3, Instagram at LaurenBlakelyBooks, Facebook at LaurenBlakelyBooks, or online at LaurenBlakely.com. You can also email me at laurenblakelybooks@gmail.com

Made in the USA
Middletown, DE
06 April 2024

52558024R00215